I0571902

A Novel

IJ Goldman

Neeman House Publishers
Seattle, WA

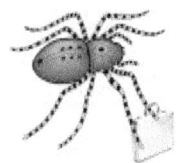

One

Mrs. Klondike must have been an owl in a previous life. It was a good imitation anyway, the way she would swivel her head flawlessly at the slightest disturbance, her eyes blinking smoothly like lens shutters. This made Dillon's stealth mission all the more complicated. At any moment those luminous eyes could lock on their target, piercing the middle of his back as he inched past the grungy slide windows of her office. Some really intense but muffled classical music was reaching a crescendo inside her antique radio. It was the kind of dull blowing and banging that orchestras did that somehow inspired people to standing ovations. Usually it depressed him or put him to sleep. Now it seemed like horror film music and he was Norman Bates, his heart pounding along with the orchestra as he made his way cautiously to the room at the end of the hall. He was grateful, though, that an errant squeak of his sneakers could easily be passed off as the cheerful chirp of a flute. He imagined the conductor madly flailing his arms at the flautist, who calmly obliged him with snippets of sneaker squeaks.

Suddenly, Mrs. Klondike's amplified voice filled the hallway, every hallway of the entire school, in fact. Dillon's heart did a loop.

"Mitchell Carmichael, Mitchell Carmichael, please come to the front office. Mitchell Carmichael."

It wouldn't be long before Mitchell Carmichael, whoever he was, would show up. He'd be appearing in, or somewhere near, this hallway. It was now or never. Dillon sprinted quickly down the rest of the hall and burst into the principal's office. He closed the door, which produced a fleeting squeak that traveled up Dillon's spine. He remembered to breathe and looked around him. He had been in this office a few times before, but this was the first time unsummoned. Mr. Rigler had left wrinkles in his leather chair. A half-empty coffee mug stained a piece of paper he had been reading. He had left the office only moments earlier, but his presence still seemed to linger.

Dillon had twenty minutes to get the job done before Mr. Rigler would return from his meeting with the superintendent. He had Mrs. Klondike's meticulous organizational skills to thank for this information. She had the principal's weekly schedule all neatly typed out and posted with a bright yellow butterfly-shaped thumbtack to a moldy chalkboard next to her desk. While in her office the other day so generously volunteering to help her move some heavy desk files, Dillon had so easily availed himself of the information he needed to snoop around Mr. Rigler's office.

Dillon's eyes went to the flat-screen computer at the center of the desk. He sat himself down in the imposing chair, rearranging the wrinkles in the leather. The computer had not yet gone to screensaver. If it had, there may have been some password protection preventing him from accessing it. He grabbed the mouse.

"Inbox," he tried to whisper to himself, but produced no more than a dry gurgle. "Where's the email inbox?"

His ears were on high alert for even the slightest sound. If he was discovered now, that would be it for his schooling.

He found the inbox. It had been minimized. He enlarged it. Now he had to search by Sender. "Carter Construction," he said without sound. He scrolled down the names looking for Carter.

"Carrie Smith.... Carson & Burrows.... Cavennaugh, Josephine."

Dillon sighed nervously. It wasn't there. Ah! But if Mr. Rigler wanted to keep it secret, perhaps it was in the deleted files?

He checked his watch. Fifteen minutes to go. He clicked on the deleted files and searched the emails according to sender. Here it was! He couldn't believe it. His heart was in his throat. Fingers trembling, he opened the email. "Invoice. Improvements and repairs to Westridge High gymnasium." There was a lot of detail but the final total at the bottom was what mattered.

"Eighty-seven thousand, four hundred ninety-six dollars, and thirty-two cents." He reread it to make sure, to seal Mr. Rigler's downfall. It was just as Dillon expected. He had not known the exact figure but he was pretty sure that it would be less than Mr. Rigler claimed it to be. $200,000 was what the principal had told the school was the cost of the repairs. Some people had expressed their surprise at the high cost, but no-one had taken the initiative to investigate it. Until now. There was probably a fake invoice somewhere that Mr. Rigler had generated for the records, but this email was the real thing. What had happened to the other $113,000 the fundraising committee had raised for the cost? Only Mr. Rigler would know the answer to that. It had been sharp thinking on the principal's part, Dillon had to admit. It wasn't millions of dollars that would have afforded him a life of luxury. That would have been so obvious and would have landed him in jail right away. No, he still had the same poky house, still drove the same run-down car. He'd kept the figure to a relatively modest, unremarkable amount that slipped so quietly into the laundry list of sundry school expenses. And he'd have a hundred grand to take home and play with at the same time. The figure would lie low, beneath the radar range of a bored auditor. But not escaping the attention of this kid, who had grown weary of adult misbehavior.

Now for the print function. He had to walk out of here with proof. "Print," he uttered in quiet triumph, which was shattered by the opening of the office door. It was hard to tell who was more shocked, Dillon or Mr. Rigler.

"You're back early," Dillon found himself saying from somewhere in his brain, all other functions completely numb.

"The superintendent cancelled," Mr. Rigler answered him in his own stupor. They continued to stare at each other, Dillon comfortably ensconced in the executive chair, and Mr. Rigler hanging limply in the doorway in a most bizarre moment of role reversal. Until Mr. Rigler got his wits about him and began yelling at the top of his lungs. To which Dillon responded by leaping, printout in hand, over the desk, knocking the computer to the floor and dodging Mr. Rigler out the office door faster than his brain could command it.

"Come back here immediately!" Mr. Rigler raged, stumbling after him, ignoring his computer's plunge to the laminate floor where it sighed briefly before expiring.

Mrs. Klondike was on the scene in no time. Her hand reached for Dillon but missed. The principal and the office manager were both rooted to the spot. They both glared through the window at Dillon's departing figure as it raced down the grass bank.

"Who was that?" Mr. Rigler demanded, breathing as though he'd just returned from a track meet.

"That was Dillon Appleseed," Mrs. Klondike replied, tapping her fingers against her folded arms.

"A troublemaker?"

"No, not typically." She pursed her lips. "I think you know all the troublemakers quite well, Mr. Rigler."

"Rotten Appleseed," Mr. Rigler mumbled.

They both turned to check on the status of the fallen computer. "I think your computer is no longer with us," Mrs. Klondike remarked. "Yup. Gone up to the big Hard Drive in the sky."

"That will be enough of your commentary, Mrs. Klondike," Mr. Rigler snapped. "Get hold of Appleseed, and bring him here."

"Should I call the police?"

"No."

"But he br...."

"Don't question me, Mrs. Klondike. Just do as I say."

"But it was too late," Dillon said, chewing methodically on his peanut butter and jelly sandwich in the musty cafeteria as several riveted eyes bore through him. "I just called the police myself."

7

"What did the cops say when you busted him?" Steve asked wide-eyed, crushing his empty Styrofoam cup. "I mean, how could they believe you? You're just a kid."

Dillon shrugged. "They didn't at first but when I gave them the exact figures of the invoice and everything, they started asking me more questions. Then they must have gotten hold of the contractor to question him about his invoice. Next thing I know the cops were here going through everything."

"That's so sad," Amy commented, and they all lowered their heads to half-mast. "Can you just imagine Mr. Rigler being lead away in handcuffs? Did anybody see that?"

"I got a picture of it on my cell," Tommy declared with glee, flashing his phone.

"No way!"

"Way cool!"

"Let me see that."

The animated group then descended on Tommy, clamoring for a glimpse of some fuzzy photos of their principal in disgrace. Dillon was once again alone again in his usual spot where few people sat, except for his friend, Cal, of course, whose earphones seemed permanently glued to his head. He hardly ever took a break from them, except to ask questions like, "Wanna shoot some ball?" - then returning the phones to his ears without waiting for the answer. Cal's mother reported that he even slept with them on. Dillon once imagined Cal's wedding day:

"Do you, Cal, take this woman as your bride?"
"Huh?"

Dillon munched in silence, his thoughts returning to Mr. Rigler's wife whom he'd met once. She had offered him a ride home from school when he'd stayed late. She'd even given him a couple of packets of Doritos that had been left in her car. Now he was reciprocating by getting her husband thrown in jail.

"Dillon." Apparently he hadn't been left completely alone. It was Samantha, probably the most popular girl in the entire school, outranking her nearest rival by several layers of mascara.

To hear her actually call his name was startling.

"Yeah," he responded, swallowing.

"I think what you did was really cool."

"Yeah?" Dillon said again.

"Yeah," she confirmed. "I like the way you risked everything, and everything."

Her chewing gum tumbled about like laundry on slow wash.

"Well," he cleared his throat. "I mean I didn't do it just for the risk."

"Oh, sure, you're just saying that," she smiled.

"No, really. I did it because embezzlement is…wrong, actually. When I see injustice and nobody is taking action, I feel like I have to do something."

Samantha's smile stagnated. Her chewing continued unabated.

"I mean," Dillon continued. "Don't you often feel like everyone knows they have to do something to fight for what's right in society and yet no-one's doing it?"

She had no answer for him, her eyes dimming.

"Don't you?" Dillon pressed.

"Uh, sorta…." she shrugged her shoulders.

"All you have to do is think about this gym thing. I mean everyone rolled their eyes when they heard the figures Mr. Rigler presented to the school – we all knew it was excessive, but it's the next step that everyone was missing – putting objection into practice. A lot of people

9

like to complain. Very few actually do anything about it. My Grandpa says that this has been a pattern throughout history. In pre-war Germany, for example..."

"OK," she slapped her hand on the table. "You're weird." She jumped to her feet and left.

"Do you think I'm weird, Grandpa?"

"What do you mean? Why do you ask?" Grandpa Harley said, extending his hand to stroke the nose of Thomas Edison.

"Please do not touch anything, sir," A security guard appeared like a genie. His pasty white face made him look as if he were a wax model himself.

"I'm sorry," Grandpa replied, his moustache curling into a submissive ball.

"No problem." The guard walked off.

"Quite remarkable," Grandpa said, as he stared after the guard. "They say you begin to look like the environment you work in, but that was extraordinary. I wonder if I'd held a match close to his face whether he'd begin to melt."

Dillon laughed. "Anyway, Grandpa, back to my question..."

"What question? Oh, about how strange you are."

Dillon grimaced. "It sounded like you just answered my question, Grandpa."

"Well, you do know, my boy, that you take after me quite a bit," Grandpa said in an apologetic tone, smiling warmly at every historical icon they passed.

"Oh, so you do think I'm weird then," Dillon said dryly.

"In the most wonderful way imaginable," Grandpa responded.

"Great."

Amelia Earhart seemed to give a disapproving stare through her thick flying goggles.

"Why do you ask, anyway?" Grandpa turned to him.

"Well, Samantha said that I'm weird."

"Samantha? You mean *the* Samantha? The one you said has been invited to the prom of every school in the state?"

"Yup."

"Then I'd take it as a compliment."

Dillon rolled his eyes. "Just because she spoke to me? According to that, she could have called me an ugly goofball, and I should still take it as a compliment."

"Certainly. It's all in your attitude." Grandpa stared into the eyes of Thomas Jefferson. "Liberty and the pursuit of happiness is a subjective thing."

"Yeah, well. Sometimes I wish there were more people who think like I do."

"You want them all to be weird?"

Dillon restrained himself from jabbing his Grandpa's arm. He couldn't help laughing, though.

"At least she was impressed that I raided the principal's office," Dillon said.

"Really?" Grandpa's thick gray eyebrow arched like a parametric curve. "Well that's a lot more impressed than your parents were."

"No kidding."

"They almost canceled your birthday party."

"I wish they had."

Grandpa squinted at his grandson as he walked. "So you're not in the mood for a dinner party?"

"Oh, sure. I'm turning sixteen and I'm having my aunts and uncles over for a four-course dinner at 5 o'clock in the afternoon. What else can I ask for?"

"The flu'," Grandpa quipped, and they both chuckled.

"Your Dad did say he was getting you something special," Grandpa reminded him. "Last year he got you that alien machine you keep in your pocket all the time."

"It's called a PDA, Grandpa. A Personal Digital Assistant."

"You can call it what you want, but it's an alien machine. I half expect it to one day to spawn mutant orbs of radioactivity. It's just another example of the infiltration of science fiction into society, and its degree of domestication as if it were as natural as the trees in the field," Grandpa pontificated.

"Well, to me it's cool," Dillon responded. "And when Dad does this, it kind of makes up for things a little bit. I wonder what he has in mind this year. I hope it's a car."

Grandpa chortled. "You haven't even got your license yet!" he slapped his side. "Kids these days," he muttered. "I didn't get my own car until I was twenty-eight."

"That's because cars weren't invented before that."

Grandpa had no qualms about jabbing his grandson's arm.

"Grandpa." Dillon slowed to a stop.

Grandpa stopped and turned to face him.

Dillon's eyes traveled to the floor. "Seriously. Do you think I'm weird?"

Grandpa raised his hands and settled them squarely on Dillon's shoulders.

"Dillon, you are an incredibly perceptive, sincere and caring young man, who is not daunted by adventure when it leads to meaningful discovery. If other people think that's weird, that's their business. Right, Ludwig?"

Beethoven was indifferent, a little detached.

"I think this is an accurate depiction of Beethoven's emotions," Grandpa remarked, returning his hands to his sides. "He was a complex person. What a great man."

"Grandpa, you act like you know him."

"Well," Grandpa sighed. "It does feel as though I've met him through his music. He may be dead for hundreds of years but some part of me tells me he's alive."

"Sure. Maybe you'll run in to him some time."

Grandpa laughed. "Now that would be something, wouldn't it? That would be utterly spectacular, in fact."

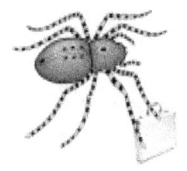

Two

"Y̶ou are so ugly," Grandpa Harley murmured, clenching his jaw in fierce concentration. "So exquisitely ugly."

"Grandpa, did you say something?" Dillon asked from the other corner of his bedroom, his own attention captivated by the screen in front of him.

"I was just talking to the Jug," Grandpa said, meticulously putting the final touches to the underbelly of the model P-47 Thunderbolt. It had been his gift to his grandson, but he was clearly invested in the pleasure his own gift provided. "Looks can be deceptive. A flabby belly, but powerful. Just like me," he quipped.

His moustache twitched as he held the plane in one hand and guided a spoonful of custard, strawberries and lemon juice into his mouth with the other.

"Grandpa, maybe we should go downstairs," Dillon suggested, although he showed little enthusiasm for the idea.

"I hate dinner parties just as much as you do," Grandpa said, licking his lips and testing the firmness of the landing gear. "They talk about politics, and that's dangerous."

"Dangerous?"

"Yes, because it bores me to death."

Dillon chuckled. "Grandpa, come over here and check this out."

Grandpa reluctantly set the Jug down and moved over to Dillon's corner. He pulled up a chair, swiped off a pile of clothing and sat down.

"So tell me, what's this contraption?" he said slowly as he twirled his strawberries in the custard goop, his eye on the birthday present Dillon's father had given him.

"Come on, you know what it is, Grandpa."

"Well, yes. I know it's a computer like I know what Einstein's theory of Relativity is. I've heard of both of them. That's about it."

Dillon snickered. "Ok, well what would you like to know?" he said.

"Can it make you a cup of coffee in the morning?" Grandpa asked, his eyebrow slightly raised.

"Great," Dillon muttered. "I've got a lot of explaining to do."

He began by showing his Grandpa how to use the mouse.

"Where do you fire?" Grandpa asked.

"Fire? What do you mean?"

"Well, you just move this control stick around and around without doing anything?"

Dillon shook his head. "Grandpa, this is a computer, not a World War II fighter aircraft. You don't fire, you click."

"What difference does it make? So where do you click then?"

Dillon wanted to explain but a voice from downstairs was calling his name.

"I guess you'd better go," Grandpa said with a slight smirk.

"I'm sure Mom wants you to come down too," Dillon retorted.

"She didn't call my name," Grandpa said, shrugging his shoulders and swinging the mouse to and fro across the pad.

"Dad!" the voice rang out again.

Dillon sported a satisfied grin, one which his grandfather was apparently too distracted to notice.

"Let's go, Grandpa." Dillon stood up.

"Tell your mother I'll be there in a couple of seconds," he said. "She did call you first."

Dillon rolled his eyes. He sailed down the railing of the dark staircase to the dining room which was lit only by candlelight, and decorated with multi-colored balloons in every corner.

"Dillon, this is your birthday party and you're not even at the table," his mother said wide-eyed as she carried roast duck from the kitchen. When her eyes were wide, it was her way of yelling at him without actually yelling at him.

"Hey, Dillon," his father called, as he chewed on a very long asparagus stick and was trying to make his point about presidential veto power and the need to reform it, to Dillon's Uncle Tony who was gearing himself to tear the point to shreds. Dillon came over to his father's side, who held him around the waist with one hand, the other repeatedly aiming a greasy fork at Uncle Tony as if it was ready to launch.

"Where's Grandpa?" his mother asked on her way back to the kitchen.

"He'll be down in a second."

Dillon sat down next to his baby sister who had gathered everyone's party napkins together, shaped them and given them each a name, and was conducting animated conversations with each one.

"Which one is me, Nicole?" he asked.

"You're the bad guy," she replied without blinking.

"Oh." He dug into his tuna and rice salad. "But you love me anyway, right?"

"I guess."

The duck lay in the center of the table on its ornate silver dish, surrounded by potatoes. It was enshrouded in its own steam, clouding the view between Dillon and his great Aunt Babette, or her acronym "GAB" as Grandpa not-so-fondly called her.

"Dillon," she purred, setting down her champagne glass and adjusting her wide-brimmed mauve hat that seemed permanently glued to her head.

"Yes, Aunty."

"What are your goals this year? What are your dreams?" She whispered the last word eerily and allowed it to stretch as long as her breath would allow.

Dillon's first reaction was to laugh her off, but he resisted it. She often punctuated drab conversations with a melodramatic question or comment, which was pretty zany but cool at the same time. He especially appreciated the fact that she took an interest in him. Grandpa saw things differently. They had gotten along as any brother and sister – mostly congenial with the occasional spat – up until the point that Great Aunt Babette's husband, Walter died. Ever since then, Grandpa and GAB were either loudly or silently at war with each another.

"Um, I haven't really thought about that," Dillon replied, tapping his fork against his plate.

Her eyes widened as if they would become a full screen. "Dreams, my boy, are the stuff of life. The mind soars, the heart yearns and the world calls."

Dillon stopped tapping.

"Oh, Dillon. If it were not for dreams I do believe this stale blood that courses through these antique veins would cease its puerile course. I am alive because of dreams, I am the victor of time because of dreams."

"Stuffing, Babbette?" Dillon's mother interrupted from the other end of the table.

GAB's eyes dimmed. "No, thank you."

Dillon watched his great aunt pick a tissue from her purse and dab the corners of her eyes. His Uncle Tony's voice was now the centerpiece, thundering and urgent, still going on about the most dangerous subject in the world.

"No, it's not a matter of partisanship. It's a matter of guts to stand up for what is right. If the popular vote puts a person in power, the people have spoken. They can't turn around and argue with their own choice!"

To Dillon, this was like getting excited about the rules of classroom behavior. His father, a lawyer both by profession and by social disposition, seemed to crave every word.

"Dillon," his mother called. "Why aren't you eating? You're still on your tuna and rice salad and the duck is getting cold."

"Give him a sweater," Dillon retorted. Nicole giggled, but their mother was not amused. It was a rather serious business, this birthday party of his.

"Dad!" Eileen Appleseed shouted again in the direction of Dillon's upstairs bedroom. A series of indiscriminate groans and muttering ensued, and finally

Grandpa Harley appeared at the bottom of the staircase his bowl of custard in hand.

"What have you been doing?" his daughter asked above the litigious din her husband and brother-in-law were creating.

"Playing with that new contraption."

"What contraption?"

"The computer, Mom," Dillon answered for him.

And then it all started, the first familiar signals of battle, beginning with GAB's loud cluck of disdain. Her eyes impatiently searched the ceiling.

Grandpa set his eyes on his sister. "What was that about?" he growled.

"I did not say anything," GAB responded, her hand clasping her heart.

"It's what you didn't say," Grandpa insisted.

GAB's jaw dropped as if to combat his low-flying comment. "Next you'll write a book about what I didn't say." She began fanning herself with her napkin.

"You were clearly trying to make a fool of me, as if I didn't know what a computer was," Grandpa protested. "As if you were the world's expert computerist."

GAB burst out laughing. Even Dillon snorted. Thankfully his Grandpa didn't notice. GAB's unbridled laughter was really the center of his attention.

"A computerist," she repeated, wiping away some fake tears. "Your honor, I rest my case."

"And what a case it is. Filled with nuts."

GAB's jaw swaggered as if she were intoxicated. "You always resort to that, Harley. It's because you have nothing intelligent to say. You never have. It's what happens when your breadth of knowledge is derived from the TV guide." She reached for her lipstick in her purse.

He leaned over the table.

"I learned more about history from PBS and the Discovery Channel than you ever you did from your meditating chants and your silly yogisms."

Dillon couldn't help chuckling, but it was overshadowed by his mother's furious voice. "Stop it! All of you!" she yelled at the top of her lungs.

Her husband and brother-in-law paused mid-discussion to take in her expression for a moment, but then continued in a lower (but not less urgent) tone. GAB carefully painted her lips and Grandpa sat down with his custard bowl still firmly in hand.

"This is Dillon's birthday party," she continued. "Please, let's not ruin it."

Nicole had been humming something throughout the various altercations that only became audible now that there was a brief respite.

"That's a pretty tune," said Eileen's sister, Marjorie, whose bangs of hair all but obscured her face. "What is it?"

"Happy birthday to you," said Nicole as she firmly flattened a particular napkin.

"Oh, well. What do you know?" Marjorie smiled through strands of hair, her hands clasping the stem of her champagne glass. "I've never been an aficionado of the classics." Her voice was like velvet.

Dillon smiled at his little sister. Some disturbed part of him surrendered to the sadness of the moment and he began putting words to the tune. Before long, everyone joined in, and Dillon's birthday party continued late into the evening, the champagne flowing, the fruit punch fizzing and the duck still lying there getting cold. At last, when some of the guests had fallen asleep at the table, Dillon could be excused.

Classes at Westridge High seemed to be intentionally dry and stuffy, taking even the most fascinating of subjects and snuffing out all the life of then until they were just a semblance of stale textbook words. The first moon landing, for example, could have been relayed in the same spirit of excitement it had engendered in living rooms across America in July of 1969. If Dillon had been the teacher, he would have made sure that the black-and-white scene would play in vivid Technicolor in the students' minds as they relived every momentous minute of history-making. It was his Grandpa who had nurtured in him a profound respect and fascination for world history, a passion for intriguing facts that had the affect of blasting away false perceptions and narrow-mindedness.

Instead, Mr. Groll, their history teacher, preferred to invoke the stiffness of Old English poem recitals, effectively suffocating the subject. He would talk mostly to himself, pacing back and forth and reciting dates, names and events for thirty-five minutes. It seems he had no interest in inspiring his students, who in turn, could not be blamed for describing the subject as "like, you know, dead."

Dillon was thankful that he had Grandpa, who frequently opened up whole paradigms for him, history that inspired him.

The other subjects were not much different, except for Computer Science, which was like a different universe, especially because of the new teacher, Mr. Halfinger. Mr. Halfinger was tall and scrawny, with wiry hair and box-shaped glasses. He moved about the classroom very rapidly and had a deep booming voice that jolted even the most sleep-deprived students in the class. Not only were his movements rapid but he spoke so fast that his teeth moved like car pistons on an

21

incline. Cal, who wasn't usually the type to show interest in an educational authority, once told Dillon between songs on his earphones, that he thought of Mr. Halfinger as the difference between cable and dial-up. Coming from Cal, this was a major endorsement. The students didn't stop to pinpoint what exactly it was about Mr. Halfinger that so effectively grabbed their attention. All they knew was that when he stood in front of them ready to teach, they became absorbed in his bulbous eyes which seemed to draw energy from some extraneous source. Whereas binary numbers could so easily have fallen into the same dull category as laborious mathematics, Mr. Halfinger was somehow able to make 1's and 0's come alive, digits switching on and off before their very eyes.

He would also throw in the very latest developments in the computer world, which seemed right at his fingertips, having scarcely left the keyboard of those journalists reporting from the edge of technology.

Today he actually mentioned Star Trek in class. You could hear a pin drop. Apparently there had been a breakthrough in something called Image Particle Transfer, or IPT, technology that would one day allow actual organic forms to transfer across domains and dimensions.

"Are you saying, people would disappear from one place and suddenly appear in another place?" Stacey asked in astonishment.

There were several groans of cynicism and disbelief sounding throughout the class.

"Make Stacey disappear," someone suggested, basking in the peals of laughter that followed.

Mr. Halfinger's eyes bulged so large they could have passed for boiled eggs.

"Would I ever say an untruth?" he admonished them in almost imperceptible whisper. The class was abruptly silent again.

He turned to Stacey. His lips parted smoothly like electric gates of a large estate. "Yes, Stacey," he breathed, his words singeing like steam. "Yes. What you say is correct."

He paused, then addressed the whole class.

"So, tell me. All of you. Which line in Star Trek might actually become possible?" he asked calmly, his eyes illuminating each face they met.

"Beam me up, Scotty!" a few of them responded in unison.

Dillon was transfixed. His mind flooded with the endless possibilities were this concept to become a reality. He struggled to focus on anything else in the lesson and for the rest of the school day. He imagined the end of conventional transportation as the world knew it. No more need for cars, bikes, airplanes, boats and trains. No more roads and traffic lights. No more pollution problems, no more traffic congestion. The whole world would be transformed. He couldn't wait to tell his Grandpa.

Dora, the housekeeper opened the door for Dillon.

"Hi," she said, which was about one quarter of her English vocabulary. The other three quarters was "No speaka English" which she always said smiling before disappearing with her broom into some other area of the house.

The way Dillon saw it, she was freaky. At one point he'd thought she genuinely couldn't speak the language. But one day he had arrived home unexpectedly early from school with a fever and overheard someone speaking on the phone in perfect English. He could have sworn it was Dora's voice but when he came into the living room to investigate, she was holding her broom looking a little flustered. "Dora, was that you on the phone?"

"No speaka English," she'd said, smiling as always and disappearing into the kitchen.

She had puzzled him ever since, some part of him hoping that his fever had caused his mind to play tricks on him.

He dropped his bag against the door of the coat closet and skipped downstairs to the basement which was fitted out as an entire apartment for Grandpa.

"Grandpa!" he shouted as he jumped over the bottom few stairs to the landing.

The small carpeted living room was empty as was the (mostly unused) kitchenette and large master bath.

"Grandpa!" he yelled again. This time he heard a faint response from somewhere else in the house. His own bedroom.

Dillon scampered up both flights of stairs to his bedroom and found his Grandpa seated at his desk in front of the new computer.

"What you doing?" Dillon asked him out of breath.

"Playing with the contraption," he responded, without taking his eyes off the screen.

Dillon hunched himself over his Grandpa's shoulder, and began to laugh. "Grandpa, you're just moving the mouse back and forth."

"So what? I'm watching how it disappears at the one end and reappears at the other. Somehow it doesn't get lost in real life."

"Funny you say that, Grandpa," Dillon said. "You can't believe what my Computer Science teacher told us today."

Grandpa's eyes widened after Dillon finished relating the news from class.

"No more staircases!" He declared. "No more back pain."

"I guess so," Dillon said, smiling.

"But what if part of me gets lost in the process?" Grandpa asked. "Not that it would be such a bad thing." He patted his substantial stomach.

Dillon shrugged his shoulders. "Let's find the news reports on it. The world must be going crazy about this."

"I don't see a newspaper anywhere" Grandpa said, eyes searching the desk.

"Don't need it. I can look it up on the Internet."

"Oh, I've heard of that too," Grandpa nodded.

"Just like Einstein's theory of Relativity?"

"Exactly."

Dillon could not imagine having no idea what the Internet was.

He sat down alongside his Grandpa and checked the news on the Internet. Political controversy, celebrity squabbles and stories of a cat saving its owner's life.

"That is something," Grandpa remarked. "How does the computer know the news?"

But Dillon was oblivious to his Grandpa's words.

"This can't be," he said, his eyes chasing every tidbit of news the screen manufactured.

"There's nothing here about Image Particle Transfer. Surely there's something in the news about it, even just a mention."

He performed a number of searches and still nothing at all turned up.

"Weird."

"Do you think your teacher was making it up?" Grandpa asked.

Dillon sat back in his chair. "I don't get it. Why would he do that? He's supposed to be teaching us about Computer Science, not fiction."

"Maybe it's a government cover-up," Grandpa Harley suggested.

"Then how would he know about it?" Dillon argued. They both looked at each other without anything to say. Dillon felt let down. If there was any teacher in the school who had gained his respect and admiration, it was Mr. Halfinger. The prospect of being misled by him was difficult to accept. But then why would he tell them about a revolutionary development in computer technology that didn't seem to exist?

The following day, school seemed to drag more than ever. Dillon had his eye on the wall clock in each classroom, the countdown towards Computer Science causing him to gloss over T.S. Elliot, the cross-section of the human eye and everything else that was supposed to be occupying his attention. Even Thomas Edison, whose true-to-life wax incarnation he had pored over together with his Grandpa just the other day, was no more than a dull rendering of the facts of his life.

He was called on in Math to solve a basic algebra problem and he had to jumpstart his brain in order to process the question. Finally, when the time came for Computer Science, Dillon felt his heart accelerate and his nerves tingle. Mr. Halfinger made his trademark grand entrance, practically leaping to the center of the room, his eyes popping wide open, ready to scan each student. Dillon held his breath. Should he confront his teacher now in front of everyone? What would Mr. Halfinger do to him in response? He had never seen Mr. Halfinger become angry before in class. But that was probably because his style was so riveting that there was rarely any need for a show of authority.

Dillon decided he would wait to see if his teacher would bring the subject up on his own anyway, and then he might have the courage to question him on it. But Mr. Halfinger delved immediately into the subject of flowcharts – with an unconventional twist, of course. Each student would represent a box, and everyone in the class would be required to organize themselves into a human flowchart that would be representative of a computer program. It was only a few seconds before a predictable chaos erupted, students happily wreaking havoc with the desk and chair arrangements, debating each other and shouting commands in all directions. Throughout all of it, Mr. Halfinger continued to stand in the center with a satisfied smile, basking in all the noise and activity which he had so effortlessly orchestrated.

Should he approach him now while everyone was organizing themselves? Dillon wondered. But before he could think any further, Linda Ferrimore called him over to assume his position as an "if" string.

After the class, Dillon picked up his bag and again deliberated whether or not this was the moment to approach his teacher. He knew he had to move fairly quickly in order to get to Spanish on time. Maybe he should....

"Dillon," Mr. Halfinger called.

Dillon turned towards his teacher, his heart accelerating again.

"Yes, Mr. Halfinger."

"Could you stay a couple of minutes? I'd like to talk with you."

Dillon swallowed. "Ah, sure."

He slowly approached his teacher's desk. Mr. Halfinger closed a couple of books and straightened his desk before inviting Dillon to take a seat opposite him. His eyes made a sweeping check of the classroom to ensure privacy.

"I'll get right to it," he said. "Dillon, I am aware that you performed several Internet searches yesterday in order to investigate research Image Particle Transfer."

Dillon jumped up in fright.

"Don't worry," Mr. Halfinger said. "I'm not going to...."

"How'd you know I did that?" Dillon breathed. He backed away from the desk.

"That's not important right now, Dillon. What is important is...."

Dillon shook his head and started walking towards the door. "No, no, this is.... I can't....I need to go."

"Dillon, please. Don't go. I have already spoken earlier this morning with Mrs. Mendoza to tell her you will be a few minutes late for Spanish class."

Dillon stood very still, his eyes unblinking and his skin almost as white as the wall behind him.

"I'm sorry if I have scared you. Dillon. That is certainly not my intention." He shrugged his bony shoulders and smiled broadly.

Dillon remained stock-still.

"Look, I realize that this is a little strange for you, but I want to assure you that no harm will come to you. Come on, do you think that I would risk such a thing?"

Dillon studied his teacher's face: the patches of pale-skin and the dark whiskers that protruded from them. His eyes then returned to the floor. "What is ...." he croaked. He cleared his throat. "What is this about, Mr. Halfinger?"

"Well, Dillon," Mr. Halfinger lowered his voice. He briefly checked the room.

"When I mentioned IPT to your class yesterday, I wanted to discern who amongst you would be most fascinated with the concept. Not those who reacted simply because it conjured up the 'Beam Me up, Scotty' line. I was looking for those amongst you who would be hooked by the idea, hooked enough to explore it further in their spare time, hooked enough to spend their entire day wrapped up in thought about it. And I believe you are that person. Not merely because of your interest in this particular topic, but because throughout my continuous evaluation of all my students, I have noticed your singular interest in certain subjects that transcend the academic to embrace the real, living, and joyous chaos of intellectual exploration."

Dillon shook his head in confusion and disbelief and managed a smile. "Yup, that would be me. I think."

"Oh, I know, Dillon. I know. Now, please sit down, and let me explain a few things." He motioned to the chair. Dillon had trouble moving his legs, but eventually made his way to the chair.

Mr. Halfinger opened his laptop computer. Again he checked the room. He shifted the computer so that Dillon could see the screen and typed something in the address bar of his web browser. "Dillon, memorize this address. I cannot write this down for security reasons."

The address was nonsensical and 11 characters long, consisting of both numbers and letters.

"I – that's a long address, Mr. Halfinger. I don't know if I can memorize it."

"It's simple. There's a formula. The address you see is

f7h4565wg4p.com. Locate each character on the keyboard and identify the key that lies immediately South West of it."

Dillon was puzzled. "South West of it?"

"Yes. For example: The first character is f. If you look on the keyboard, any keyboard, immediately to the South West of f is c."

"Oh," Dillon smiled. He completed the translation for each key and came out with C-Y-B-E-R-T-R-A-V-E-L.

"Cybertravel!" he announced enthusiastically, his fear temporarily at bay.

"Shhh!" Mr. Halfinger cautioned him, his face turning a little pink. "This must be done very, very discreetly."

"Ok. What is Cybertravel?" Dillon whispered.

"You'll see now."

The web page that surfaced was very simple with a small digest of daily news and commentary.

"I don't get it," Dillon said. "There's nothing special about this site."

"Patience," Mr. Halfinger said. "This is a fake cover-screen. Now watch this. You see this harmless looking little flower in the bottom corner. Click three times on that." He gave Dillon control of the mouse.

"Three times?"

"Three times."

Dillon obliged, and up came an almost completely black screen, except for two white strips in the center.

"Now enter the word, 'transfer' and my password, 'half1'. Then hit enter."

Dillon hesitated. "I'd prefer if....will you do it?"

Mr. Halfinger smiled. He pressed enter. What Dillon saw next left him somewhere between the states of fascination and terror, where the thrill of discovery and the fear of the unknown danced wildly together along every nerve of his body.

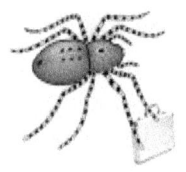

Three

Gerald Appleseed worked in a tall glass building that had so many interesting angles, it looked like some giant hand had twisted it around several times before setting it down in its place. Dillon often heard his father talk about the various lawsuits filed by the occupants of the neighboring buildings who found the sunlight being refracted by the glass to be inescapable no matter which way they arranged their furniture. Rather than becoming daunted by their claims, his father seemed to become inspired by the challenge. He thrived on conflict and would regale his family with every detail of his game strategy against these claimants.

Dillon stood in the lavish lobby of the building, the dimmed lighting creating a haze of red and gold colors. His mother, Nicole and Aunt Marjorie stood beside him as they waited for his father to emerge from the elevator. It was one of those times Dillon fervently wished that he had his driver's license already. His test was scheduled for two weeks' time and it could not come sooner. The knowledge of his impending license made it all the more difficult to endure unnecessary group trips like this, when all he wanted was to speak with his father alone.

"Why didn't you just call Dad?" Nicole asked, frustrated that she wasn't at home playing with her Barbie collection.

"I did, Nicole," Dillon said. "He always puts his phone on voicemail, remember?"

"Not always," his mother corrected him, yet not quite convincingly.

"Yes, always," Nicole said.

"Eileen," Marjorie nudged her sister, brushing some hair away from her face for a moment before it fell right back again. "Don't let your kids talk back to you like that. Why do you let your kids talk back to you like that?"

Eileen rolled her eyes. "Marjorie, please."

"Respect. No respect. That's why I didn't have any kids."

"But you told me that you never had kids because you couldn't find a husband," Nicole protested.

"Nicole!" Eileen admonished her. "That is inappropriate."

"Finally," Marjorie mumbled.

Eileen sighed. "Look, can everyone please just behave and be quiet while we wait for Daddy. Dillon really wants to speak with him."

"About what?" Nicole asked.

"About some computer thing," Eileen said.

"For some computer thing?" Nicole whined. "That's not fair. It's just a computer thing and we all have to come here just for that."

"I had to bring you here because there's no-one to watch you at home, Nicole."

"And this is really important," Dillon added.

"Obviously more important than my therapy session which we will miss if we wait any longer," said Marjorie, not bothering to brush the hair from her face.

"Why couldn't Grandpa look after me at home?" Nicole persisted.

"Because I've told you many times that Grandpa likes to take a nap in the afternoon and I can't leave you at home with him."

Dillon turned to his mother. "Can you take Aunt Marjorie to her session and come and pick me up again afterwards?" he suggested in a drone.

Eileen sighed. "Fine. At least then we won't have to rush. I'll meet you here in an hour. Nicole, Marjorie, let's go."

Dillon sat down on an antique bench that smelled thickly of varnish, and waited. After a number of minutes, the lady at reception called him up to her moon-shaped granite counter.

"Young man, your father would like to speak with you." She handed him a receiver.

"Dad?"

"Dillon, look. I have been trying to come down but every time I try to leave the office something else happens. Now I have back to back meetings until 7pm. Is it that urgent? Can't it wait until I get home later?"

Dillon sighed. "What time will that be?"

"Well, let's see....Around....10. Or 10:30pm."

"Dad, that's late." He felt his muscles tighten.

"Well, can't you tell me now quickly over the phone?"

Dillon brought his hand to his forehead. "No, I.... I can't. It's really...." He dropped his voice to whisper, which ironically made the receptionist perk up.

"It's really top secret."

"Oh, come on, Dillon. What nonsense is that?"

"No, really, Dad. My teacher told me something at school that I need to talk to you about because it's so unbelievable and, like, scary. I need your advice, being a lawyer and everything."

"Well, what did she tell you?"

"It's a he. And I told you, I can't say on the phone. I need to speak to you in private and it can't wait."

Gerald sighed. "I don't know, let me see what I can....one second, Dillon. Just one second....What, Anne?....Ok, tell him I'll be right with him. What? No, I need to look at the contract again....yes.... I know he's not going to like it, but he signed the darn thing.... Ok, Ok, I'll be there in thirty seconds....Dillon?"

"Yeah."

"Listen, Dillon, I just can't do this right now. It's impossible. There's so much going on. I'm sorry, boy, ok? I need to go."

"Bye. Dad," Dillon mumbled.

He let the receiver dangle by its chord.

"I'll take that for you," the receptionist offered, her smile creating wedges in her thickly smeared make-up.

Dillon returned to the antique bench to wait for his mother. He pulled out his hand-held PDA from his pocket. He traced his fingers along its smooth silicone edges. The year before, his father had handed it to him with a grin and a quick ruffle of his hair. Now he had the computer which had also been unveiled with a flash of a smile and accompanied by an obligatory pat on the shoulder. Sometimes he wished he wouldn't like the gifts. The problem was they were simply awesome.

He was about to select "games" when he was struck by the urge to explore what Mr. Halfinger had shown him earlier. The thought of it made him tremble, but if his father was not available to advise him, he would just go ahead with it anyway. He would get a glimpse of it right there and then. He looked to the left and right of him and with unsteady fingers began to type the alphanumeric code into the address bar. Just as he pressed enter and the fake cover-screen came into view, a man with a briefcase sat down next to him on the bench. Dillon quickly closed the PDA, but not before the man had managed a glance at the screen.

"<B> Hi there</B>" the man said with a smile.

It was a frightening nonsensical, almost non-human utterance. Dillon bolted from the bench and headed for the doors. The low garbled voice of the man continued to reverberate in his mind as if the sound had latched onto him, digging his claws into him as he left the building.

Standing outside of the revolving doors in the pedestrian traffic, the wind lifting his hair, he scanned the street for his mother's car even though he knew it would be a while before she arrived. Things were turning weirder by the minute. What was he getting himself into? Maybe he should just try to forget what had happened today, forget what Mr. Halfinger had shown him, forget the surge of excitement and wonder he'd felt upon discovering something that was sure to revolutionize the world....

As he stood there, though, allowing his thoughts to churn about in his head, things began to change. The more he thought about it, the more the fear began to evolve into the thrill of adventure, his skin rapidly transforming into a minefield of goosebumps, the lure of a hidden dimension quite quickly trumping any concerns for his safety.

He even plucked up the courage to turn around and gain a glimpse through the opaque glass at the person who had frightened him. The man continued to sit there, an otherwise innocuous figure sitting amongst everyone else. Only Dillon knew of the hidden dimension, what seemed to be a monstrous one. It reminded him of that story his Grandpa had read to him when he was a young kid: Beauty and the Beast – only in this case, the beast was hidden inside the beauty.

By the time his mother picked him up, the fireworks inside Dillon's mind were almost ready to explode. He was just bursting to tell Grandpa about this, about everything. Grandpa would be amazed, just as amazed as he was. Grandpa would understand.

"Dillon," his mother was calling him, as they merged onto the freeway.

"Yeah."

"You seem quiet. Did you sort everything out with Dad?"

Dillon smiled, not unlike the smile of Mr. Halfinger.

"Yup. All sorted out."

"Good."

Whatever Dillon wanted to unload on Grandpa, it had to wait. When they arrived home, sounds of chaos greeted them. From the kitchen came a cacophony of dishes shattering, machines roaring and voices yelling. Everyone raced toward the kitchen to find Dora and Grandpa engaged in a raging culinary battle that involved every available cooking implement and food item within arm's reach. They were both doused in flour, ketchup, and strands of egg, the occasional popcorn kernel clinging to the goop. Weapons included a rolling pin, a mixer, and a large Duncan-Hines—coated wooden spoon.

After Eileen's jaw returned to its original position, she yelled above the din for order, just as Dora shouted, "Imbecile!"

Imbecile, Dillon thought. Pretty sophisticated word for someone who doesn't speak English.

Both Dora and Grandpa halted their battle and turned to face the family.

"What on earth is going on here?" Eileen demanded.

"No Speaka English," Dora said, instantly composed.

Grandpa threw his hands in the air. "She wouldn't let me put popcorn and cake in the blender, so I..."

"Popcorn and cake in the blender?" Eileen and Dillon said in unison. Nicole twisted her lips in disgust.

"Yes, I've had it before," Grandpa insisted, a splotch of ketchup hanging from his moustache.

"Dad, you've never had it before," Eileen said, exasperated.

"Of course I have. You even made it for me."

"What? When would I have done such a thing?"

Dora followed the conversation like a tennis spectator. She tried to wring her hair which was soaked in cooking oil.

"When we were in the old house and you made a cake for your mother and me for our twentieth anniversary."

Eileen titled her head and frowned. "Your twentieth anniversary?" As she spoke, it dawned on her that today would have been her parents' fiftieth wedding anniversary. She discerned the tenderness in her father's eyes, even through the web of flour, ketchup and egg. It also dawned on her that her father had made a slight error in recollection.

"Poppy seeds, Dad," she said with a smile, some moistness developing in her own eyes. "Not popcorn. Poppy seeds."

There was a brief pause before everyone began to laugh, including Dora who could not apparently "speaka English."

"What was Grandma like?" Dillon asked later as he helped his Grandpa scrape dough off the wall.

Grandpa Harley said nothing for a while, chipping away at a clump of hardened dough. "Dillon, have you ever had a particularly magical dream where you're actually aware that it's just a dream?"

"Yeah, I've had those. It's cool when that happens. It's like you're standing outside of yourself, watching yourself. I try to make the dream last as long as I can."

"Well," Grandpa said, turning briefly to his grandson. "That's pretty much what it was like spending time with your Grandma. I never wanted the dream to end."

That was all he said, and Dillon sensed that he ought to wait until a bit later to tell his Grandpa everything that had happened that day.

He waited until after dinner to call Grandpa up to his room. Grandpa carried with him a bowl of fresh custard, strawberries and lemon juice.

"You want to show me something on that new contraption of yours?" he asked as they climbed the stairs.

"Uh....yes, I do." He was trying to restrain himself, although it was like trying to stop the champagne from exploding into the crowd at a Formula 1 victory celebration.

They sat down at Dillon's desk, the sound of Grandpa's custard-munching accompanied by the whir of the computer's boot-up.

Grandpa perked up at the little jingle the computer played as the screen loaded. "Oh, I like that," he said. "It plays music too."

Dillon smiled but his mind was racing ahead to the screen with the flower, even before his fingers began to enter its alphanumeric address. When he got to the site, he swiveled his chair towards his Grandpa.

"Grandpa, remember yesterday when I told you about Image Particle Transfer?"

"Sure. Beam me up Scotty? No more staircases, no more back pain."

"Yeah, well…." Dillon took a breath. "Mr. Halfinger knew that we checked on-line about it."

Grandpa frowned. "You mean he knew that we were sitting here in front of the contraption and typing it in?"

Dillon nodded.

"How did he know?"

Dillon shrugged his shoulders. "He must have hacked into my computer."

Grandpa inspected the surface and sides of the computer. "I don't see a dent," he said.

Dillon suppressed a laugh. "Grandpa, that's not what hacking is. Hacking means someone has accessed your computer from their computer."

"Of course," Grandpa said, slapping his side. "Why would I think that hacking means what it has always meant for thousands of years?"

"In any case," Dillon continued. "He showed me what IPT really is about. It's not about transporting people to different places on Earth. It's about transporting people into Cyberspace."

"What space?"

"Cyberspace." Dillon pointed to the website. "You see this? This is an access portal that lets you travel into the domain of the world wide web, into the computer, where you'd be able to see websites come alive and explore them. Picture it as being right inside the computer world." His breath was short and his eyes wide.

Grandpa was not impressed. "That's a fairy tale if you ask me. I remember when I was a kid, I thought there was a person inside the transistor radio because a person's voice was coming from inside it. The image of Billie Holiday being all cramped up in there as she produced the perfect soft sound, was particularly troubling to me. As I grew older, of course, I realized it wasn't true, although don't ask me how it works with all that sound wave business."

"No, Grandpa, it is true." Dillon insisted.

"About Billie Holiday?"

"No, Grandpa," Dillon rolled his eyes. "About getting access to Cyberspace."

"How do you know? Because your teacher told you? I remember I had a teacher by the name of Ms. Wengrove who told us that talking to plants makes them grow better."

Dillon cocked his head. "I also heard that."

"Well, maybe she taught you too. Hang on, she was about thirty years old when I was in the sixth grade, which would make her about ninety-nine years old today – which is not impossible considering the advances in…."

"Grandpa!" Dillon urged. "Please, let's concentrate on this." He pointed again to the computer. "Mr. Halfinger actually showed me how to do it."

Grandpa's expression began to change. "He did?"

"Yes, he did." Dillon swallowed. "If we wanted to, we could go into Cyberspace right now."

"Right now?"

Dillon nodded, an adventurous twinkle illuminating his eyes.

"You said, 'we'."

"Yes, Grandpa. I want you to come with me."

Grandpa Harley shifted in his chair and raised his finger to his cheek as if considering a serious business proposal.

"That would be irresponsible," he said.

Dillon looked down.

"But also irresistible," Grandpa added, still with the same seriousness.

Dillon smiled. He lowered his voice to a whisper. "Let's do it, Grandpa. Let's explore Cyberspace together. We'll see all sorts of amazing websites, computer characters that until now are just things you see in a text book. Now everything will come alive and we'll be in the middle of it!"

Grandpa twirled the custard about with his spoon.

"And we'll come back ok?"

"Yup. He showed me how to get back – pretty much the same way we go in."

"How long will we be away?"

"Well, that's the coolest part, Grandpa. Time stands still for us in Cyberspace. So we can take as long as we like and we'll be back the same second we left in real life."

"Well," Grandpa sighed after a long pause. "I am the adventurous type. I can assure you that. Ask anyone who saw me chase an Anaconda away from our picnic table one summer in the mountains."

"Mom told me that was a garden snake."

"Your mother was too young to remember properly, Dillon."

Dillon fidgeted with his wristwatch. "So, Grandpa, what do you say?"

Grandpa looked away. "I don't think we should do this," he said softly.

"Why not?" Dillon said.

"It sounds so dangerous. I mean one minute you're here, the next minute you're not. It's one thing to play a game, it's another thing to completely disappear into the game. I mean, what if we don't come back alive? Your mother would kill me!"

Dillon would have laughed, but his disappointment prevented it. He stared at the computer screen for a while.

"I guess you're right, Grandpa," he mumbled. "It's different to busting Mr. Rigler."

"Yes," Grandpa agreed. "That was a matter of principle."

Dillon snickered. "A matter of principle? Did you mean that really bad joke?"

Grandpa's eyes scurried about. "Uh, yes. Now I do."

They both laughed.

Grandpa patted Dillon's shoulder. "Still, I continue to admire your eagerness to assist in the advancement of humankind. We are so much alike, you and I."

Dillon sighed. "I guess that's what makes me weird."

"I suppose so," Grandpa said with a smile. "I think it's time for me to get ready for bed now." He rose from his chair. "Don't be sad, Dillon. Think of it this way. One day you will be able to take that enthusiasm for exploring new frontiers and use it to exponential effect."

"Right, Grandpa."

"Good night, boy."

"Good night, Grandpa."

Dillon slowly prepared for bed. He hadn't done his homework but at this point he just couldn't bring himself to do it. In any case, he found he could easily do it on the bus to school in the mornings. Usually at that time of the day nobody around him was in the mood for talking much and he could settle down with his books and a pen. He shut down his computer and put away his PDA. After switching off the light and climbing into bed, he stared at his posters and the shadowed figures they contained. He listened to the sounds of distant late night traffic as well as the occasional bark of a dog outside or a door shutting somewhere in the house. Some time after he heard his father's car pulling up, he drifted off to sleep.

"Dillon!"
The boat he was driving began to fade because....someone was calling his name?
"Dillon!" the voice said again in a stronger whisper.
Dillon sat up in fright. "Grandpa?"
Grandpa Harley was hovering over his bed. "Shhh," he said.
"Grandpa, what's wrong? What happened?"
"Nothing's wrong," Grandpa assured him, a hand on his grandson's shoulder. "Be quiet or your mother and father will wake up."
"Ok," Dillon croaked. "What....What's happening?"
"Well," Grandpa sighed. "I couldn't sleep. And I was sure you couldn't sleep either."
He kept his stare on Dillon awaiting his response.
"Well, actually, I was able to...."
"In any case," Grandpa said quickly. "I want to do this."
"What?"

"I want to go to the Decipher-space or what ever you call it."

"Cyberspace?"

"That's it. You got it."

Dillon blinked away what little remained of his sleep. "Really?"

"Yes."

"When?"

"Now is as good a time as ever."

Dillon could not believe he was hearing this. His heart jumpstarted and immediately embarked on a whirlwind tour of all the undiscovered regions of his chest. .

"But....it's the middle of the night."

"And therefore?" Grandpa shot back without a second's hesitation.

"Well....for one thing we are both in our pajamas. We can't go into Cyberspace in our pajamas."

They both laughed, their cupped hands trying to stifle the sound .

"Shhh," Grandpa warned again.

"What made you change your mind?" Dillon asked.

"Well, let's just say sometimes my heart pummels my brain into sawdust."

"What?"

"It means I can give you all the logical reasoning in the world why this is a foolish idea, and in the end I get consumed by the magic of it, the idea of exploring uncharted territory. You know, Dillon you may be seeing a man with only a few hairs left on his head, and those hairs that remain are white – but my boyhood dreams have never left me."

Dillon nodded.

"Besides," Grandpa added. "I had acid reflux and couldn't sleep."

Dillon laughed out loud. They both froze as they heard someone stir in one of the bedrooms. A few seconds went by and there were no further sounds.

"Alright," Grandpa whispered. "I'll go downstairs and get dressed, and you do the same, Dillon. Okay?"

Dillon took a breath before nodding his consent.

"Should I bring anything with me? My passport? What about some food?"

Dillon laughed nervously. "No I…. I don't think you have to worry about that, Grandpa."

Grandpa Harley tiptoed out of the room and down the stairs. Dillon jumped out of bed and got dressed in anything he could pull out of his closet. As he was loading the computer again, Grandpa entered the room panting.

"Wow, that was quick, Grandpa."

Grandpa stretched his arms and rotated his ankles. "I'm roaring to go," he said.

"What's that shirt you're wearing there, Grandpa?" Dillon looked closer. "Oh, it's a Star Wars shirt!"

"I thought it was apropos."

"G-r-a-n-d-p-a," Dillon growled in a poor imitation of Darth Vader.

Grandpa grabbed hold of Dillon's hockey stick and assumed the laser-beam duel position.

"Whoah!" Dillon said. "Let's remember what we're here for."

"Okay, okay. Tell me where I'm supposed to stand."

"That's actually a good question, Grandpa. One second, let me go through the steps here."

He entered Mr. Halfinger's username and password, and the screen went black.

"Welcome to Biteflite Cybertravel Services," a rosy voice began.

"Shhh! Can you tell her to speak a little softer," Grandpa urged.

Dillon lowered the sound.

A question appeared in the center of the page.

"If you are Cyberian, click here. If you are human, click here."

"What's a Cyberian?" Grandpa asked.

"I tried to ask Mr. Halfinger that but he told me there wasn't any time to go into that."

Dillon clicked on the second box.

"Thank you. How many humans will be traveling on this cyberflight?"

Dillon pressed "2".

"Will either passenger be carrying along any items?"

Dillon clicked "Yes."

Grandpa looked at him in surprise. "What are we bringing?"

"My PDA," Dillon said. "Mr. Halfinger told me I should definitely bring it with. I guess that's in case I need directions or something."

After Dillon described the PDA, the screen went to a long, dense paragraph of legal writing. At the end was a box that Dillon checked affirming that he accepted all the terms and conditions.

"But you didn't read any of that," Grandpa protested.

"Nobody does," Dillon said casually.

"No wonder everyone is suing everyone else these days," Grandpa remarked.

"Both passengers must adhere to the following instructions exactly," the computer said. "For your own safety, Biteflite will not allow travel unless your transfer position is 100% in place."

"That's nice of her, whatever she meant," Grandpa commented.

"It means they won't allow you to leave unless they've got your whole body in focus," Dillon explained. "Mr. Halfinger explained that the program uses very advanced body heat sensors that size up your entire body and that information is entered into the system."

"I give them permission to leave this part behind." Grandpa pointed to his belly.

"Passenger Dillon, please stand directly in line of the screen, one foot away."

Dillon took a breath and obliged.

"Please move 2 inches forward."

Dillon moved ever so slightly forward.

"Thank you. Please hold very still."

After about ten seconds, the computer again thanked him and called for Passenger Harley.

Grandpa stepped up to the plate. He held his breath.

"There is no need to hold your breath," the computer said.

"Ha!" Grandpa exclaimed. "I hope she can't read my mind too. She'd figure out it was me who stole the bathroom towels from the Hyatt Hotel in Florida in 1973."

When Grandpa was done, the computer advised them, "Please do not move more than 500 feet from your original positions before transfer."

"Fine, we're not going anywhere. Now what?" Grandpa asked.

"We are ready for transfer," the computer said. "If you would like to proceed with this transfer into Cyberspace, press enter. If you would like to cancel this transfer, press cancel."

Dillon and his Grandpa looked at each other. "We could cancel this whole thing right now," Dillon said.

"We could," Grandpa agreed.

"And it would be an ordinary night."

"Yup, an ordinary night."

"We could think about it a little mo…."

"Let's go," Grandpa said matter-of-factly.

"Let's go!" Dillon repeated, his trembling finger hitting the 'enter' button.

"Thank you. You will be transferred momentarily. For further inform…."

But it was like the anesthesiologist telling the patient to count backwards from five. Neither Dillon nor Grandpa Harley could hear the rest of the lady's sentence. They were gone.

Four

People were brushing past Dillon as he stood outside a concrete and glass skyscraper that rose so high he could hardly make out the top. Several other buildings hugged this one in each direction. His mind was groggy and his vision blurred as if he had just awoken from a long luxurious nap in a hammock on a hazy summer afternoon. In his confusion Dillon thought he was downtown near his father's building, until he saw the large corporation logo for Biteflite Cybertravel Services emblazoned in silver above the revolving doors to the skyscraper.

Wiping his eyes, Dillon suddenly understood where he was. His immediate thought was, if this was Cyberspace, where was Grandpa?

"Your attention please. This is a security announcement. Cyberian Anti-Viral Enforcement has raised the security alert level to.... *Orange*. Do not leave file attachments unattended. Any unidentified file attachments will be removed and destroyed."

Dillon searched frantically around him but saw no signs of his Grandpa. The area he was in was a square plaza with walls and curves of granite, dotted with boxes of greenery just like the downtown parks.

"Excuse me." He stopped a man in a suit passing by. "Have you seen an older man, balding? His name is Harley."

The man shook his head. "Sorry."

Dillon ran back and forth between the plant boxes. He kept tripping and having to catch his fall. The ground was cobbled and uneven. His mind filled with images of his Grandpa stuck somewhere between real life and Cyberspace, his arms flailing and his moustache twitching wildly. He immediately felt the guilt for dragging his Grandpa into this. His breathing became heavy and rapid. What was happening to his Grandpa?

"Your attention, please. This is a security announcement. Cyberian Anti-Viral Enforcement has raised the security level to…." This time the recorded announcement was interrupted by a live one.

"Passenger Dillon Appleseed, Passenger Dillon Appleseed, please come to information in the Arrivals Terminal to meet your party. Passenger Dillon Appleseed."

His party. Dillon sighed with immense relief. Everything was so strikingly similar to the airports and malls back home. Now, how to get to the Arrivals Terminal?

He entered the building through the revolving doors and immediately spotted his Grandpa talking to a lady at the information desk. Dillon ran up to him and gave him a bear hug. "Grandpa, I was so worried."

"Ah, that's so sweet," the lady said, her teeth and her earrings sparkling.

"So if Marjorie has no kids yet then Dillon and Nicole are your only grandchildren, huh?" she asked

Grandpa. "They must be spoiled," she said with another gracious smile.

"Yup, they sure are," Grandpa replied, obviously already comfortable enough to divulge a lot more than the average banter with a complete stranger typified.

"You know, Dillon," Grandpa said holding him around the shoulder, "this lady was so helpful and easy to talk to, even though she isn't human." He and the woman laughed together. Dillon was baffled.

"I'm Cyberian," the woman explained. "The vast majority of the people you see around you are Cyberians. I enjoy telling all the arriving humans all about us. There really isn't much difference between us except that Cyberians don't eat or drink. We recharge our batteries at night before going to sleep."

"Hey, I like that idea!" Grandpa exclaimed. "That way you never overeat and never get fat!"

The lady laughed. "Yes, I guess we're fortunate in that way. I've toured some websites while on vacation that talked about how humans diet, and I saw different health food studies. I counted my blessings that we don't have to worry about that. I said, 'Lorraine, count your blessings.' At the same time I found it very intriguing. I always enjoy learning about different cultures. It gives one a broad perspective on things."

At each point she made, Dillon's jaw dropped slowly open like a drawbridge, and stayed there. While he was speechless, Grandpa was not.

"So there are no restrooms then?" he asked her.

"Oh, we do have restrooms," she said, holding her palm to her mouth to hide her giggle. "I mean, Cyberians also have waste – all the chemical toxins we absorb from being constantly on battery power. But I don't want to get too graphic here." She let out a stray giggle.

Dillon's mind, though, had no trouble resuming where she left off, launching into spectacular visions of corrupted zinc bursting from an abdominal Duracell.

"Oh, by the way," she turned to Dillon, eager to change the subject. "I want to apologize on behalf of BiteFlite for having diverted you to outside the terminal for landing. We occasionally run out of memory space and have to divert incoming transfers. Sorry about that."

"That's okay," Dillon croaked. He wanted to ask her what would happen if a Cyberian forgot to recharge at night, but he was afraid to do so.

"So you speak English, obviously," Grandpa was saying.

"Oh, yes. It's interesting. English is not really our native tongue. But computer programming has advanced so rapidly with so many different variations and versions that it just became easier on everyone to speak English."

"What is your native language?" Grandpa asked.

"HTML," she replied. "There are still some die-hards who speak it because they moan about culture erosion." She rolled her eyes.

"W-o-w," Dillon stammered. He immediately thought of the man with the briefcase sitting next to him on the bench in the lobby of his father's office building. That strange-sounding greeting he'd given him must have been in HTML.

"Uh, what is HTML?" Grandpa asked.

Dillon answered for the lady. "It's Hyper Text Markup Language, a special language for website programming."

"Still sounds Greek to me," he remarked.

Lorraine laughed again. "You have a wonderful sense of humor, sir. The thing is, I know that HTML is like a code that is used to build computer programs and make them work, but to be honest, I don't quite understand it myself." She grinned sheepishly. "You know, when you're born into something , you don't always question it. I remember asking my Daddy, bless his soul, about HTML, and he just shrugged his shoulders in his adorable, even-tempered way and said, "Lorraine, there's so much you need to know. Why spend time on what you don't need to know?"

"That is quite wise," Grandpa agreed.

"Umm, ma'am," Dillon addressed her.

"Yes, young man."

"You said something about touring websites. Can we do that too?"

"Of course," she said, bringing out some tourist brochures from underneath her counter. She opened up a pamphlet.

"You see, we are here, at the Biteflite Arrivals Terminal. If you want to visit websites, you'll need to go to the Noogle Search Station, which is located here, a short ten minute walk from the terminal." She circled a point on the little map." Just go along Silicone Valley Road East, keeping to the sidewalk, until you get to the station on the left. It has a big sign saying Noogle Search, so you won't miss it."

"Thank you," Dillon said.

"Yes, thank you very much, Lorraine," Grandpa said. "It has been wonderful talking with you."

"Likewise," she smiled. "I hope you both enjoy your time here in Cyberia."

They left the counter carrying a couple of brochures and headed for the street.

"She's a nice lady," Grandpa said as they exited the building. "But when she said 'Cyberia', it gave me the shivers."

"Yeah," Dillon admitted. "I hope this Cyberia is different from that Siberia. It must be the name they have for Cyberspace."

"Well, in my day," Grandpa began, but couldn't finish because he tripped and fell onto Dillon and they both came crashing to the ground. No sooner had they fallen than a man with copper-framed glasses and similarly colored wisps of hair helped them both to their feet.

"Are you alright, sir?" the man asked Grandpa.

"Me? I'm fine," Grandpa said slowly, steadying himself. "But my grandson - he was my cushion – the question is, is he okay?"

"Yeah, my side hurts some," Dillon said, brushing himself off, "but otherwise I'm okay."

The man switched his briefcase to his left hand and adjusted his glasses.

"My name is Morton McAfnee," he said, extending his hand. "Welcome to Cyberia."

Grandpa thought of slave labor camps, and then quickly brushed the thought aside.

"How did you know we were visitors?" Dillon asked.

"Oh," the man said, ruffling his fingers through his thin strands of hair. "One can always tell who's from out-of-system." He grinned. "Besides, Cyberians wouldn't wear a Star Wars shirt. Most of them don't relate to it because it is pre-Cyberian."

"What?" Grandpa said, a little miffed.

"Well, Cyberia is a relatively new domain, as you can imagine. It emerged along with the advancement in computers and the worldwide web. Cyberians that are older than thirty are immigrants from the real world, most of them naturalized Cyberian citizens."

"Cool," Dillon said, scrutinizing all the passersby. He wondered what the Cyberian Pledge of Allegiance might constitute.

"Oh, so it's my age that really gave it away," Grandpa muttered. "You just didn't want to say so." Morton continued to grin.

"Why is the ground so uneven?" Dillon asked. "I kept tripping earlier, even before this fall with Grandpa."

"Yes, unfortunately tripping is very common here, even amongst the most seasoned Cyberians. There is actually a class action lawsuit that never seems to end, in which the public is claiming damages from the government. The Supreme Court of Cyberia can't seem to come to any conclusion on the matter."

"Well, why don't they just replace the cobblestone?" Dillon asked. "It's so rough and jagged."

Morton laughed. "It's not cobblestone," he said. "Take a closer look."

Dillon and Grandpa bent down to examine the ground. Dillon traced the surface of the stones with his fingers.

"It does feel a little different," he said.

Suddenly the stone he was touching vanished. Dillon recoiled. "Aaah!" he cried in fright.

"Don't worry," Morton said. "You see, these stones are really what we call cookies."

"The ground is made of cookies?" Grandpa cried, straightening up. "And, wait, don't tell me, you're made of French Fries!" he scoffed.

Dillon chortled. "No, Grandpa. I learned about cookies. They are like bits of information that store the tracks of where you're going."

"Yes, basically," said Morton. "Cookies are like little sensors that gather every detail about computer users and what they're doing on the Internet."

"Little spies, then?" Grandpa suggested.

"One could say that," Morton nodded reticently.

"Spooky cookie," Grandpa added.

Morton blinked away the humor. "Anyway, in Cyberia, the ground is entirely made up of cookies, all of them built from human experiences on the Internet."

Grandpa mumbled something inaudible.

"But how come the cookie I was touching just disappeared like that?" Dillon asked.

"Well, you studied cookies, so you may have learned that cookies don't last forever. The information they gather is not typically stored permanently. They usually have an expiry date on them. The one you touched happened to expire as you were touching it. Happens all the time."

"Cool!" Dillon said, glancing at Grandpa who looked a little peeved, his arms firmly folded across his chest.

"And that's why the ground is uneven," Morton explained. "New cookies are added as you move along to different places, and they disappear as they expire. So you can have piles of cookies in one area and gaps where cookies used to be, in another."

"I don't know about any of this," Grandpa said. "Where I come from, when cookies expire, it means they've gotten old and wormy."

"Speaking of worms," Morton said, "Let me give you my card."

"Huh?" Grandpa said, arching an eyebrow. "Now you're going to tell us that you're actually a worm."

"No, no," Morton chuckled, brushing rivulets of sweat from his forehead. "I'm no worm. I fight worms. Read the card."

Dillon read it out aloud. "Dr. Morton McAfnee, Case Specialist, Department of Worms and Spyware, Cyberian Anti-Viral Enforcement."

Dillon stared up at Morton. "I get it. These are worms that infect computers. They're bad."

"Bad?" Morton sneered. "When you've seen one with your own eyes, you won't use such mild language."

Dillon squirmed. Grandpa huffed. "I think I've heard it all."

"Anyway," Morton said with a polite smile. "It was nice to meet you both. I hope we meet up again some time."

Dillon shook his hand. "Thank you, Dr. McAfnee...."

"Just call me Morton."

"Thank you Morton. You've been really helpful."

If you call talking about cookies and worms helpful, Grandpa was itching to say.

"Call me if you need anything," he said as he walked off.

"Uh, how do we do that? With a phone?" Dillon shouted after him.

"No, we don't have that. Send a web-form."

"A web-form?" Grandpa repeated.

"Yes," Dillon said. "It's a message you can send from within a website. You just type it in on the web page and press send. And it goes off – a little bit like an email."

Grandpa groaned. "I don't understand a word you and that guy are saying. You're probably speaking that HBO native tongue."

"HTML," Dillon corrected him.

"Whatever."

They walked to the intersection of Silicone Valley Road East and Circuit Circle, and stood spellbound by the continuous whirl of energy about them. The pedestrian traffic was so dense and fast it was more like a raging river than a throng of people. It rushed through the streets at breakneck speed, so fast it appeared as a series of streaks, as in those night shots of city freeways.

"How can they move so fast without bumping into each other?" Grandpa wondered out aloud.

Dillon shrugged his shoulders. "How can they move so fast in the first place?" he said.

"Well, let's ask them," Grandpa decided, stepping immediately into the traffic.

"Wait, Grandpa! You'll get hurt."

But Grandpa was already in the street. Even as he stood still in the street, the traffic seemed to stream effortlessly around and above him. All he felt was a continuous rush of wind as people brushed by very closely.

"Hee-hee!" Grandpa cheered above the wind. "New Yorkers could learn a thing or two about how to deal with congestion from these people."

"Good day, sir."

Grandpa jumped, the stream adjusting accordingly.

A man in royal garb, scattered with numerous diamond pendants and fine gold chains had stopped right next to Grandpa. He wore a crown engraved with the words "Nobel Prinse".

"Hello," Grandpa replied hesitantly, somewhat disenchanted by the enchantment.

The man flashed an array of gleaming white teeth that would have been the envy of every Hollywood superstar.

"My Dear Sir. Allow me to introduce myself. I am the Noble Prince Bob. I am contacting you because of a business concerning a huge sum of money from a deceased deposit in the Security and Finance company where I work. Though I know that a transaction of this magnitude will make anyone apprehensive and worried, but I am assuring you that all will be well at the end of the day.

I discovered an abandoned deposit in my company owned by one of our foreign customers who died along with his entire family as a result of an automobile crash...."

Grandpa grimaced. "How can you keep smiling through all of this?"

The prince didn't seem to hear him. "....He actually deposited this funds amounting to twelve million US dollars for safekeeping in my company. Company file records...."

Noble Prince Bob was interrupted by the sound of Dillon slapping his forehead. "Oh, I get it!" he exclaimed. "I bet this is one of those email scams. Lots of people get them all the time. Which means, this guy is an email! All these people streaming past us are emails being sent. Cool!"

Prince Bob's smile didn't lose any of its steam. He seemed delighted to see that Grandpa Harley remained quite intrigued by the story.

"How do I fit in?" Grandpa asked the prince, oblivious to the jargon Dillon was spewing, and envisioning for the first time in years that he might actually spend his retirement years in luxury.

".... I am turning to you as a safe-keeper for this money because I see that I can trust you, and in turn you will receive twenty percent of...."

"Grandpa!" Dillon interjected. "Don't listen to him. He's a fr...." Dillon noticed a gem-encrusted sword handle peeking from the prince's robe.. "He's a fr.....

He's a friend." Dillon smiled broadly. "But it's time for us to go."

Dillon grabbed his Grandpa's hand and pulled him back onto the sidewalk. Noble Prince Bob was forced to continue on his speedy and illustrious way.

"Dillon, why did you that? Can you imagine all those millions of dollars?"

"Grandpa, he's a fraud. Everyone gets these emails."

"I don't."

Dillon rolled his eyes. "Grandpa, if you had email, you would get them."

Grandpa shrugged his shoulders, not entirely convinced that letting the prince go had been as wise a decision as his grandson was implying.

"Grandpa, c'mon. Trust me," Dillon said, noticing his grandfather's disappointment. "Look, let's try this again and I'll show you how common this is."

They both walked right into the path of the emails, Dillon's mop of hair taking flight in the wind. Sure enough, an employee of United Bank in a crisp grey suit stopped directly in front of them. "Dear customer," she began with a crooked smile. "After reviewing your records we have found that the security of your account information may have been compromised...."

"She's not really from United Bank," Dillon whispered to his Grandpa.

"How do you know?" Grandpa replied, not quite in a whisper.

"Well, I don't have an account at that bank."

Grandpa laughed. "All right, I suppose you are right again young man." He turned to the young woman who was rattling something off about internal security procedures."

"Does your mother know you're working for charlatans?" he scolded her.

The woman did not reply. She merely repeated her message and seemed she would do so for eternity.

Dillon and his Grandpa were about to return to the sidewalk when a boy in jeans and baggy sweatshirt and wearing headphones approached them. Dillon blanched. "Cal, what are you doing here?"

"Hey dude, what's up? Wanna shoot some ball later? Let me know." Just as in the real world, Cal had no need for an answer and zoomed on his way.

"Friend of yours?" Grandpa asked, following the kid's rapidly disappearing trail.

"Yeah, well, kind of, I guess. I mean, it's not really him. It's obviously an email sent by him," Dillon tried to explain.

Grandpa shook his head. "Life was a lot simpler when I was a kid."

Dillon began to walk briskly ahead. His eagerness to get to the station was pulling him forward. "Come on, Grandpa let's go."

But Grandpa had already begun wading back into the thick of the email stream, eager to catch the next apparition.

"Come on, Grandpa."

"Now, just hang on a minute. This is quite ridiculous but quite fascinating at the same time. It's not very often I get to have conversations with phantom people." He turned briefly toward Dillon. "Although people do accuse me of doing that all the time." Grandpa laughed at his own little quip, but was interrupted by the visage of a young lady with flowing chestnut hair.

"Excuse me," she said with conviction, her expression somewhere between stoic and fierce. She was armed with a clipboard and oversized pen which she juggled between her fingers and her teeth.

Grandpa raised an eyebrow. "Let me guess. You're a mermaid who's lost and needs my social security number to get back to sea."

Before the young woman could say anything, Grandpa attempted to wave his hand clean through her head, expecting nothing but air. Instead, his hand met real skin and real cheekbone, and hence the real indignation of his victim. She gasped along with Grandpa, who shrunk back in fright.

"You're....not fake," he stammered.

"You bet I'm not fake!" she yelled. "The police officer who will arrest you will not be fake either!"

Grandpa's eyebrows arched to a puppy-dog plea. "I am so sorry. Please don't call the police. I have never struck anyone in my life. I really thought you were a ham."

"Spam, Grandpa! Spam!" Dillon corrected him quickly.

"Spam!" Grandpa exclaimed. "Yes, spam."

The judgment rested with this girl who was rubbing her cheek and glaring at the odd pair in front of her.

"Let me explain," Dillon ventured. "You see, we're...."

"I didn't ask you for your resume," she snapped. "You need to know whom you are dealing with, both of you. I'm Susan Dandelion from MemFriends."

"MemFriends?" Dillon gave her a blank stare.

"Yes, MemFriends. Don't tell me you've never heard of MemFriends," she clucked, slapping the clipboard against her knee as if in the midst of an argument with her baby sister.

"S-s-sorry, I haven't. You see I'm...."

"I don't want to hear it," she snapped, holding her palm in the air toward him. "I've heard it all. There's no excuse you can give me for why you've never heard of us, that I haven't heard before."

Dillon didn't quite know what to say. He kept staring at her raised palm which wasn't going away.

"Uh.... madam," Grandpa Harley intervened. "Perhaps you'd like to start again and kindly explain your mission, which I'm sure is a very honorable one."

Susan's tone softened. There was something about Grandpa Harley's gentle, yet unrelenting conviction that kind of took the wind out of all things bloated.

So Susan sighed and began to recite what she seemed to have had engraved into her heart a thousand times. "MemFriends is an organization committed to the preservation of memory in Cyberia. Thousands of new websites go up every day, devouring precious memory space. More than ever before, systems are seizing up and malfunctioning. There is so much out there now that it's become a breeding ground for viruses and hackers. Cyberia is polluted with renegade bloggers, spammers, and junkmail and nobody seems to care."

Her blood pressure seemed to rise very rapidly as she came to the end of each sentence.

"So MemFriends is organizing a petition that would encourage legislation to stop the domain tycoons from their unrestricted website expansion."

She scanned their faces for signs of empathy for her mission.

"Well," Dillon began, "maybe I should introduce myself first. My name is Dillon Apple...."

"Yes, yes, yes," she interjected. "You don't have to tell me anything. You can just write it down over here."

She pointed to her clipboard, handed him her whale-shaped pen and actually smiled. Dillon took the pen and held it away from him, as if were a live flailing creature.

Grandpa's eyes narrowed. "What do your parents say about this?"

Susan's smile evaporated. "That's personal," she hissed. "My mother would support me on this."

"Would?" Grandpa's eyes remained steadily focused on her.

"Whatever," she said in a low rumble, almost a growl.

There was a long silence before Grandpa spoke.

"You know what?" he said, his eyebrows arched. "I like what you're doing. I think you're a good soul."

Dillon squinted at his grandfather. What kind of ploy was this? He didn't see the expression on Susan's face, though. She had a peculiar reaction, as if she was stung by the tenderness of Grandpa's words. Although she showed no emotion, the lines on her face dissolved and her stare was no longer like iron.

"So," she swallowed. "You're going to uh....I mean, would you please sign it?"

Grandpa took the pen from Dillon, scribbled his signature and then handed the pen back to Dillon. Dillon obliged and signed his name even as he continued to squint up at his grandfather and then back at her.

"Let's go," Grandpa said summarily after Dillon handed the clipboard back to Susan. She slowly took the clipboard back and her eyes settled on this old man as he walked away, straining to catch the last glimpse of him as he disappeared down the road. Dillon stared back after her.

"Grandpa, did you know what you were signing?" Dillon asked as they made their way through the thick stream of Cyberians and emails.

"Not a clue," he said.

"Ok, so what am I missing here?" Dillon pressed.

"Dillon, I've been on this Earth for eighty years now…."

"Well, this isn't exactly Earth."

"Oh, hush!" Grandpa waived a hand at him. "I've been alive for eighty years anyway. And I've seen a lot of things. I've met a lot of people. I've seen a lot of pain. And there have been many times, my boy, that I've wished I can do something about that pain, to help those people in pain." That was all he said.

"Now it's my turn to not understand," Dillon said with a frown.

Grandpa Harley laughed. "Yes, but the difference is, you will in time understand what I am talking about. I, however, don't think I'll ever understand this computer world. The other day you had tried to explain some computer jargon to me, but to be honest, a virus will always mean a cold or the flu; boot will always be a type of footwear; and ram will always remain an animal."

When Lorraine had said that they wouldn't be able to miss the search station, she was not exaggerating. Noogle Search Station took up what seemed like hundreds of blocks along Silicone Valley Road East.

"It's like a city!" Dillon, exclaimed, beaming.

"My back," Grandpa groaned. "And there I thought all this transferring business would help my back. Just getting to this station is a journey in itself."

The station was comprised of numerous buildings, each with many entrances.

"How would we know where to go?" Dillon asked no-one in particular.

As if to answer his question, a sign to his left seemed to pop out of the ground, proclaiming, "For inter-website travel, please see a ticket agent at any one of our millions of gates."

"What was that?" Grandpa recoiled. "A jack-in-the-box road sign?"

"I think that was a pop-up screen," Dillon said, smiling. "That happens on my computer where screens just appear from nowhere. Now I can see them in three dimensions. Cool!"

"Well, whatever it is, millions of gates is quite impressive," Grandpa acknowledged. "Grand Central Station doesn't quite have as many."

They entered the building closest to them. It was a long, narrow structure, white and cream colored, spartanly furnished except for a row of ornate blue and gold ticket counters. Agents dressed in matching uniforms manned the counters. Even though the agents were serving several customers, there was very little sound, which seemed odd for such a mammoth operation.

Dillon and Grandpa Harley cautiously approached the only available agent they could locate. She didn't seem too pleased to see them.

"Not like Lorraine," Grandpa said under his breath, hardly moving his lips.

"Destination, please?"

"Umm. I'm not sure." Dillon peered up at his Grandpa. "Grandpa, where do you…" He was interrupted by Grandpa Harley directing him to the woman's fingers which were busily typing every word that Dillon uttered.

"Umm. What are you writing?" Dillon said quickly.

"Your destination, sir."

"B – but I haven't told you that yet."

"Yes, you did, sir. Your destination is 'Umm, I'm not sure. Grandpa where do you'". She gave a mild smile. It was her lunch break soon.

Dillon frowned. Grandpa Harley chuckled. "That really is quite funny," he said approvingly.

But the woman's expression remained as stoic as the steel clock-face of her wristwatch.

"Let's see now," she continued unhindered, punching a few keys in a rhythm she clearly enjoyed.

"Alright. In QM, there are no trains, I am afraid. But without QM, take train #58 on platform 3."

"What's QM?" Dillon asked.

"Quotation Marks."

Dillon's eyes darted back and forth, summarizing and surmising.

"I get it!" he exclaimed to his Grandpa.

"What?"

"You know, Noogle is a search engine. One second. Ma'am?" He turned to her.

"Yes, sir."

"How many stops does this train have?"

"109,000 sir."

"I knew it!" Dillon's fist went into the air. "Grandpa, there's a train for every search query you type in. If you put "Umm, I'm not sure. Grandpa where do you" in quotation marks you get no results, so there aren't any trains. But if you remove the quotation marks you get 109,000 results, so there's a train with 109,000 stops!"

Grandpa's moustache twitched about 3 times a second. "Look, my boy. As you know already, I have absolutely no idea what you're talking about. What I do know is that if I get on a train with 109,000 stops I will spend my last days lounging on a vinyl seat looking wistfully out a window....which doesn't actually sound like such a bad idea, now that I think of it," he mused, eyebrows raised and a fingertip pressed into his moustache.

"Grandpa, wait. We're not going to take that train."

"You're not?" the woman asked, midway through printing out the tickets.

"Yes, umm. Sorry." Dillon blushed. "Grandpa, let's check out what the websites look like from the inside. Let's go to a giant site like Congo."

"We have to be dressed properly and well armed to visit a jungle, Dillon," Grandpa Harley warned.

Dillon shook his head. "Grandpa, Congo is a bookstore."

"It is? What do they sell? 'Getting *a head* in life?'" Grandpa laughed heartily at his own quip.

"Umm," Dillon turned to the lady who was shredding the printed tickets in exact little squares. "Could you issue two new tickets to Congo.com?"

"Yes, sir," she said.

"How many stops does that train have?" Grandpa asked.

"Thirty-two million, one hundred thousand," she said eyeing her watch and the lunch bag tucked just under the counter.

"W-o-a-a-h!" Dillon said, his eyes wide open, as opposed to Grandpa's eyes which narrowed in contempt. "This is ridiculous. How could a train have 32 million stops? The train would take several lifetimes of its passengers to reach its destination!"

"We switch crews, sir," she answered without flinching.

"You switch crews, huh? Ha-ha-ha. You crack me up, as my grandson would say."

"Wait, Grandpa. We probably get off on the first stop. Am I right, ma'am?"

"Yes, sir. 99% of the passengers will be getting off at the first stop."

Grandpa mumbled. "I'm not even going to attempt to understand this."

The small printer whirred and spat out the tickets.

"That will be 400 Cybercents please."

"400 what?" Grandpa asked.

"400 Cybercents." It was lunchtime now.

"That must be the currency," Dillon said. "Do you accept American dollars?"

"No, sir. We do not accept American dollars. You will have to exchange them for Cyberian dollars and cents first."

Grandpa sighed. "Now how do we do that?"

The lady brought out a large plain gray box from under the counter right next to her lunch which was waiting for her. She removed the lid and pushed the box along the countertop towards her customers.

Dillon and Grandpa looked into the box and saw a smaller second box flashing on and off with yellow lights. Suddenly a voice began in monotone. "Please place your money to be exchanged here and push enter."

Dillon looked up at his Grandpa whose eyebrow lifted again.

"I suppose you'd like some money," he said grudgingly.

Dillon nodded with a smile.

Grandpa Harley pulled out his wallet and dropped a ten-dollar note into the box.

"Is that going to be enough?"

"Oh, yes. That is more than enough, sir."

The enter button was like a green pincushion. Dillon pressed down on it. No sooner had he done so than the note completely disintegrated, and several black square chips appeared instantly in its place.

"Your transaction is complete," the voice announced. "Please take your money."

"W-o-o-w!" Dillon bent over the box. "Now that's what I call exchanging money. The American dollars actually morphed into Cyberian dollars. Isn't that cool, Grandpa?"

"That is quite spectacular," he admitted.

Dillon picked up the chips. There were ten chips, each engraved with a giant 'C' and the number 100 cutting across its center.

"1000 Cyberian Dollars?" Grandpa asked in surprise. "For 10 American dollars I get 1000 of these dollars?"

"Yes, the exchange rate is 100 to 1, sir. The Cyberian dollar lost a lot of ground when the dotcom bubble burst a few years ago."

"Oh, yeah," Dillon nodded. "Remember that Grandpa?"

"Uh. Yes, well…." Grandpa cleared his throat. "I don't really watch the news."

"We lost a lot of sites at that time," the lady continued, a trace of emotion entering her expression for a very brief moment. "Entire domains were wiped out."

"Hmmm. I'm sorry," Grandpa said, although he hadn't a clue what he was sorry about.

"So wait a minute," Dillon said, turning aside to process something in his head. "You said these tickets cost 400 Cybercents?"

"Yes, sir."

"But – how many Cybercents are there in a Cyberian dollar?"

"1k, sir."

"1k?" Grandpa queried.

"1k is 1000 Grandpa," Dillon informed him quickly before resuming his line of questioning. "So if it's 100 to 1, then 1 Cyberian dollar is …1 American cent, and 400 cybercents would be like… 0.4 of 1 cent."

The lady nodded slowly. Was the math lesson over?

"That is so cheap!" Dillon exclaimed.

"Not for hardworking Cyberians, it isn't," she said, not quite successful at disguising her bitterness.

"Well, Dillon, you know," Grandpa began in that tone that always prefaced a lengthy story from yesteryear. "When I was a boy, that's about how much it cost to…."

"Excuse me," the lady interjected with artificial calm which was beginning to fray at the edges, "but I think your train is about to download." *And I would like to have my lunch*, her mind protested rather loudly.

"Remember, train #58, Platform 3."

They followed the signs to platform 3, making their way through thick crowds of Cyberians and emails.

"Grandpa, did you hear her? She said our train is downloading. Isn't that neat?"

Grandpa Harley was huffing, struggling to carve a path through people and their briefcases. "People use silly slang all the time today. The correct term is boarding."

"No Grandpa, it's…."

Dillon could not finish because his jaw was hanging at the sight before him. There must have been thousands of passengers gathered on platform 3 stretching as far as his eye could see. There were more people here than spectators at the Superbowl.

"All these people are getting on the train?" he asked finally.

"Getting on what train?" Grandpa retorted. "There's none to speak of."

No sooner had Grandpa spoken than a long gleaming white train appeared on the tracks out of thin air. It didn't arrive. It just....appeared.

"Download complete," a voice thundered from the speakers and the entire mass of people moved at once towards the numerous opened doors of the train.

Dillon was spellbound. "I....how...."

Grandpa stopped one of the passengers at his right.

"Excuse me. Can you tell me how are all these people are going to fit on this train?"

The man smiled sympathetically. Or out of condescension, Grandpa thought. "Don't you worry about that," he said. "This server can handle millions of users at one time."

Grandpa stared at him blankly. Why couldn't everyone speak English?

The seats were the standard no-frills material that stuck to your skin after sitting for a while. Grandpa sat at the window peering out at the remaining thousand or so people crowding at what seemed like an equal number of doors stretching into the distance.

Something beeped and a melodic voice began. "Good morning, ladies and gentlemen and welcome aboard Noogle 58 with service to Congo.com and related sites. There will be over thirty two million stops on this line, so please remain seated until your stop is announced." Grandpa rolled his eyes. "For your convenience, detailed web privacy statements and anti-viral safety brochures can be found in the seat pockets in front of you. In the case of a server malfunction, please contact a system administrator. On behalf of the train driver and all the staff onboard, we wish you a pleasant journey."

"What was she trying to say?" Grandpa turned to Dillon.

"Basically, welcome on board," Dillon said with a shrug of his shoulders.

"Good morning," a pleasant but not quite human voice said to Dillon.

Dillon turned to his right and immediately screamed at the top of his lungs, jumping from his seat. The giant spider also let out a piercing screech and leapt from the spot that he had taken next to Dillon.

"Giant spider!" Dillon yelled frantically to everyone else around him. Grandpa was removing his shoe. "I'll take care of him," he said. "I've taken out a few spiders in my life."

"What's the matter with you?" an old lady whined from the row behind them. "You never seen a web crawler before?"

"Yeah," her five-year-old grandson added disapprovingly, his eyes almost disappearing into his baseball cap that had a big Cyberian Huskies logo in front.

Dillon and his Grandpa stared at each other, at the annoyed passengers around them and then at the web crawler whose furry eyebrow was raised on his equally furry face, four of his especially furry legs – or perhaps hands – clasping the pages of the daily newspaper, The Cyberian Express.

His other legs were folded comfortably each on top of the other, the practiced position of the typical executive on his early morning commute.

"I'm sorry if I startled you," he said over his silver-framed eyeglasses.

Grandpa squinted at the web crawler. "What kind of spider are you exactly?" he asked.

The web crawler chuckled, his suit-clad abdomen almost bursting at its buttons.

"I'm not an Arachnid, if that's what you mean," he replied. "Although, I have the greatest respect for them. Some of my best friends are Arachnids."

Grandpa squirmed. He thought about how many spiders he had encountered in his life that had gotten anything but his respect.

"Then what are you?" Dillon asked.

"Well, my boy, as you heard before, I am a web crawler. Although my wife prefers that I go by the title, Intelligence Agent. It's what she can tell her friends, you know. Anyway, I spend my time traveling the worldwide web visiting websites and collecting data."

"That sounds cool!" Dillon said, his fear dissipating.

The web crawler chuckled again. Those suit buttons must have been welded on.

"You know, the life of a crawler is both exciting and lonely," he said. "You're on the road all the time. You're exploring new vistas, sampling different cybercultures. But at the same time, you wish you could just stay in one place and have some permanence." He averted his gaze for a second.

"Do you have a family?" Grandpa found himself asking much to his own amazement.

Some grayish mucous started oozing from the crawler's tiny eyes. "Yes," he said. He removed his glasses to wipe his eyes and then clicked open the latches of his briefcase. Rummaging through his papers, he withdrew a tattered photograph and showed it to Dillon and his Grandpa.

"This is my family," he sighed with half a smile.

The photo showed a whole cluster of spiders smothering a beach log, against a brilliant blue sky.

"This was three years ago in the Inpedia travel brochure."

"The Inpedia brochure?" Dillon asked.

"Yes, it was a pdf, or maybe an html, I can't remember. Whatever it was, it was beautiful. We had such a good time together." He sighed again. "Unfortunately, I don't get to see them as often as I would like."

Dillon peered at the picture. What would normally have given him a cold shiver looked remarkably, well....cute, right now.

"H- how many children do you have?" Grandpa asked.

"Oh, about 4,500," he replied. "And each and every one of them has a special place in my heart."

"But do you uh.... have a heart?" Dillon pried. "I mean you're a spider. Actually not even a spider, but a web crawler. And web crawlers wouldn't necessarily, I mean....actually have hearts, I mean, right?"

The crawler peered into Dillon's eyes. "It's just an expression," he said.

"Wait a minute!" Grandpa objected. "Did you say you have 4,500 children?"

"Thereabouts," the crawler replied.

"Well, how do you remember all their names? – and your poor wife. How does she cope with you gone all the time?"

"Those are good questions," the spider said, nodding. "The truth is I don't know all my kids' names, but they're ok with that. They understand. As for my wife, what can I say, she is an angel of the highest order."

Grandpa shook his head. The image of a spider and an angel together didn't sit well with him at all.

There was another beep. "We are entering Congo.com Interweb Port. If this is your stop, please check your surroundings to make sure you have all your belongings. Anything left on the train will be permanently deleted. Thank you for traveling with us."

The doors opened and people poured out onto the cookie streets right in front of a large sign that welcomed them to Congo.com. Dillon and his Grandpa stared at the vast chamber ahead of them. It was like an airport hanger, or perhaps even an entire domed city with walls and ceilings so high and remote they were only vaguely discernable. It contained its own hive of activity, people, and interior chambers, intricately interlinked and intertwined. As Dillon stepped through the entrance, he heard a voice, so close to him he could almost feel the breath in his ear.

"Welcome, Dillon T. Appleseed."

Dillon turned sharply to face the origin of the voice, but there was no-one there.

Before he could say anything, the voice continued.

"If you are not Dillon T. Appleseed, please push here." A door to his left began to flash yellow, the same sort of flashing he saw on the money exchange box. There was a green pincushion button on this door too.

Grandpa was scratching his chin. "Now how do you like that? First it seemed to recognize you, and then it wasn't sure. It sounds to me like senility exists even in the computer world. You just can't escape it. No matter how hard you try."

Dillon managed a laugh, although he was engrossed in thought. He spilled a few thoughts loud enough for Grandpa to hear. "It must have matched me with my IP address....but how?....my brain functions, heat sensors....?"

"Dillon," Grandpa Harley interrupted him.

"Yes?"

"There's a bright light around your feet."

Dillon looked down to see two round beams like car headlights sweeping the floor around him.

"Ah! Of course," he exclaimed. "The site is reading my cookies!"

"Reading your cookies," Grandpa muttered. "Maybe we both need to have our cookies read."

Dillon sighed. "Remember what Morton told us, Grandpa? The cookies store information about where you go on the Internet. When I go on Congo.com at home and look at stuff, and buy stuff, the computer stores that information and recognizes me the next time. That's why I got that greeting."

"Really polite," Grandpa remarked. "Probably the politest cookie I have ever come across."

Dillon surveyed the area. The walls of this cavernous entrance hall were lined with giant mahogany doors, gold-plated plaques affixed to the center of each one. The writing on the plaques was flowery and bold, prompting Grandpa to remark, "Is this a jungle or the Waldorf Astoria?"

Dillon read aloud what was inscribed on each plaque.

"Books, DVD's, Magazines, Music, Textbooks, clothing, Jewelry, Office products, toys, food, pet supplies, shoes, lawn mowers...."

"Wait a minute," Grandpa interrupted him. "You said this was supposed to be a bookstore, as in a store that sells books. Which bookstore have you been in lately that sells lawnmowers?"

"Well, the thing is, Grandpa, websites have the advantage of having as much space as they want because cyberspace has no limit. So they figure why not...."

"Watch out!" Grandpa yelled suddenly, but it was too late. A baseball traveling at lightning speed struck Dillon in the cheek. Grandpa closed his eyes as it made impact. When he opened them Dillon was looking confused.

"Did something hit me?" he asked, stroking his cheek.

"What do you mean, did something hit you?" Grandpa said, flustered. "Yes, a baseball – it came flying out of nowhere and crashed right into you. Are you alright?"

"Y-yeah, I'm fine," Dillon replied. "I didn't really feel anything. Just a rush of air." He continued to stroke the skin of his cheek, which Grandpa examined closely.

"I don't understand how you didn't feel anything," Grandpa said, continuing his inspection. "A baseball just slammed into you but there's no sign that it did. I really had all sorts of images of you needing a hospital right away, and me having to explain to your mother that you got hit by a baseball inside an elegant bookstore jungle that sells lawnmowers in Cyberia."

Dillon stood back and searched the ground around him. There was no ball to be found. "Who would swing a ball at me?" he wondered.

Just then they saw a stodgy man with bushy eyebrows, in a loose, striped shirt walk towards them. He adjusted his baseball cap and bent down to pick up the ball a few yards away.

"Grandpa," Dillon stammered. "I – I think that's....that's...."

Grandpa's face froze. "Yes...yes, I think it's...."

"Babe Ruth," an overhead voice sounded, completing the thought that both of them were too astounded to express on their own. "An Inspired Life. Paperback, 367 pages. Publisher: BubbleBay. Language: English. ISBN-13: 928-0X222877. Product Dimensions: 8.4x5.5x1.1 inches. Shipping weight: 15 ounces. Average Customer Review: 4 stars. Congo Sales Rank: 8,765."

Dillon tried to swallow but his throat muscles were not responding. If felt as if a fizzy drink was careening through his blood stream. Eventually he tugged at his Grandpa's arm and managed to string a few words together. "Grandpa let's talk to him. Let's go say hi to Babe Ruth!"

Grandpa shook off Dillon's hand. "Dillon, I might be getting a little senile in my old age, but I don't talk to dead people. Not just yet."

"The thing is," Dillon swallowed, keeping his eye on the baseball star. "I think he's alive but not alive."

"Oh, here we go again," Grandpa snapped, tapping his feet.

"No, really, Grandpa. Look at the sign on the billboard above us. Grandpa squinted up at the sign which read, 'You recently looked at'.

"On Sunday, I was on Congo.com at home and looked at this book. I was going to ask Dad if I could get it, but didn't get the chance. The site knows what I looked at because of the cookies."

"Because of the cookies," Grandpa repeated with an empty expression.

"Yeah. And so what is super-cool about this is that now that we're in Cyberspace, it looks like we get to meet what's inside the books. It's kind of real but not real at the same time. Isn't that just so cool?" He was grinning from ear to ear. "Now, let's go see if we can talk to him."

Dillon started moving and Grandpa trudged along behind him.

"Mr. Ruth?" Dillon said nervously.

There was no response. The man didn't even look up from the bench he was sitting at.

"Maybe call him the Big Bambino," was Grandpa's suggestion, but Dillon shrugged it off.

He sighed. "It looks like we don't get to communicate with the people inside the books. We can only watch but we don't get involved. Maybe that's why I didn't feel the ball hitting me."

At that moment, Babe Ruth lifted his head and addressed nobody in particular.

"Baseball was, is and always will be to me the best game in the world," he declared with gentle conviction. Then he took the ball and disappeared into the shadows.

"Wow," Dillon breathed. "Wow."

Out of the corner of his eye, Grandpa noticed a group of people in the distance huddled together and chatting excitedly amongst each other.

"And who are they?" Grandpa wanted to know, bringing the group to Dillon's attention.

Dillon shrugged his shoulders. "Let's go find out."

Even as Dillon and Grandpa approached, this animated group of yappers remained oblivious to their presence.

"They can't see us either, can they?" Grandpa remarked.

Dillon shook his head. They both tried to catch a few phrases here and there amidst the clamor.

"Eloquently written....quoting the right sources....other Babe Ruth books....never been so disappointed....finished it in one sitting....slow and tedious."

It was a while before Dillon picked up on the clues. Then he exclaimed excitedly, "Grandpa, these are the reviewers of the book! They're all saying whether they liked or didn't like the book."

"Hmm," Grandpa said. "None of them can agree with each other. Now that is the most realistic scene I have witnessed so far in this whole cookie land of Cyberia."

Dillon chuckled. "It's not really a land, Grandpa."

"Oh, well, then, this whole cookie kingdom of Cyberia," Grandpa retorted, lightly tap-dancing on the uneven ground, which caused Dillon to emit an embarrassed laugh.

"Grandpa," he said, wincing at the spectacle. "I think you're starting to enjoy this."

Grandpa Harley stood tall and proud. His moustache twitched rapidly. "I think you're right, my boy. There is much potential here in this secret galactic backwater to which you have drawn me."

Sometimes Grandpa spoke in a way that reminded Dillon of Mrs. Henderson, his English teacher, who frequently stretched her lips in order to fully enunciate some very flowery and strange words.

"It is liberating to know," Grandpa continued, "that there exists a domain where conventional boundaries dissolve as the imagination begins to take off." He turned from his soliloquy to face Dillon. "You know what tune is playing in my head. Right now?"

Dillon shook his head.

Grandpa continued to tap his feet and click his hands. "Doo-be-doo-be-doo."

Dillon smiled. "Why that tune, Grandpa?"

"My boy, I'm not just singing the tune because I like Frank Sinatra. I'm singing the tune because I want to go see Frank Sinatra." His eyes swelled with glee, locking on his grandson.

"Yeah!" Dillon said slowly, his own eyes meeting his grandfather's.

They headed through the giant door labeled "Music" and immediately found themselves on some sort of pedestrian highway that snaked through a city of concert halls, open air theaters, stages and recording studios. Every building, it seemed, was a venue for music of one type or another. Thousands of people walked this highway, popping in and out of each building.

Dillon was speechless. Grandpa was too, only for a short while, though. Grandpa had been dealt quite a few challenges in his life, but a lack of words was not one of them.

"Something's not right here," he commented after drawing everything in. Dillon nodded, although still spellbound by this exclusively music-oriented wonderland.

"What sort of music department is this if there is no sound?" Grandpa mumbled.

It was true. The silence was like the vast stillness of barren countryside. They could see miles into the distance, over the heads of people and structures, yet were swathed by a blanket of silence.

"Let's find out why," Dillon suggested, leading the way.

They stopped at the entrance to a concert hall and peered inside through small glass windows. Hundreds of patrons sat in plush seats surrounding a well-lit stage. An orchestra was clearly in the midst of playing something and the audience was clearly lapping it up. Yet Dillon and Grandpa couldn't hear a sound.

"Can I help you?" A bald man with glasses hanging off the edge of his nose asked them in a bored tone.

"Umm....well," Dillon began.

"Why is there no sound?" Grandpa took over for him, getting right to the point.

"Well, of course there is sound," the man said, almost laughing but instead managing to clear his throat.

"Do you hear it? We don't," Grandpa responded.

"No, of course you can't hear it," the man said. "Look where you are standing."

Both Dillon and Grandpa stared down at the cookies around their feet.

"This is website white space. There isn't anything on it. You have to position yourself right up against the product in order to be able to experience the sound of it. Otherwise you won't get anything." He gestured to them to move a few yards closer through a doorway.

"It's like the mouse I showed you, Grandpa," Dillon noted. "You have to position it on the actual icon to gain access to it."

"Well, as far as I'm concerned, my boy, mice shouldn't be positioned. They should be trapped."

They moved closer. Still nothing. They inched even closer. Suddenly, their ears were filled with the collective roar of horns, violins, cymbals and piano in the thrust of a dramatic finale. Dillon jumped even though he should have known what to expect. Grandpa, on the other hand, was closing his eyes and soaking in this sudden magical invasion of notes and vibrations.

The bald man spoke up. "Well, then, that's enough. If you wanted to stay you'd have to pay and if you wanted to pay you'd have to book, and in order to book you'd have to send a web-form two years in advance." He seemed satisfied with his Dr. Seuss-styled announcement.

"Two years?" Dillon stammered.

"Well, how often is it that you get to see Beethoven in action?" the man replied smugly.

Grandpa's eyes snapped open. "What did you just say?"

"I don't repeat things simply for the sake of sensationalism," the man declared. "I do believe you heard me the first time."

Grandpa adjusted his jaw as if to lock it in position.

"Did you say, see Beethoven?"

"Grandpa," Dillon tucked at his shirt and pointed to a short stocky man whose hair rose in waves as he pranced around the stage madly. "That must be him – the guy whose hair is flapping up and down as he's directing the orchestra."

"The g-g-u-y?" was all Grandpa could say, his quivering mouth wide open.

"Ok, the proverbial party is over," the bald-headed attendant insisted, trying to lead them back through the doors. "Let's put an end to the salivating and get mov...."

He was interrupted by Grandpa's brazen bellow in the direction of the stage. "Ludwig!" Grandpa called to him with abject fondness. Almost under some sort of spell, he began rushing towards the stage.

"Security!" the attendant yelled. Almost immediately two uniformed men sprang from the shadows and threw themselves on top of Grandpa who flopped to the floor face first. Ludwig Von Beethoven did not flinch at the sight nor the sound of the scuffle. However his indifference had nothing to do with his preoccupation with his task at hand. Rather, it was because he wasn't really, well... alive. This detail is what Dillon wanted to remind his grandfather as he watched him lunge for the stage in front of hundreds of people, but sadly didn't get the chance. Now his Grandpa's face was smothered in cybercookie crumbs and was being led out of the concert hall area with his hands held behind him. Dillon, too, was shoved along towards the exit and onto the pedestrian highway.

"What do we do with them?" one of the guards asked the bald-headed man.

"Just put them on the first train out of here," the man snapped, fluffing his hands as if to dust the two of them off.

"But I want to see Frank Sinatra!" Grandpa protested after him, bits of cybercookie crumbs falling from his moustache.

"Looks like you're not going to have it....*your way*," one of the guards sang, to the great amusement of his colleague.

Grandpa Harley sneered as he was led through the Music doors.

"Comedians," he muttered, although there was an irrepressible curl in his lips.

A train downloaded in front of the exit and before they could get a good look at it, Dillon and his Grandpa were shoved through the open doors and onto the seats of an empty coach.

The doors closed quickly and the cheery voice began with all the departure instructions. "....non-stop service to North Pole Weather Report."

Both of them went as pale as the snowy wilderness they were about to meet.

Five

Dillon banged against the window. "No, No, let us out! Get us out of here! Aaargh!"

Grandpa had some choice expletives for the bald man and his henchmen and had to battle hard against his tongue to keep the words from spilling in the presence of his grandson.

"That's why there's no-one else on this train," Dillon said, shrinking into his seat. "Who would want to go there?"

"I would," a slight voice said.

Dillon and Grandpa yelped in unison.

"Who…. said…. that?" Dillon stuttered.

"Oh, I'm sorry I scared you," the voice said, and then they saw a small creature emerge from the back row.

"You're a web crawler," Dillon said, sighing in relief.

"In training," the spider corrected him. Dimples appeared on each edge of his smile, rendering him an oddly cute creature. "I'm a junior web crawler. Guess what? I get to go the crumby places that no-one wants to go to so that I can earn my colors. But that's ok." He took a breath and pushed out his abdomen. "One day, when I qualify, I'll get assigned to some place magical, like a Hollywood film web site, where I can rub shoulders with the rich and famous."

Grandpa shuddered. I have news for you, he thought to himself, no celebrity is going to want to rub shoulders with a creepy spider.

"Can you help us?" Dillon burst out, his stomach sinking at the notion that they were about to be stranded at the North Pole.

"With what?" the junior web crawler inquired.

"We don't want to go to the North Pole. We're going to freeze. How can we stop this train?"

The web crawler laughed, so that his feelers appeared to be dancing.

"You're not going to the North Pole. You're in Cyberia, remember? You're going to the North Pole Weather Report."

"Oh," Dillon said. "So it's different."

"Not really," the crawler quipped and burst into laughter. "You're still going to freeze like an ice cube."

"Immature little rascal needs a good paddling," Grandpa huffed. "Where are your parents?"

The little crawler's demeanor changed instantly. "Oh, no, please don't tell my parents. They'll take me off the training course."

Grandpa gave a wry smile.

"Um," the crawler said. "What you need to do is go to the pay station as soon as you arrive where you can book your next trip back electronically."

"There'll be no-one there to help us?" Dillon asked.

"Um, you're going to the North Pole weather report," the crawler reminded them, not quite able to abstain from precociousness altogether. "There's, like, no-one there. You have to use the machine."

"Grandpa, can you get some money ready so that we can buy the tickets quickly when we arrive?"

"You mean the Monopoly money or whatever?" Grandpa asked.

Dillon nodded. "Yes, the Cyberdollars."

"Good idea," the crawler commented.

When the doors opened, a blast of frigid air immediately conquered the inside of the coach, and as they stepped outside a thick wall of snow pummeled at them, dropping a blanket of dry powder all over them within a matter of seconds.

Then a pleasant and crystal clear voice sounded, somehow penetrating the barrel of snow without any difficulty.

"Overcast early with heavy storm system developing. Blizzard conditions will persist throughout much of the day. Temperatures around -18 degrees Fahrenheit. Dangerous wind chills may approach -40 degrees."

The spider took each hand of Dillon and Grandpa in the clutches of his furry legs and pulled them towards an enclosed booth.

"The booth is heated," he yelled through the driving snow.

After they all squeezed into the booth, the snow simply slipped off them. There was a reason for that.

"Cripes!" Grandpa cried. "It's boiling hot in here."

"Sure is," the crawler said, his slimy skin squished right up against Grandpa. "It has to be, otherwise this booth would be buried a mile deep in snow."

"Well, my skin is going to crack with all these instant temperature switches," Grandpa moaned.

"Oh, it looks pretty cracked to me anyway," the crawler retorted, scrutinizing Grandpa's wrinkles.

"Kinda like my Uncle Theodore's skin that he molted last week."

"Why you little…." Grandpa growled, but Dillon interrupted him. "Grandpa, quick, give him the Cyberdollars so that he can book our tickets out of here!"

Grandpa handed money to the crawler, who punched a few buttons in rapid succession.

"Where do you want to go?" he asked them.

"Well, I'm kinda hungry," Grandpa said, now regretting the fact that he hadn't brought along a healthy supply of custard.

Right away Dillon recalled the lady at the first ticket booth typing in as a destination whatever tumbled out of their mouths. "Oh, wait!" he stopped the crawler. "Don't type anything yet. We don't want to go to 'well, I'm kinda hungry.'"

Grandpa laughed. Sure enough the crawler looked surprised. "That's not where you want to go?" he asked, his feelers swaying like loose windshield wipers.

"Uh, no." Dillon assured him.

"Why not? I have cousins on the Budapest government website. They tell me it's really nice and cultural over there. They've invited me to come and crawl their site some time – when I qualify of course." He grinned.

Grandpa frowned so hard that the cracks in his skin became crevices. "What the….?"

Dillon chuckled. "I get it." He turned to his Grandpa. "He thinks we said Hungary, as in the country."

"Well, what other type is there?" the crawler asked, perplexed.

"Never mind," Dillon said. "Let's go to Mc Ronalds. You can type that in."

After they bolted through the blizzard and through the open doors of their train, Dillon and his Grandpa brushed off the cakes of snow and ice that had gathered in those few seconds of running. This time the train was packed with passengers, although Dillon and his Grandpa had been the only ones to board at the North Pole Weather report.

They squeezed onto a bench next to a group of boys all wearing Cyberian Huskies shirts and caps. The boys were raising their voices in an excited exchange of comments and quips, sparring with each other without regard to whom their elbows might be poking.

"Ouch!" Grandpa exclaimed, more annoyed than hurt. "It just goes to show that boys will be boys even in cookieland."

"Grandpa," Dillon said, staring through the window and oblivious to the happenings around him, "did you notice that the spider didn't get it when we said 'hungry'? He could only think of Hungary, the country."

Grandpa turned to Dillon. "Yeah, well. Maybe spiders don't get hungry. And, hey, we learned that everyone here recharges themselves with batteries, remember?"

Dillon was silent. He bit his lip and looked down, his head bobbing with the gentle rocking of the train.

"What's the matter?" Grandpa asked.

Dillon sighed. "Well, Grandpa. I owe you an apology. I don't think we can eat here in Cyberspace. You wanted to bring food and I told you I didn't think it was necessary. Now we'll need to go back right away."

Grandpa fluffed Dillon's hair. "Don't worry about it, boy. It's been fun. Hey, we can always come back. First, let's get up close with a burger at McRonalds and see what it looks like anyway."

The aroma was more than stirring. It was suffocating. The air was swimming with bubbling fat and juices, hot splashes of meat raining down around them. Thick juicy steak sizzled so loudly it sounded like a crackling bonfire. All the senses were attacked and all the sounds and flavors were amplified. Even the dripping, freshly sliced tomatoes exuded a raw, earthy smell so pungent one could easily imagine oneself on a farm, pinned to the damp soil that gave rise to them. Both Dillon and Grandpa stared at the spectacle, sticky sweat collecting on their skin.

"This is like Miami in the summer," Grandpa Harley remarked.

"I don't think I'm that hungry anymore," Dillon said, the nausea creeping up his throat.

"Yeah, I agree," Grandpa said. "No wonder these Cyberians choose not to eat. I'd also rather plug myself in if I were them."

"I don't think they can eat, even if they wanted to," Dillon said. "If we wanted to eat, we'd have to figure out a way to get hold of the food." He pointed to the different cubicles holding the menu choices. A single burger encased in thick security glass sparkled under a spotlight as if it were a museum piece – quite a reasonably priced museum piece at $2.50. "It's like Babe Ruth and Beethoven. It just appears here but you can't access it."

"Let's go home and get some custard," Grandpa suggested, the mere memory of his favorite dish putting a broad smile on his face.

"Ok. But Grandpa?"

"Yup?"

"Can we make one more stop?"

"Where?"

"Well, did you know that I have my own website?"

"What? You have one of these fancy rooms?"

Dillon smiled. "Yeah. It's really primitive. I don't have my own domain name and I use a host that's cheap, so it has pop-ups and banner ads."

"Yes, well, you go on talking gibberish and I'll just think about my custard."

Dillon laughed, swallowing some fat-saturated air as he did.

"Grandpa, I have a photo album on the site with our family pictures. Wouldn't it be neat to see everyone as if they were standing all around us?"

Grandpa raised his eyebrows. "Forget the custard for now. It's got so many calories anyway. Let's go to your work site."

"Website," Dillon corrected him.

"Right." As they walked to the ticket counter, Dillon could hear his Grandpa mumbling something about website, shmebsite.

Dillon knew something was different about this train the moment he and his Grandpa stepped onboard. It appeared to be an older train, the seats worn and the walls stained and scuffed. When it moved, the wheels squeaked and everything rattled as if parts were about to break loose. Even the announcement was gruff and abrupt instead of the usual sugar-coated melody, and didn't seem to be concerned with any safety and security procedures.

"I don't know about this train," Grandpa murmured, echoing Dillon's thoughts. "These are the type you never ride alone or at night."

The passengers, too, seemed the perfect fit for this train. They ranged from disheveled and disorderly to onerous-looking and shady.

"What destination did you tell the lady?" Grandpa whispered.

"I-I just gave her my name," Dillon replied, gripping his seat nervously.

The train came to a stop at a dark underground station. There was no light at all except for some obscure flashing signs. Immediately, Grandpa put his hand across Dillon's eyes.

"Grandpa! What?" Dillon shouted, his heart almost skipping a beat.

"Don't look!" Grandpa urged him. "This is disgusting. This area is not for children. In my opinion it is not for adults either!"

Grandpa was almost trembling with rage. "We need to get off this train, but not here. We can't risk walking around in such filth."

Dillon understood what his Grandpa was referring to. His parents had warned him about certain parts of the Internet that could disturb him. Attraction to the opposite gender was confusing enough anyway, they had told him. The last thing they wanted was for him to be lured by deeply disturbing images and ideas.

The doors closed and the train moved on, emerging from the darkness. Grandpa removed his hand from Dillon's eyes but he wasn't any less enraged.

"Now it truly is time to go home," he huffed. "I've had enough."

Dillon was troubled by how his name as a destination would lead them astray. "I guess because I use a free host for my site, it doesn't offer much protection and it attracts all the rougher, lower-class elements of Cyberspace."

"Whatever," Grandpa said. "Let's go home."

No sooner had he spoken, then the doors slid open. This time the announcement was more civil.

"Welcome to Dillon. T. Appleseed's Home Page...."

Dillon perked up. "This is it, Grandpa. This is my site. Let's go!"

Before his Grandpa could object, Dillon was out of the doors. Grandpa Harley had no choice but to follow suit.

They stood in the small blue welcome room that Dillon had chosen from a template. A colorful flashing line served as a threshold in either direction. Dillon was grinning from ear to ear. "I can't believe we're standing inside the homepage of my own website," he beamed.

Grandpa said nothing.

A voice came on, one that was obviously quite familiar. "Hi, welcome to my page. My name is Dillon T. Appleseed...."

Dillon chuckled. "Isn't that crazy, Grandpa? That's me talking."

Grandpa Harley managed a smile.

"....my mother's name is Eileen and my father's name is Gerald. I guess you could say I have an older mind, considering the fact that my Grandpa Harley is my best friend. I could say a lot about him, but the bottom line is that he is just the coolest Grandpa in the world."

Grandpa Harley's mood turned a corner.

"....We do everything together, from model-airplane building to playing Mastermind. We also delve into detailed discussions of philosophy and history. We sometimes end up debating each other , and the reality is, it's hard for Grandpa to admit he's wrong."

Grandpa's eyebrow lifted as if caught in the hook of a building crane. Dillon smiled sheepishly. The voice continued.

"I've always wanted to have my own site where I can write about so cool microwave surfer and she said hospital...."

Dillon frowned. "Wait a minute."

The voice continued but slowly mutated into a deep, distorted sound, syllables merging and disappearing.

"....complexity office ice cream sharing oast ife bbnzzznll."

The blue walls started to change color.

"Grandpa!" Dillon shouted. "Something's wrong with the site! I think it's corrupted. Let's get out of here."

They both darted towards the exit, but the exit began to hop around as if made of rubber, the doorposts bouncing along effortlessly.

Dillon made a dash for the ticket counter which passed him in the air, but he missed, falling flat on the vibrating floor.

"Not so fast!" a thunderous voice erupted from behind them. Dillon and his Grandpa whirled around in terror. There, in full site of them, was an enormous worm with bloated bulbous slick skin, dripping whole globs of luminous slime, slithering towards them, smashing and crushing everything in its path, advancing very quickly on the two cowering figures staring up at it.

Six

Ever since he was a young kid, one of Dillon's worst recurring nightmares involved being chased by a voracious lion, and somehow, inexplicably, he couldn't run from the spot no matter how hard he tried. Either the ground would turn to jelly or his legs would simply fail him. He would be gearing himself to sprint away from the animal and find himself crumpling to the ground instead, directly in the path of the animal. In every case, the terror would be sufficient to tear him from his sleep and he would sit up with a silent scream. Although jolted by the experience, he would always take immediate comfort that he was leaving the animal behind him in a world that had vanished in an instant.

As he and his Grandpa slipped and skidded towards the elusive exit, he thought of the lion, the sensation of everything turning to blubber and also that sense of relief on waking. Would the same thing happen here in this netherworld? Even as this grotesque pulsating worm was bearing down them, Dillon couldn't help but view it with a certain skepticism. How real was this worm? How real was Cyberia anyway? Would it dissolve into nothing? Within these few split-seconds his head filled with doubts even though his body trembled in fright and he and Grandpa continued to scramble for stable ground.

The worm lowered its giant pumpkin-shaped head towards them and expelled a lime-green ball of fire which dropped between Dillon and his Grandpa. As the foul-smelling goopy fireball hit the ground it created a seemingly bottomless crater, the surrounding ground smoking in the aftermath. Dillon yelped and pulled his Grandpa from the spot.

"Pleased to delete you today," the worm sneered. "You will be infected. You will be corrupted. You will be wiped from the hard drive."

Dillon saw that the fireball, rather than sink down the crater it had created, edged away from the hole and began to grow, bubbling with grey-yellow mucous. They both watched Dillon's photo album rapidly erode as the green fireball's toxic flames licked at it.

Dillon tried to pull his Grandpa towards this bouncing exit, but Grandpa Harley was struggling for breath, unable to keep up.

Dillon glanced up to see the worm lower its head again. This time he could feel its sulfur-smelling breath against his skin. Dillon and Grandpa ran into the blue wall of the room. They were cornered. Dillon heard a great whooshing sound as the worm drew up its saliva, preparing to expel another fireball right onto the two of them. Dillon closed his eyes. Grandpa raised his arm above his face.

Suddenly a loud chime sounded, like a magnified doorbell. Then a calm, pleasant voice came on, similar to the voice that made the announcements on the train.

"Warning! Your system has been infected. We recommend you isolate any potential viruses now. Would you like to isolate now?"

Dillon looked frantically about him. The worm had frozen, the green fire that had just left it was also suspended in mid-air. Grandpa too appeared to be frozen. But Dillon saw his chest heave once. "Grandpa!"

"Yes," Grandpa barely breathed.

"Are you alright?"

"Just swell." Grandpa's face was whiter than his moustache. "I was just imagining my obituary. "Harley Wilson. Overcame many odds to live a productive and full life, only to be burnt by a worm in Cyberia."

"I don't know what to do," Dillon swallowed. "It's giving us the choice of isolating the virus. It sounds like the right thing but I don't know what it will do to us."

"Maybe we'll become like lepers," Grandpa said blankly, resigning himself to a dismal fate no matter what the options. "We'll never have any contact with other people because our disease is so contagious. Whatever disease it is. I'm not even going to ask you what disease we have, because it's likely to be mumbojumbo."

Dillon's breathing accelerated as the seconds passed. How long would this remain on pause? The worm hovered over them, completely paralyzed, its noxious fire-breath defying gravity. Dillon had to decide now.

"Grandpa, I think we should go for the isolation."

Grandpa shrugged his shoulders. "Sounds fine to me. I've never been much of a socialite anyway."

"Yes!" Dillon shouted finally in reply to the voice.

Nothing happened.

"Don't you have to press that green pincushion?" Grandpa asked nonchalantly, as if he had spotted a pretty souvenir in a tourist shop.

Dillon followed his Grandpa's direction. There, crossing the elevated underbelly of the worm, was a little grey box containing the warning and question they had heard moments earlier. The "yes" box was flashing, awaiting his selection.

Dillon gulped. He knew that the worm was immobilized and that anything dangerous or threatening was put on hold for the moment, but the idea of approaching the viscous underbelly of this giant creature in order to make the selection, both frightened and repulsed him.

"I...." he croaked.

"Do you want me to do it?" Grandpa offered. "I mean, if you really give it any thought, it's just a worm."

Dillon gawked at his Grandpa.

"Granted, it's not your common-or-garden earthworm you bring to school to show your friends. But you know, my father used to say, 'big people can be small-minded sometimes'. Don't let size intimidate you. And as for that green ball of mucous, just because it's icky doesn't mean it's gonna kill you. You should have seen what our soup looked like back in boarding school."

With that he sauntered over towards the box, smiling politely up at the worm's head as he passed underneath.

"Grandpa!"

Grandpa Harley gave the 'yes' button a firm nudge with his palm, turned around and gave his grandson a look of triumph.

There was a loud thud on the other end of the room right next to the "Contact Me" icon. A thick glass booth seemed to have dropped from the sky onto the "Contact Me" box, immediately sealing it in and severing it from its environs. Dillon and his Grandpa then whirled around to see another glass booth drop onto the introduction section behind them, muting his own words of welcome. Another glass booth attempted to lock onto the worm's head, but its slimy skin wouldn't allow the booth to take hold. It came crashing to the ground, splintering into thousands of tiny pieces. Glass isolation booths began storming down everywhere now, one narrowly missing Dillon.

"Grandpa, let's get out of here!" he yelled. Grandpa started in Dillon's direction, but just as he stepped out from underneath the worm's underbelly, a glass booth dropped from above and landed squarely on top of him, trapping him.

"Grandpa!" Dillon yelled, rushing toward the booth. Grandpa's palms were pressed against the glass. He was saying something but Dillon could not hear a sound. Dillon quickly scanned the area around him in search of something sharp or heavy that he could use to smash the glass, but all he could see was broken glass fragments scattered on the cookie ground. In desperation he took a few steps back and charged the booth, lunging his body shoulder-forward into the glass. He gasped as a searing pain tore through his shoulder and back. His right hand clutching his shoulder, he looked up to see Grandpa still in the same position, although he was pale and seemed to be gasping for air, his body slowly crumpling to the ground.

"No! Grandpa!" Tears immediately collected in Dillon's eyes. "Somebody help! Please! Somebody!"

He continued to cry out until his own voice was muted by another glass booth dropping over him and sealing him in. He and Grandpa stared at each other through their booth walls, although Grandpa's eyes appeared so droopy they were ready to close.

All of a sudden the glass in front of Dillon vanished. The booth had simply disappeared in an instant. Grandpa's booth was also gone. Dillon spun around. All the other booths were still there and others yet were falling from the sky. He was about to go over to Grandpa, who lay in a heap on the floor, when he was seized by three men in space suits, carried in the air and strapped onto a stretcher. The swiftness of their actions and the strength of the bonds on his arms and legs made it pointless to protest. He managed to gain a glimpse of his Grandpa who was also laid out on a stretcher alongside him. He appeared to have an oxygen mask attached to him. If they were going to trouble of providing them with air, these people couldn't be that bad, Dillon thought. He was wheeled at high speed through the badly corrupted site exit and straight onto a waiting train.

"Dr. Chomberg, Dr. Chomberg, Code yellow on Coach 3."

Dillon tried to look around but the restraints would permit him to see only the side wall of the train and a machine with myriad controls that had the word CAVE printed in bold on front.

A muffled voice spoke. "Hmmm. Now we're in a cave. How'd you like that?"

"Grandpa!" Dillon shrieked with delight. He couldn't see his Grandpa but the familiar voice brought immense relief.

Another figure in a space suit hovered over him now. "Nurses, prepare de-radiation units," she said. Her actions were hurried, pressing buttons and snapping clasps. But her demeanor was calm and self-assured.

"Hello, there young man," she said, smiling through the window of her headpiece.

"Hi," Dillon said.

"My name is Dr. Grace Chomberg and we are just going to do a quickie procedure here to decontaminate you."

Before Dillon could say anything, he was wheeled away from her and slipped into a tight, funnel-shaped chamber. An alarm sounded, followed by a large grinding noise, like that of a lawn-mower. It grew in intensity until he felt his body vibrating against the walls of the chamber.

To his right he saw a little notice pasted to the wall. It took him a while to read it as the letters were dancing with the vibrations:

"A friendly message from CAVE: Please be aware that decontamination should not be regarded as a substitute for a healthy diet and regular exercise. While decontamination is highly effective at removing all toxins, it will not ensure healthy living. Only you can do that." A caricature of a smiling doctor waved a finger at him. At the bottom, it was signed by Andy Belhauser, the Public Relations Officer of CAVE, Cyberian Anti-Viral Enforcement.

"Cyberian Anti-Viral Enforcement," Dillon repeated to himself as the noise and the vibrations began to subside.

He tried to think back where he had heard that before. He traced his steps all the way back to the point that he and Grandpa arrived in Cyberspace. Then it dawned on him. He reached into his pocket and drew out a business card. Yup! That was him.

"Morton!" Dillon exclaimed as he was removed from the machine and saw the man in question standing right there waiting for him.

"Hi, Dillon," Morton said, his index finger pushing his glasses up the bridge of his nose.

The restraints keeping Dillon to the stretcher were removed by three navy-blue-uniformed workers, now no longer in space suits.

Dillon sat up on his stretcher. He could see Grandpa emerging from a decontamination machine of his own.

"Morton, you and these CAVE guys saved my life and my Grandpa's life," Dillon said in awe.

Morton smiled like a cashier about to wish him a nice day.

"You're a very lucky, young man. We at CAVE have saved a lot of people trapped in the isolation mechanism. But not all have been so fortunate." He patted Dillon on the shoulder.

"Ow!" Dillon grimaced.

"Oh, I'm sorry. Didn't mean to you hurt you."

"No, it's ok. I tried to slam into the booth to rescue Grandpa and got hurt."

"Oh, we'll get a nurse to take care of that for you."

"But how did you just get rid of the glass booth around us like that?" Dillon pressed.

"It's called BoothTooth technology. Don't worry about trying to understand that now. It's taken us many years to develop and perfect the system, and will probably take just as long to explain it to you."

He laughed in short spasms like there was something stuck in his throat. Dillon thanked him. "Where are we headed?" he asked.

"We're going to CAVE headquarters," Morton replied. "I thought we'd give you and your Grandpa a private tour of the facilities."

"Cool!" Dillon exclaimed, imagining entire rooms filled with cockpit dashboard lights.

"Tremendous," Grandpa moaned from his bed. "Do they serve custard in your cave?"

As they pulled into the underground station at CAVE Cyberworld Headquarters, Dillon could see tens if not hundreds of other trains simultaneously pulling in on different tracks. Each track arrived at a different underground elevation. Dillon pressed his face against the window in order to get a glimpse of the roof of the station, but so many different track levels wound around the conical walls that it was impossible to see the roof.

"Wow!" he uttered, blowing fog onto the window.

Grandpa Harley was snoring in his seat. "Grandpa, wake up!" Dillon nudged him. "Grandpa, it really does look like a cave. A giant cave."

"Giant?" Grandpa said, one eye wide-open.

"Yes. It's so cool."

"Is this where the giant worms live?" Grandpa asked, still with only one eye wide open.

"No, no. Of course not. It's...."

Good." He promptly fell back asleep.

The large reception area looked like a hotel lobby, rich colors and shimmering patterns dazzling the eye. There were numerous fountains sprouting from various pockets around the large facility and waterfalls streamed down the rocky walls. The lights were like icicles, thousands of thin tubes shooting downwards several feet from the glass ceiling.

Morton noticed Dillon and his Grandpa peering up at the lights.

"They're made to resemble stalactites," he told them. "You'll notice all about you that several of the interior features simulate cave living."

"Cool," Dillon said.

"Cool is definitely the word," Grandpa remarked, rubbing his shoulders. "Why is it so cold in here?"

"We keep it slightly cooler than comfortable because warmer air creates a breeding ground for viruses," Morton responded with a smile.

"How far underground are we?" Dillon asked.

"About one mile."

"A mile!" Dillon exclaimed. "That's awesome."

"A mile of cookies deep," Grandpa commented.

"Sounds good to me."

"Wait until you see the rest of this place. Let's first get you both registered for the tour."

Jan at the front desk took down their information and registered them. "Are you ready?" she asked them when she was done.

"Ready for what?" Dillon asked.

"Ready to hit enter." She pointed to a green pincushion on the counter. "You are now registered. All you have to do is hit enter."

No sooner did Dillon and Grandpa press the button than Jan's face began to dissolve before them. In her place, large gold letters appeared: "Welcome Harley and Dillon. Please wait while your tour loads. Do not hit enter twice or all your body stats will be lost."

Dillon gulped. He gave Morton a frightened stare.

"Don't worry," Morton laughed, even as the rock walls around them gave way to firm white plastic. "We're fine. It's not as ominous as it sounds. Even if we do accidentally hit the button twice, the chances are we'd recover all our body parts pretty easily."

"How comforting," Grandpa retorted.

The room they were in now came into focus. It had high white ceilings and tiled floors, and was mostly empty except for a few displays positioned at various intervals along the walls. Large, vibrant paintings also adorned the walls here and there.

"A museum!" Grandpa declared with great excitement.

"Grandpa likes art," Dillon told Morton.

"Well, these are portraits of some famous Cyberians," Morton said. "Many of them were founders of Cyberian security systems. They did this in the early years of Cyberia when life was still quite primitive and you had guerilla bands easily hacking into people's bank accounts. It was like the Wild West. Chaos ruled. These people were the pioneers of Cyberian security Thanks to them we have CAVE today. Let's look at a couple of the paintings."

They stopped at the first portrait. A white-haired man with a gaunt face stared blankly at them. He was seated in a plush chair in front of a construction site. The description below read:

Gill Bates, innovator and philanthropist, is seen here in front of a website under construction. Bates was the first person to fund a site dedicated solely to Cyberian website security. Initially called the Hacker Police Initiative, it later became known as Cyberian Anti-Viral Enforcement, the name the organization still bears today. With the help of others, Bates was able to secure billions of bytes in memory for a new CAVE headquarters that could serve as the center of operations for all of Cyberia.

"Amazing man," Morton said, pushing back his glasses. "But let me show you this guy. This is my favorite." He lead them to a smaller portrait of a teenage boy with thick braces on his teeth.

"Wait a minute," Grandpa protested. "This young boy?"

"Yup," Morton chuckled. "I just love this story."

They read the description:

Sixteen year-old Warton Weltzheimer made history as the youngest systems engineer to develop Cyberian security systems. Formerly the most wanted hacker on the net, Weltzheimer turned himself in and underwent an extensive rehabilitation program before joining CAVE as the mastermind of anti-viral operations. After a short while of working for CAVE, Weltzheimer succeeded in apprehending many of his former partners in crime.

"Wow!" Dillon said.

"Isn't that neat?" Morton echoed, beaming.

"What's so bad about being a woodchopper?" Grandpa wanted to know.

"What?" Morton said, puzzled.

Dillon snorted. "Grandpa, I told you before that hacking means accessing one computer from another."

"That's right, you did," Grandpa replied. "Someone also spoke to me in Russian once at a restaurant in 1981. But I don't remember what he said either. How'd do you like that?"

"Anyway," Morton breathed. "Let's show you some of the displays here."

They approached a model of a weapon that appeared to be some sort of canon.

Morton laughed as he began to describe it. "You have to give these guys the credit for trying," he said. "The early strategists believed that the way to fight worms was to launch fireballs at them – kind of like, fighting fire with fire. They soon found out that the worms not only were unharmed by the fireballs, they actually thrived on them. It was like giving them a shot in the arm. They ingested them and grew in strength and vigor as a result. Talk about a failed experiment. But you know, they had to learn somehow."

"It's like those enthusiasts a hundred years ago who wanted to make flying machines," Grandpa said, recalling the filmed scenes of embarrassing early flying experiments. "But look where they are today."

"Exactly!" Morton enthused. "I laugh now, but all sophistication must have humble beginnings."

"All sophistication must have humble beginnings. I like that," Grandpa repeated, reserving a modicum of respect for this man whose mannerisms otherwise irritated him on many levels.

"What else is there?" Dillon asked eagerly.

"Well, we could spend the whole day here," Morton said. "But there are a lot of things I want to show you so let's move on in the tour. Dillon, would you step on that green pincushion on the floor in that corner?"

Dillon ran over and happily jumped onto the pincushion. When he bounced back up, the pincushion was gone and they were standing in the center of a room full of spiders. Thousands of spiders.

Both Dillon and Grandpa Harley squirmed.

"Web crawlers?" Dillon inquired, shivering.

"That's right. Very good, Dillon!" Morton exclaimed. "You're learning. These are web crawlers trained in every aspect of web security. We send them out to patrol the net and report any suspicious activity to headquarters. We receive millions of data bits about security every day based on their hard work."

He stopped one of the crawlers as it passed by.

"Harold, do you have a minute?"

"Sure, Mr. McAfnee," Harold said, clutching documents with three of his legs.

"Harold, this is Dillon Appleseed and his grandfather, Harley."

"Hi there," Harold said, extending one leg to Dillon and another to Grandpa at the same time.

Both Dillon and Grandpa went pale. Dillon shut his eyes and gingerly extended his hand.

"Don't worry, I don't bite," Harold assured him with a smile.

A spider that doesn't bite? Grandpa mused. It reminded him of the fox in The Gingerbread Man.

Harold took Dillon's hand. The prickly furry feeling made Dillon's hairs stand on end. When Grandpa didn't extend his hand, Harold withdrew his other leg.

"Harold is chief dispatcher," Morton told them. "He does an excellent job of sending agents out all over Cyberia in a timeous fashion."

"Why thank you, Mr. McAfnee. You've made my day."

"You're welcome, Harold. Keep up the good work."

Morton pressed another green pincushion and the spiders began to dissolve. Both Dillon and his Grandpa breathed a sigh of relief.

Vast rocky terrain gradually took shape in front of their eyes. The contours and crevices of the rock became more discernable as each portion of landscape solidified. Dillon tried to turn himself in order to survey their new surroundings but found himself unable to budge.

A pleasant voice chimed in. "Movement is not permitted until your domain transferal is fully complete. For your protection, temporary movement resistance fields have been engaged to block significant body movements until transfer is complete."

"What did she just say?" Grandpa asked impulsively, whether or not the answer made any difference to him.

"Basically, moving can be dangerous for your health," Dillon replied.

"Well," Grandpa scoffed. "That's a surgeon general's warning I've never heard before."

"Shhh!" Morton urged. "A lot of essential and sensitive dialogue occurs here and it would be better if we talked quietly so that we don't disturb them."

"Who's them?" Dillon whispered, as the scenery around them finally emerged in full resolution.

"The Monitors of Electronic Networking, or M.E.N. They form the communications backbone of CAVE, intercepting communication signals and highly classified data, and then decoding it, allowing CAVE to be a step ahead of all security threats to Cyberia."

"Wait a minute," Dillon said. "That's pronounced MEN? As in CAVEMEN?"

"That's exactly right. That's how we refer to them here," Morton smiled, taking the liberty of fluffing Dillon's hair, which to Dillon felt as if a bunch of lizards had been set loose over his head.

"You don't miss a beat," Morton said.

"Unlike his grandfather," Grandpa Harley quipped. "I've missed so many beats it's a wonder my heart remembers to work."

Morton chuckled. "I don't know, Harley," Morton said. "I think you have your self-deprecation down to a fine art."

"Wow!" Dillon exclaimed suddenly, as the lighting level increased, revealing the profiles of hundreds of people seated ahead of them in a crescent shape amongst the rocks.

"Those must be the CAVEMEN," Grandpa said.

Morton nodded. "And that large holographic screen you see in the center is the hub of intelligence monitoring, detecting security breaches and capturing signals from all over Cyberia."

It was hard not to stare at the screen. It was like a glittering neon casino sign, millions of little lights flickering and pulsating, continuously appearing and disappearing. Streaks of glowing red would shoot across the screen seemingly at random, alerting groups of

CAVEMEN who gathered immediately to investigate and strategize.

"This is awesome!" Dillon exclaimed, his own eyes glowing with the reflection of tiny lights.

"Shh!" Morton insisted again.

"Isn't this cool, Grandpa?" Dillon whispered.

"It certainly is something to look at," Grandpa replied casually, belying his exhilaration at experiencing the stuff of his boyhood dreams.

"Have a look in that corner there," Morton directed them. "You can see that those CAVEMEN have picked up the trail of a particular virus. Hmmm, I can tell by their procedures that it looks like a bad one. It could be the Best Friend Virus that has been striking lately."

"The Best Friend Virus?" Dillon inquired.

"Yes – what it does is identify the most frequent recipient of email messages in a human's sent email box. Then it composes a fake toxic email from that recipient and sends it to the human. The person doesn't think twice about opening such an email because it purports to be from someone they trust. The person opens it and, wham! Wipes out their hard drive."

Dillon grimaced. "That's mean."

"What if you don't have a hard drive?" Grandpa asked.

"And, that's only the half of it," Morton continued, ignoring Grandpa. "That's what humans experience. But for Cyberians, a fake toxic email that implodes can be deadly. Many Cyberians have been maimed or killed by these seemingly harmless encounters in the email streets. Innocent men, women and children. You read about it daily in the Cyberian Express."

Both Dillon and Grandpa looked horrified.

"Yup, I'm afraid things are not as safe in Cyberia as they could be," Morton sighed. "Which brings me to the real reason I wanted to bring you here."

Dillon snapped to attention. Grandpa raised an eyebrow.

"I thought you just wanted to show us around," Dillon said.

"Oh, come on," Morton said. "My title of Chief Case Specialist at CAVE comes with vital duties and obligations that make my time far too valuable to be a mere tour guide. You didn't realize that?"

"I have a bad back, but otherwise I would bow down," Grandpa quipped.

Morton bristled. "Come with me," he snapped, gesturing to them. "I'd like you to meet with someone."

Dillon and Grandpa trailed behind Morton. Dillon's nerves felt as if they had escaped his skin and were crawling all over him. Was it too late to go back? What had he gotten himself and his Grandpa into?

They crossed a bridge spanning a rocky valley. A sparkling stream rushed several feet below them. At the end of the bridge, the scenery changed dramatically. The floor was suddenly carpeted, and they found themselves in a neat but sparse conference room. Aside from the table and the woman seated at it, there was barely anything else in the room.

"Commander Burdock," Morton cleared his throat.

The woman looked up from a chart.

"Morton," she said coolly.

Morton seemed unsteady on his feet. "They're here, Commander."

A shiver went up Dillon's spine. This had been thoroughly planned out.

The woman rose from her chair and approached them. She smiled broadly, infusing her face with warmth, instantly reminding Dillon of Mrs. Saffer, his kindergarten teacher.

"Well, hello, there," she said warmly. "I'm Sharon Burdock, and, well...." She gave a self-deprecating shrug. "I guess I run the show around here."

Morton laughed nervously.

"Hi," Dillon volunteered, a pipsqueak sound that seemed far away.

"Good day, Commander," Grandpa said, standing stiffly at attention.

Commander Burdock giggled. She turned to Dillon. "He's funny, your Grandpa, isn't he?" Each of her wrinkles seemed to smile.

Dillon wasn't sure how to respond.

The Commander invited them to take seats around the table. The seats were plain wicker chairs that were suited more to a garden than an office. On the table were a couple of photographs of young children.

"This is Tyler and this is Kaden," she said proudly. "My adorable grandchildren."

"They are," Grandpa agreed. "Do they go to school?"

She nodded. "Weltzheimer Elementary over on Seedy Drive."

"It must be so cool to be in school in Cyberia," Dillon remarked. "I wonder what the classrooms look like. Do the rooms have doors or do you just download yourself into class?"

Commander Burdock laughed. "We ought to bring you over some time as special guests from the human world. I'm sure the kids would love that."

"That would be neat!" Dillon enthused.

"But for now we really need to discuss the purpose of your visit," the Commander said in a solemn yet strangely sweet tone.

113

Dillon glanced at his Grandpa whose eyebrow remained raised like an aqueduct arch.

Morton swallowed. He had paid no attention to the small talk about grandchildren and schooling. Dillon wondered why Morton seemed unable to relax in his superior's presence. He kinda liked her himself.

"Let me give you a little background," the Commander began. "Do you recall, when you first arrived in Cyberia, hearing a special security announcement at the BiteFlite station?"

"Yes," Dillon replied. "It said something about Code Orange, but I don't remember the rest because I was busy looking for my Grandpa. We got separated when we arrived."

"Yes, I heard about that," the Commander confided.

Dillon's eyes darted around. "You did?"

Commander Burdock and Morton exchanged glances. Dillon observed this with a growing sense of uneasiness. He had no idea the extent to which their plan was contrived. It had seemed purely coincidental that Morton had been there to help Grandpa to his feet when they had arrived. What kind of trap was this?

"Yes, I'm sorry you had to go through that," Commander Burdock said quickly. "Now, let me tell you that you're correct about what you called Code Orange. As you may know, we at CAVE are responsible for the security of all of Cyberia, which is no small task. We recently had to raise the security level to Orange. This means that there is an unusual threat to the security of all Cyberians. In this case it is being generated by an organized syndicate of destructive forces, possibly including viruses, worms, Trojan Horses and Spyware, that is bent on destroying the entire nation of Cyberia as we know it."

As the words left her mouth, the blood seemed to drain from her face. This smiley, jovial lady seemed to reveal the terror that was gripping her.

"The whole of Cyberia?" Dillon asked quietly. "I mean all the websites and everything?"

"Everything."

"All of this will be gone," Morton reiterated.

Grandpa sighed deeply. "I'm really sorry to hear that. I thought it was only our world that suffered from sick demented people."

"Yes, thank you for your sympathy," the Commander said. "The thing is we would normally have the capability of dealing with such a threat. We have state-of-the-art technology and intelligence systems set up, with all the manpower we needed. The problem is that this threat is unlike any other we have experienced. The coding that accompanies it is so deeply encrypted that even our veteran experts can't even begin to decipher it. So we are at this point unable to trace the origin of the threat, nor identify in what form the attack is going to take place. All we know is that the CAVEMEN are unanimous that a catastrophic attack is imminent. We cannot predict exactly when, where, how or by whom."

She smiled at the end of her presentation of doom.

Dillon grimaced. "Maybe, I'm thinking that...." He glanced at his Grandpa before continuing. "....That it's time for us to go back home now."

Grandpa appeared to have no objections to such a notion.

"Well, just a second," Morton said hastily, sliding his glasses quite forcefully back up the ridge of his nose. "I think you might find Commander Burdock's proposal to you quite interesting."

Dillon's eyes locked on Morton who was playing roughly with some loose strands of wicker on his chair.

115

Commander Burdock cleared her throat. "Morton, please try to remember not to intimidate our guests."

"Oh, don't worry about that," Grandpa retorted. "We are not easily intimidated. Especially after surviving a ferocious worm and a suffocating booth."

Morton forced a smile, his lips quivering a little as they stretched.

"So let me explain what Morton is referring to," the Commander said, her textured reassuring voice triggering a memory of Mrs. Saffer about to explain the habits of a female black widow spider.

"You see, there is one possible way we could dramatically reduce the fallout from such an attack. And the answer, Dillon, is in your coat pocket."

Dillon instinctually raised a hand to his chest, as if about to take an oath.

"You have a PDA in there, am I right?" she queried.

Dillon squinted at his Grandpa before answering quietly in the affirmative.

"Well, that PDA may seem to be an ordinary piece of electronic equipment to the average human in the outside world. But to a Cyberian, its value is inestimable."

"Why?" Dillon asked with a frown.

"Because, if you think about it," she leaned forward, as Mrs. Saffer did about to reveal the part about the black widow's murderous instincts. "A PDA, or any such outside computer, can create websites and destroy websites in a matter of seconds, simply by pressing a couple of buttons. This is something we can't do here because we live inside the world of websites and cannot control their existence or their removal from the inside. We would be trying to control the outside from the inside, like the characters of a novel trying to extract themselves from the novel. Only the author can do that.

In that sense the PDA is the author of all of Cyberia, with the ability to create and destroy in a way that far exceeds our capabilities inside this world."

Dillon stroked the edges of his PDA through the fabric of his coat. This sundry item he lugged with him had suddenly transformed itself. Now he was reluctant to withdraw it from his pocket.

"But, I still don't get it," he protested. Morton shifted impatiently in his chair.

"No problem," Commander Burdock assured him. "All this information can be confusing. What part do you not understand?"

"Well, you can get a PDA from a website that sells it right here in Cyberia. Can't that do the same thing?"

Commander Burdock nodded approvingly. "Great question, young man. It's not that you don't understand. It's that you're not satisfied with a half-answer. You see, the problem is we can't buy the darn thing." She had an embarrassed smile.

Dillon was puzzled.

"We just can't proceed to checkout," she shrugged. "No Cyberian can actively engage in a website transaction. If you have visited some sites on your trip thus far, you will have noticed that you can interact with the items on the website, but you will be unable to acquire or extract them because they are part of the ingrained structure. Only humans can do so from the outside."

"Babe Ruth and Beethoven," Grandpa said to Dillon. Dillon nodded slowly.

Commander Burdock peered at Grandpa Harley and giggled. "I heard about that incident with Beethoven. So yes, I think you get my drift."

Grandpa blushed.

"All we can do really is watch the process occur. It can be exceedingly frustrating, but on the other hand, you learn to live with your limitations and accept yourself for who you are. My mother used to say, 'Who is wealthy? One who is happy with one's lot.'"

"That is very true," Grandpa attested.

"So you need the PDA in order to destroy the attackers?" Dillon inquired.

"Yes, basically," the Commander replied. "As I said earlier, we are still not sure how or where this attack will occur, but armed with a PDA like yours we would have a much greater chance of eliminating the source of the threat in an efficient and timely manner. It may give us that upper hand against our enemies, something that has always been our trademark here at CAVE. It's what enables Cyberians to live safe and peaceful lives."

"So, in other words, you want me to give you my PDA," Dillon said, cupping the hidden instrument with his palm.

"Well, not exactly. I mentioned the difficulty in obtaining a PDA, but there is another caveat to this whole thing. It is actually against the law for a Cyberian to be in possession of a PDA. It is one of the founding principles of Cyberia and it is extremely difficult to obtain an exemption, even if it means the safety of Cyberia is compromised."

"Why?" Dillon asked.

"For the very reason that it is so useful," the Commander explained. "A PDA in the wrong hands could have disastrous effects as you can imagine. The whole of Cyberia could vanish within no time at all. So PDA's were made unconditionally illegal for Cyberians, and even if it were somehow possible for a Cyberian to obtain a PDA, we would be obligated to destroy it immediately."

Dillon shook his head in disbelief.

"Some shady Cyberians have tried to bring in PDA's from the outside world, but weren't able to do so. The Image Particle Transfer system that brought you both here is automatically programmed to deny access to Cyberians returning from the human world with a PDA in their possession. Only humans can do so. Cyberians are forced to leave the PDA in the outside world and return empty-handed. And that is why technically we would not be violating the law by having you operate the PDA on our behalf. It's a perfectly sound legal loophole. It's not something we would resort to under ordinary circumstances. But then again, these are not ordinary circumstances."

Dillon glared at her.

"I have a question," Grandpa said. "You know I am not so familiar with all these fancy highfalutin expressions you're using, but I have to ask you: what is so terrible and ominous about the Parents Teachers Association?"

The room was interminably quiet. As he was getting only baffled looks, Grandpa tried to explain his question.

"I've been on many PTA's in my time. My daughter was valedictorian and gave a lot to her school, and I felt it my duty to have a say in the every day running of things. I did find these groups full of politics and destructive in that sense. As Dillon will tell you, I think politics is very dangerous, because...." He nudged Dillon to continue.

Somewhere between amused and embarrassed, Dillon said, "Because it bores him to death."

Grandpa continued. "But I don't see how a PTA could be so...."

Commander Burdock's uncontrolled laughter interrupted him. "Oh, Harley, you are a hoot. I am so glad you are here. You relieve so much of the tension. That is sorely needed around here." She continued laughing and wiping the tears from her eyes. In the meantime, Dillon whispered the definition of a PDA in his Grandpa's ear.

"So!" the Commander gave the table a gentle pat. "The bottom line, gentlemen, is that you could be of tremendous help to us in Cyberia by agreeing to serve as support strategists in our war against Cyberian terror networks."

"You mean you want us to stay here?" Grandpa gawked.

"Well, yes, if you would, until we've at least made some progress against the threat."

"But we can't," Grandpa Harley protested without conferring with his grandson. "We'll starve. You people, or…. creatures, I suppose, don't have any food here – you just plug yourselves in, apparently. We don't do that. We eat. And I must say, I in particular, do a darn good job of that. In fact, now that I think of it, my stomach is rumbling so loud it'll cause an earthquake and this cave will fall in."

Commander Burdock's giggle was more like a cat's purr. Morton smiled, his Adam's Apple rising as if on a pulley.

"That's a good point," the Commander noted. "I don't know how I could have forgotten about that. You actually have meal times, too, don't you? Hmmm. Morton, any suggestions?"

"Well, yes, Commander. I could take them to Mc Ronalds. Dillon could use his PDA to order something on the website and then proceed to checkout. Since he's using a PDA that humans use to buy things on the web, I bet it would allow him to do that and he would end up with actual food."

"You're right!" the Commander enthused, her eyes sparkling. She stood up from her chair. "Now that would be spectacular. Quite an unprecedented event in the annuls of Cyberia. Perhaps we should notify *The Cyberian Express* and...."

"Perhaps, not...." Morton interjected. "With all due respect, Commander, it's probably unwise to draw attention to this at all. We do not want to arouse the suspicions of lurking ears."

She saluted him with a finger. "Right again. Morton, you prove yourself time and time again. It's no wonder you are where you are today."

"Thank you, Commander!" Morton said sheepishly.

"Very well, then," the Commander said merrily, "we're all in agreement?"

Dillon's jaw hung to the side. He peered at his Grandpa, who was clearly occupied with a cerebral vision of a juicy hunk of beef with extra mustard.

"Well, I guess, we could get something to eat and then we'll kinda.....see," Dillon acquiesced, though not without a sigh. Truthfully, he did not know what to think.

Dillon and his Grandpa followed Morton out of CAVE headquarters and onto a train bound for Mc Ronalds. Dillon selected a double burger with fries and Grandpa Harley ordered the steak roll. This time they readied themselves for the overwhelming aroma of meat and oil, preparing to breathe through the dense, fat-saturated air that would fill the room when the food appeared. Dillon looked to his left and right before furtively withdrawing his PDA. Morton's eyes bulged like luminous marbles at the sight. He cleared his throat. "Yes, uh, go ahead and submit your order."

Dillon turned away to enter his access password. Morton's presence was uncomfortably close. He seemed to hover right next to him as Dillon was entering the six digits.

Dillon inched away and continued with his password submission.

"Successful?" Morton asked after a while, bouncing on his toes. Grandpa remained entranced by the menu selections.

"Well, it says it needs a delivery address. What should I say?" Dillon asked.

"Oh, ummm. Let me think about that." Morton stroked his chin and twitched his nose.

"Let's try this," he said finally. "Enter the web-host's IP address, and see if we can grab the food when it appears." He provided Dillon with the numbers forming the IP address, which was the address of the computer that hosted the Mc Ronalds website. Dillon hit "submit" and they waited.

It was quiet for a long while. Grandpa sighed. "Is it coming? Your mother never keeps me waiting when I'm starving."

Then, right in front of Grandpa, a six by three foot object suddenly materialized. "Your steak roll has downloaded," an intercom voice announced. "The double burger and fries will follow shortly. Please do not exit the site during the download or the food may become corrupted."

"Whoah!" Dillon exclaimed, holding his nose. "It's a giant steak roll."

"I like their portions," Grandpa commented.

"I guess you risk size distortion when you're trying to order across domain thresholds," Morton surmised, holding back a sneeze.

"Whatever," Grandpa said wryly. "Sometimes you shouldn't worry about the process and just focus on the results."

Dillon chuckled. "Grandpa, how are you ever going to get through that?"

"Dillon, that's why there are refrigerators in the world. Oh, yeah. Morton, you do have refrigerators in Cyberia, right?"

"Uh, no, actually, we have no need for them."

"Oh, well," Grandpa said, slapping his side. "I guess I'll have to eat as much I can right now." The thought did not seem to trouble him at all.

"Now for the taste test," Dillon announced after all the food had downloaded. But the announcement was apparently too late. Grandpa Harley was already halfway through his first morsel. "Not bad," he said between chews. "Grandma would have approved. Except that she didn't like it when I ate junk food. Although it may be that burgers in Cyberia are healthier because they come from thin air."

Morton watched as the two of them sat down on the cookie floor and tried to consume as much of the food as their stomachs would allow. Grandpa, though, went just a little over that limit, so that his stomach was forced to squeeze the excess into a vacant slot somewhere.

Morton suggested that Dillon and Grandpa retire for the night before starting on their new mission in Cyberia. He booked them into the Boldfont Plaza and Towers, a luxury hotel overlooking the Public Domain Recreation Area.

The hotel had numerous amenities, filling several pages of the guide in their room. But Dillon and his Grandpa had only one goal for the night. Now that they had satiated their hunger, tiredness overwhelmed them. Worms, Morton, websites, Beethoven and burgers mingled together to form an incoherent and nauseating profile of their day. The pillows looked inviting.

Dillon was about to lay down when something beeped. There was a flashing light on the headboard above him. Just below that light was a notice:

"Dear Guests,

We'd like to remind you to plug yourself in before you retire for the night. The plug-in equipment is located underneath your bed. The management and staff of Boldfont Plaza and Towers cannot be held responsible for illness or death resulting from failure to plug oneself in. We wish you a pleasant night, and thank you for choosing Boldfont."

A shiver went up Dillon's spine. "That is so eerie," he uttered.

He peeked cautiously under the bed, and found long black tubing with sharp metal prongs lying just under the bed-frame. He shrank back immediately, trying not to imagine where exactly on the body those prongs would be inserted.

He climbed under the covers and switched off the lights. "Good night, Grandpa," he said softly through the shadows. But Grandpa Harley was already snoring soundly. Dillon's eyes were about to close when he reached over and grabbed his PDA from the night-table next to the bed, and clenched it firmly in his hand. Just in case, he thought. After all, apparently he was in possession of the key to survival of the entire nation of Cyberia. He had better make sure it never left his side.

Seven

"Let's go home," were the first words to leave Dillon's lips upon waking the next morning. Sometimes sleeping over an issue allowed all the bits and pieces floating inside his head to settle. And when it all came together in this luxury hotel bed on a sunny Cyberian morning, it was clear to him that enough was enough. Letting the future of an entire nation rest in his hands was practically a joke. Never mind having to face off a lethal enemy, he would be responsible for restoring national peace! Meanwhile, he was a sixteen year-old kid who didn't even have his driver's license yet, for crying out loud. It was time to go back to what he knew best – which was his bedroom and his hobbies, and ordinary days spent at his ordinary school.

But immediately as he started to explain all this, his Grandpa quickly overruled him. "What? Go back? Where is your sense of responsibility, young man?" Grandpa was wetting the few remaining strands of hair that flapped over his head.

"But why is it my responsibility, Grandpa? This is just a fun thing we did. I don't even know if it's real. We could just go back home and everything would be fine."

His Grandpa turned to him. "Dillon, last night I had the biggest steak roll I have ever seen. There was nothing more real than that experience. And even if you look beyond the food...." He paused, clearly having some difficulty following through with that idea. "....Beyond the food, there is the opportunity here for us to make a difference in people's lives. Call it fiction or non-fiction, who cares? We're still able to ensure that other people can exist. And now you want to go home?"

Dillon dropped his stare. "I don't know," he mumbled. "It's just so crazy, and so dangerous, and....Grandpa, do you trust that lady?"

"Sharon?" Grandpa said, returning to his hair.

"Yeah, Shar.... I mean Commander Burdock."

"Oh, she's harmless," Grandpa said. "You could tell the way she looked at the pictures of her grandchildren. Take it from another grandparent. People who get all mushy like that have hearts of gold."

The phone rang.

"Hello," Dillon said into the receiver.

"Yes, sir, you have a message from a Mr. Morton McAfnee. He said you are to take a train to CAVE headquarters. He will meet you in the CAVE lobby at 10am."

Dillon was quiet.

"Sir?"

"Yes, I uh...." He glanced at his Grandpa who was still taking roll call of all his remaining hairs.

"I guess we'll meet him there then. Thank you."

He hung up the phone and stared blankly at the creepy plug-in sign.

"What was that about?" His Grandpa asked staring in the mirror.

"Morton wants us to meet him at CAVE at 10 o'clock."

"Oh, good," Grandpa said sprightly.

Dillon let out a long sigh.

The station platform was very crowded this morning. There was a fair number of people, but the real jam was caused by an unusually heavy volume of emails streaming past them. Spam attempted to contact Dillon and his Grandpa six times before they even got to the ticket counter.

The seventh encounter was a little different, and yet patently familiar.

"Susan!" Grandpa exclaimed.

"Well, well. If it isn't the marauding Cyberspace invaders," Susan Dandelion said with a wry smile.

"Hi," Dillon said, returning the smile.

"I hope you aren't going to slap me in the face this time," Susan remarked to Grandpa.

"Oh, no!" Grandpa boomed. "Not unless I have to, anyway."

They all laughed, especially Susan, who loosened her iron grip on her clipboard.

"So, how is your....uh group going?" Dillon inquired.

"MemFriends? Uh... great! I mean, not bad." Her smile withered.

"Not that great, eh?" Grandpa suggested.

Her eyes turned to the ground. "Well, I just need to keep working on raising consciousness," she shrugged. "So, what have you two been up to?"

Dillon and Grandpa glanced at each other.

"Well, we've been assigned a very...." Grandpa began but was quickly overridden by Dillon's loud ensemble of coughing and sneezing.

"Are you okay?" Susan asked.

"Fine," Dillon growled, his eyes blinking a thousand protests in his Grandpa's direction.

"What?" Grandpa said stupidly.

"I think we need to get going," Dillon announced, pulling his Grandpa by the sleeve. "Nice to see you again, Susan."

"Yes, uh, I wish you every success with your memory," Grandpa added as he was being whisked away.

"Thank you," she said, not having the presence of mind to correct him. She folded her arms and stared after them as they disappeared into the crowd.

Within moments of arriving at CAVE headquarters, Morton had Dillon and Grandpa Harley standing directly in front of the brilliant neon screen in the crater at the center of the rocky intelligence arena. The hundreds of CAVEMEN that surrounded them hardly noticed them, absorbed by the urgency of their task. Dillon noticed that most of the CAVEMEN wore permanent frowns, that their speech seemed hurried, and that they moved about sharply and restlessly from their consoles to the screen and back.

"There's a lot on their minds," Morton commented, noticing Dillon's distracted stare.

"Nothing like doomsday to motivate a person," Grandpa commented. "In such dire situations, nothing matters except survival. You tend to forget how tired or hungry you are." His eyes seemed to travel to a distant place as he spoke. "You can't be bothered by ordinary every day problems like 'who read my newspaper and folded it in all the wrong places?' or 'why do I always land end up behind a bus when I'm in a hurry?' These things don't matter anymore when your very life is at stake."

Both Dillon and Morton watched as Grandpa allowed some gripping scene to play out in his mind. They grimaced when Grandpa grimaced, although they had no idea what grave event was being referenced.

"Anyway," Morton said matter-of-factly, "there is reason for their determination, as you know, and it is imperative that we all do our best to deter and dissolve this threat. So, I think the best point of beginning would be to examine the bugs and viruses and so forth that are currently active in Cyberia." With an animated sniff, his glasses were thrust back up his nose. "Under normal circumstances, these might be considered your common-or-garden variety of viruses and bugs that pose at most localized threats to systems and populations, hardly on the scale that the Commander was referring to yesterday. We usually have to fight these forces head-on, which is a considerable drain on manpower and security systems. With your PDA however…" His eyes widened and his voice faltered slightly, as if the little computer in Dillon's pocket was a giant beast in hibernation. "With your PDA, however, a simple press of a command perhaps might enable us to sever these forces completely from our existence, rather than simply defeating them at battle. When you weed, you don't simply cut the weed, you uproot it completely, or else it will grow back."

"Well, the truth is," Grandpa commented, "hand-weeding is effective only if you do it before the weeds flower and set seed. What you could do, though, is plant sod which grows faster than ordinary grass seed and blocks the weeds from growing in the first place."

Morton smiled politely and seemed to lose his train of thought.

"But Mr. McAfnee, I still don't understand," Dillon said. "With my PDA, you'll be getting rid of the bugs you have now forever – that part I get. But how will you be able to know whether that big major bug that's out to destroy everything will also get uprooted? It hasn't appeared yet, right?"

Morton cleared his throat. "Yes, Dillon, that's correct. But it's a start. It might lead us to the root of the bugs which might just be a central depot of sorts. If we find the center of all bugs, there's a chance this bug might be included in that."

"But isn't it dangerous to...."

"Look," Morton said abruptly. "You are a kid. A bright kid, but a kid nonetheless. I am just a little bit older than you are, with just a tad more experience in Cyber-Security than you have. I'm telling you the plan, I'm not asking you to approve it for me."

Dillon lowered his gaze. Grandpa's eyebrow popped up like an arch again.

"So," Morton said, his hands on his waist. "Are you ready to do this?"

Dillon looked at his Grandpa who rolled his lips into a funnel as if he was about to whistle. It was his way of telling Dillon to pay no attention to a grown man's tantrum.

"I guess I'm ready," Dillon said in an undertone.

"Good! Now, let's take a look at today's map of virus threats." He pointed to various red streaks shooting across the bottom right corner of the screen. "This is an infected website over here. It could be a virus, a bug, a worm. We can't be sure. It may or may not be contagious. We don't know that either at this point. But what we do know is that this site is corrupted and a danger spot. Now, if we could visit this particular site...let's see what type of site it is. One second." He turned to consult with one of the CAVEMEN and returned. "Aha! It's a mortgage site. 0% down, paid appraisal, low rates – sometimes the people who launch such sites are shady and it can be infected from the start. So!" he rubbed his hands together. "If we could actually visit this site with your PDA ready to strike, we could, as I mentioned earlier, be lining ourselves up to eventually go where no Cyberian has gone before – to the root, to the hub of the viral syndicate."

"Will we be protected?" Dillon asked wide-eyed. "I mean we're going to the site just like that?"

Morton gave a dignified snort. "Well, there will only be a short period of time that we'll be unprotected – that's because we'll have to give your PDA a chance to show its stuff without interference from CAVE. Usually, the system will automatically offer protection. Remember the glass booths that came down on you?"

"Vividly," Grandpa replied.

"Well, that was CAVE's automatic protection response. We're going to have to disarm it, or else we'll never get the chance for your PDA to eliminate the bad guys. But don't forget, young man, that for the most part we've got the entire CAVE network behind us. If you recall how you were rescued from the worm, CAVE has at its disposal some of the most sophisticated technology in Cyberia. If we ever come into danger, I will alert CAVE to reactivate the system and the security procedures will kick in immediately."

Dillon merely stared at Morton, indifferent to his assurances. Morton's impatience, however, was reaching new levels. He snapped his fingers as if to jumpstart Dillon's excitement. "Let's go to the site! I'm alerting the Commander," he declared.

He directed them out of the center towards a downloading train and before they knew it, Dillon and Grandpa were on their way to fulfilling their mission as special agents of CAVE in Cyberia.

"This is kind of cool, I guess," Dillon said nervously to Grandpa as the train rattled along towards the mortgage website.

"It is interesting," Grandpa remarked, peering at the other passengers around them. They were an eclectic mix, ranging from sedate old ladies to tattooed wire-haired punk rockers, all of them unusually quiet for a large group of assembled people. Many of them were wringing their hands.

"Many of these people leave their fate to risky ventures," Morton whispered. "They're too trusting. You always wonder who would fall for some of the marketing traps out there, but there will always be a segment of the population who will jump aboard the glitter train, even though they know somewhere inside them that all that glitters is not gold. The sub-prime mortgage marketing machine is no exception."

Dillon wasn't sure he understood Morton's sophisticated commentary. Mortgages confused him anyway. His father had explained the concept to him briefly but he'd had trouble comprehending in the end who exactly it was who was considered the owner of the house.

But then a peculiar thought occurred to him. "Mr. Mc Afnee," he whispered, clearing his throat. "If we know that our destination has a dangerous bug in it, shouldn't we be warning these people on the train about it? That way they wouldn't get off the train and they would stay safe."

Morton shrugged his shoulders. "These people made a conscious choice to be here. You can't teach them to be responsible by removing the consequences of their actions. The only way they will change their ways is if they learn the hard way, unfortunately. They have to see for themselves exactly what they're doing to themselves."

Although Dillon vaguely understood this concept, it didn't sit right with him. He had more questions but the train was coming to a stop and the doors would soon be opening. He turned, deep in thought, to the back row of the train. As he did so, a figure that had been standing there quickly vanished through the inter-leading doors to the coach behind them.

Dillon gasped.

"What's wrong? Morton and Grandpa asked simultaneously.

The train was slowing and the electronic announcement came on.

"I think someone's following us," Dillon breathed, his skin suddenly cold.

Morton studied the back of the coach.

"What makes you say that?" he asked in an accelerated tone.

"I saw someone....watching us.... and then going through those doors there to the coach at the back as soon as I noticed them."

The three of them crouched over the back of their seats, scrutinizing the back of the train. They hardly breathed.

"That's not good news," Morton uttered slowly, his face muscles locking in a vice.

"Actually," Grandpa ventured somewhat enthusiastically. "That may be good news. In fact, that may be excellent news."

"How, Grandpa?" Dillon asked.

"Well, apparently this big mystery enemy leaves no clues, am I right? At least, that's what Grandma Burdock said."

"That's Commander Burdock," Morton said, agitated.

"Yes, right. Apparently this investigation is hungry for anything that may lead to the solving of the mystery. Well, Mr. McApplebee, ta-da! I present you with your first clue."

"McAfnee," was all Morton could sneer before the doors opened and all the passengers started filing out.

Dillon bobbed his head backwards as he stepped off the train. The figure had seemed crystal clear, but now doubt began to obscure the image. He knew that one's imagination could create things that seemed real. He'd read about mirages in deserts and UFO sightings in remote areas. Some of these things were just obviously fake. Tammy in his class was convinced that her house was built on top of a self-contained secret world whose inhabitants were now extinct. She kept trying to prove this by showing everyone bones she'd dug up from the soil in her yard. The bones looked to Dillon like chicken bones. And she'd also talked about a rambunctious dog at home that would run off with the scraps from the dining table, but that somehow didn't take the wind out of her dead-people bones theory. If chicken bones in her mind represented the remains of an extinct people, then her imagination had clearly run away with her. He wondered if what he had seen right now was conjured up from past nighttime dreams. It was not uncommon for him to experience haunting apparitions, mismatched heads and bodies, and dinosaurs in human disguise all in a night's work. He'd wake up and yawn it all off as he trudged to school to face same-old, same-old. But where he was now seemed quite dream-like. The rules were certainly not the same as the real world. Anything could happen. It was possible that there really was a figure, or maybe that there wasn't a figure, but because this was like a dream, it brought up things from other dreams he'd had, or....the bottom line was he was confused. That he was sure of.

His thoughts were interrupted by a man dressed in a pin-stripe suit. The man smiled so broadly he revealed almost all of his blinding white teeth.

"Let me ask you a question," he was saying into Dillon's face, although his distanced stare seemed to indicate that he was targeting no-one in particular. "Are you paying an unreasonably high mortgage each month? Does it just keep getting higher? Don't you think you deserve to pay less for your home?" He hardly took a breath between each question, yet didn't seem to tire. "Could you imagine a lender actually paying for your appraisal *and* offering you the lowest rates seen in years?"

His generously applied cologne was chewing up the air around them, making it quite difficult to breathe.

"You heard right. We at Never B Aloan strive to guarantee you only the best terms on your mortgage as well as outstanding customer service. We care deeply about our clients, and we promise that you will never be alone at Never B Aloan." He followed his speech with a mandatory little giggle.

Grandpa's arm swooped around Dillon's shoulders, quickly pulling him away from the man's reach. "One thing I've learned from dealing with these kind of people," he said, "is that just by spending a couple of minutes listening to them can cost you money. You think it's harmless, but the next thing you know the money is sailing out of your pockets under a snake-charmer's spell."

Dillon kept staring behind him as they walked. The man apparently had not lost any steam, continuing to spew forth golden promises non-stop as if he was powered by electricity.

Morton came to a stop ahead of Dillon and his Grandpa. "See this?" he pointed.

Dillon raised his eyes to take in one of the most dazzling sights he had ever seen. It was a giant waterfall, only it wasn't exactly water that was falling. From several hundred feet high, millions of silvery numbers cascaded downwards, crashing into a vast silvery pool below. The thick wall of numbers splashed stray digits into the air, which landed at various points around the pool. One little 8 landed on Dillon's left shoe, but popped like a soap bubble.

"Numbers soup!" Dillon exclaimed.

Morton chuckled. "Not quite," he said. "This is just another of their tricks. It's a special design effect on their site that compares the allegedly falling interest rates to a waterfall, in order to entice you to apply for a loan. It's corny and kitsch, if you ask me."

"I think it's cool," Dillon said with a smile.

"Hmmff," was all Grandpa said, although he couldn't take his eyes off the gushing digits.

"Look at that," Dillon said, pointing to a horse that trotted up to the pool of numbers on the other side. "I didn't know you had horses in Cyberia. Actually, I haven't really seen any animals."

"It must be thirsty," Grandpa suggested, as they watched the horse lower its head to the pool.

Morton was silent. He then thrust his hand into his jacket pocket and searched frantically for something.

"What's the matter?" Dillon asked.

He watched Morton's color drain from his face as if it had sprouted a leak.

"Shhh!" Morton warned. "I'm looking for my radio device," he whispered urgently. "It's happening. This is our chance. It's also very dangerous. I need to co-ordinate with headquarters the timing of the emergency systems. In the meantime, get your PDA ready."

Dillon obliged, withdrawing his PDA slowly from his pocket.

"It's just a horse," Grandpa said. "You don't see these very often here, do you?"

"You need to be quiet," Morton admonished them in an urgent whisper. "It's not just a horse, believe me." His eyes darted between the animal and Dillon's PDA.

"Well, I suppose it is kinda big," Dillon said. "But there's a lot of things in Cyberia that are kinda big."

"Yeah, I don't know what the big deal is," Grandpa said. "I've seen plenty of horses just like that in my time. My Grandpa Ray owned a ranch. We used to go down there in the summer and ride his horses. And we did it without a saddle."

"Ouch," Dillon said.

"Will you two be quiet?" Morton demanded, creating even more noise.

The horse's ears perked up and twitched.

"Oh, no!" Morton groaned.

"What's he gonna do?" Dillon asked.

But Morton was already on his radio. He spoke in a sharp nonsensical tongue, which Dillon recognized.

"That's HTML," he mentioned to his Grandpa.

"I'm glad you told me," Grandpa retorted. "I thought it was XYZ."

Dillon laughed, which enraged Morton. "Ok, listen up," he fumed, stuffing his radio into his pocket. "You both are messing up badly here. We came to this site to face the enemy, remember?" He didn't wait for their response. "Well, that, my friends, is the enemy that causes all the buttons to go off on the Intelligence screen back at Command." He pointed to the horse, which had decided to make its way towards them at a steady pace. "We needed time to prepare your PDA to the point that it can allow for elimination of the threat. Had you been quiet like I told you, we might have had the opportunity to carefully prepare ourselves. Now, it may be too late. Quickly, open it up."

Dillon flipped open the leather cover.

"Now enter your password."

Dillon began to tap in the alphanumeric characters. He stopped short of the final character when he noticed Morton's crazed stare observing every keystroke. He turned aside for some privacy.

"Whatever! Quickly!" Morton said, exasperated.

The horse was coming closer, but not at a wild gallop. Its mane picked up in the wind.

"What a beauty," Grandpa remarked.

Morton pushed some sort of sound through his gritted teeth.

"What do I do now?" Dillon asked.

"Go to the site we're on, www.neverBaloan.com. As soon as you get there...."

"Hang on," Dillon said, punching the letters into the address bar. "Ok, got it."

"Now, go to page security and click options."

"Options," Dillon repeated. By this time, the horse was clipping the cookies very close by.

Morton stared wildly at the horse and yelled, "It's too late! Run!"

They all sped off as fast as they could away from the horse, which calmly came to a stop and snorted.

"Morton," Dillon called, as they ran. "The horse isn't chasing us anymore."

"That's the most dangerous part!" Morton shouted, pushing his legs to their limits, heading for the train. Then Dillon saw why. The horse's skin suddenly burst open at its sides and other horses leaped out of it. These horses were the size of two-story buildings and were laughing maniacally as if infected with rabies. Their peculiar laugh was so powerful it shook the entire site. Their coats emitted a glaze of orange-blue vapor like that of a gas burner.

Dillon cried out and pulled his Grandpa along the jagged cookie floor. Hundreds of these horses now breathed down their necks, the heat of the vapor singeing their hair. Morton had raced way ahead of Dillon and Grandpa Harley, but now it seemed they had caught up with him. Morton stood there in front of them gripped in fear.

"We can't go any further," he said gravely. "The waterfall's been moved. It's now in front of us, in our way. That's what happens when a Trojan Horse attacks. It moves things around." He closed his eyes as he appeared to be accepting his fate. "We're trapped."

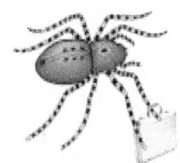

Eight

"Let's jump in!" Dillon shouted amidst the clamor of laughing horses and cascading numbers.

"What good is that going to do?" Morton snapped. "They're just going to follow us in. They're so tall they can...."

But Dillon wasn't waiting to hear the rest. He took his Grandpa's hand and pulled him with him into the pool.

It was like diving into jelly. The liquid was syrupy and thick, clinging to their skin. For a moment they were submerged, enveloped by the coarse substance that blotted out all sound, except for the dull drum of their heartbeats. But the sheer density of the substance popped them both above the surface. They found themselves bobbing rapidly along the lumpy waves towards the base of the waterfall.

Dillon squinted back at Morton and the horses but couldn't get a view. He glanced at his Grandpa who seemed to be struggling with something pasty smothering his face.

"Grandpa! What is that?"

"Hmmfff!" Grandpa Harley responded, his hands grappling at the object.

Dillon managed to reach over and pull the object with both hands. It felt like dough that had hardened around his Grandpa's facial muscles. With a great big heave, Dillon succeeded in plucking it free, and cast it into the choppy river of numbers around them.

"What was that?" Grandpa puffed.

"It was a hardened number 6," a voice shouted behind them. "Some of these numbers are of industrial strength."

"Morton!" Dillon exclaimed. "You made it! You jumped in after us. Where are the horses?"

"Well, I have to admit it, young man," Morton said, relaxing back against the chunky liquid as if he was lounging on a deck. "Your wisdom exceeds your age. I was so sure that this pool would not be a deterrent for the Trojan Horse. I thought for certain that we were trapped. I had failed to realize that this waterfall feature on this site does not have a bottom. There had been no need to create a bottom because it served no purpose – no-one would need to see it when viewing the site."

Dillon pushed his toes down through the soupy liquid.

"There's no bottom at all?"

"Nope," Morton replied with a satisfied smile. "In-fi-nite it is."

"What has this got to do with those horses?" Grandpa wanted to know, as they all floated down the rapidly accelerating river with no bottom.

"Well, the horses were not quite as light as you and I," Morton explained. "We're sort of floating on this squishy mush. But the horses, as you recall were gargantuan. They jumped right in after us and sank like stones."

"Wow!" Dillon said, at once awestruck and terrified.

"Yes, their flaming gargantuan selves will keep on falling forever because there is no bottom."

"Forever?" Dillon croaked.

Morton nodded.

"Those poor animals," Grandpa lamented.

"Those poor animals?" Morton gawked at him. "Those poor animals? You quite obviously do not have the faintest idea what a Trojan Horse is, do you?"

Grandpa puffed his chest as far as he could out of the liquid. "Well, certainly I know what a Trojan Horse is. I will have you know that I am well-versed in Homer's Odyssey. In fact, as a child, I acted in a play about the Trojan Horse. I had quite a talent for acting, I'll have you know. I was one of the Greek soldiers hiding inside the Giant Wooden Horse. Of course, ours was made of cardboard, which was a pity because it got left out in the rain after rehearsal and was all soggy. But I nevertheless thoroughly enjoyed bursting out of the horse to attack the city of Troy. I was so glad to get a part on the Greeks' side. But, in any case, what has that got to do with these poor horses that drowned?"

Morton ground his teeth as he bobbed in the liquid. "These are also Trojan Horses," he said in a low growl.

"They are? They were made of wood? I didn't see...."

"No!" Morton raged. "Listen to me! The term, Trojan Horse, comes from that story. But the parallel in Cyberspace is a program that can seem to be harmless like the horse we just saw, but harbors hidden commands that can be very malicious, and can damage and destroy everything."

"Oh, so that's why there were others hiding in the first one," Dillon observed.

"That's correct."

Dillon and his Grandpa were silent as they tried to entertain this bizarre concept, and they would have remained so for quite some time afterwards had it not been for the frightening sound of rumbling water getting noticeably louder.

"We're headed for the waterfall," he shouted. "We have to try to wade to shore, or we risk being crushed by the downpour."

They all tried to paddle towards the banks of the river but the density of the liquid, coupled with the now raging current, prevented them from making any headway.

Digits sprayed by the waterfall were now raining down on their heads. They could hardly see ahead of them. The noise was a magnified drumbeat that snuffed out any other sounds. Dillon could now no longer see where his Grandpa was. He could not even turn around. They all sailed helplessly towards the thrashing wall of numbers.

Something flashed in front of Dillon's eyes. It disappeared, then reappeared through the murkiness. It was a luminous outstretched hand held right in front of him. Without hesitation, Dillon reached out and grabbed onto it. Immediately he was lifted right out of the raging torrents. The hand seemed of normal size but had incredible strength. It dropped him gently on the river bank. Heaving, Dillon looked up at his rescuer. He reeled back in shock. There was no arm, nor body to the hand, nothing except a tangled network of strings or wires. Just then Grandpa and Morton were delivered by similar bodiless hands onto the dry cookie ground alongside him.

"Grandpa, you all right?" Dillon breathed, while trying to wring his shirt out from the sticky liquid.

"Oh, can't complain," Grandpa moaned.

"Those arms saved our lives," Dillon remarked.

"Yes and no," Morton said, wrenching globs of jelly from his hair and then lowering his head onto his arm.

"What do you mean?" Dillon asked him.

"Well, those hands saved us from drowning, but not because they care about us in the slightest."

Dillon continued to look puzzled.

Morton sighed. "Those arms prey on vulnerable people, those in distress. It's called phishing."

"Fishing? You mean they're fishing for people in order to eat us?"

"No," Morton chuckled sardonically. "They drain us of our identities. The minute we latch on to their bait, they have us, and they start the process of draining our personal identities so that we're left with just an outer shell with no inner knowledge."

Dillon gawked at him. "Why is everything so sneaky here?"

"Welcome to the world of web security," Morton quipped.

"Well, it's too late anyway," Grandpa remarked. "I beat them to it. I began losing my mind long ago."

Both Dillon and Morton had to laugh.

Suddenly the bodiless hands descended on each of their heads and began to stroke their scalps, tenderly massaging them as if motivated by profound love and care.

"Here it begins," Morton said grimly.

"It feels good," Grandpa remarked with a smile.

Dillon tried to squirm away but the hand followed him effortlessly. He tried to run, but the hand ran with him. It remained inside his hair, caressing his head no matter in which direction he turned.

"Freaky," he stammered, finally surrendering and falling to the floor, the hand merrily continuing its work.

"Now you know why I maintain that resisting this is futile," Morton muttered, the hand on his head sweeping through thin red wisps of hair. "Pretty soon we will start to lose our personal information."

"There must be something we can do," Dillon protested. "Why hasn't CAVE rescued us yet? Didn't you manage to alert them?"

Morton sighed. "As I told you before, I had deactivated the CAVE security procedures so that it would not override your PDA. I had to do that otherwise we would not have had the chance to test out your PDA. The CAVE systems would have intervened. But then when you and your Grand....uh, when we disturbed the Trojan Horse causing it to come after us too quickly, I tried to reactivate our communication with Command, but it was too late. The Trojan Horse had already corrupted the communication channels. CAVE does not know we're in trouble. As far as they see it on the screen, all the pretty lights are shining just perfectly and there aren't any red lights to speak of."

Dillon put his head in his hands, the foreign hand dipping with him, almost in empathy.

Grandpa wasn't saying anything as long as he could continue to lap up this luxurious head-rub. After all he had been through in the preceding moments, he felt he had earned a little pampering.

A whizzing sound made them turn. Something was speeding toward them at breakneck speed.

"I knew it," Morton mumbled.

"What?" Dillon pressed him.

"Here's the web-form to tell me my message to command didn't go through."

The rushing figure came to an abrupt halt in front of them. It had on a worn, checkered shirt and waterproof trousers, and was wearing hefty green tinted flying goggles over its eyes. Dillon imagined that this is what Orville or Wilbur Wright would have looked like. It stood there for only a few seconds before dropping to its knees and bursting into uncontrolled sobbing.

"My name is MAILER-DAEMON," he wailed, drying his cheeks, which were raw and calloused. "And I am so, so sorry. But I could not deliver your message. I tried. I really tried. I tried again and again and again. But in the end I had to give up. There was nothing I could do. I am so sorry."

Grandpa reached forward to console the man. "Don't worry, young man. You don't have to take the blame for...." Grandpa was trying to place a hand on MAILER's shoulder but some sort of invisible barrier stopped him.

"He can't hear you. It's pointless to attempt to talk to him," Morton advised Grandpa. "This is his job. He does this all the time."

MAILER-DAEMON rose to his feet. "Better luck next time," he sniffed, and zoomed off into the darkness.

"It's his job to be the bearer of bad news," Grandpa mused. "I relate to the difficulty of his job. During the war I knew of many tragic situations when a visit had to be made – the one that all wives, mother and fathers dreaded because they, in their heart of hearts thought it only happened to other people. Once I...."

Grandpa was interrupted by a chime. The massaging hands on their heads suddenly froze. Everything around them froze, including the numbers river and waterfall.

"Your system has been infected." The cool digital voice created a rush of warmth inside Dillon's chest. "We recommend that you isolate any invading viruses or malware immediately. Would you like to isolate now?"

The flashing green pincushion appeared off to their right. Both Dillon and Morton eagerly aimed their fingers at the "yes" button. Almost immediately those rectangular glass booths began to rain down all around them. This time, instead of a perilous threat, the falling booths were a welcome sight – even at the prospect of entrapment and suffocation.

"CAVE must have found out anyway," Morton shouted amidst the clamor. "Somebody must have alerted them."

Dillon thought briefly of that figure that had followed them on the train. The thought of a lurking mystery rescuer was both comforting and spooky at the same time.

They all tried to dodge the falling booths, especially Grandpa whose vivid recollection of his prior experience inside one of them gave him that extra boost. "Let's get out of here!" he declared, trying to charge off over some uneven expiring cookies. "Where's the train?"

Morton lead them in the race to the train station, but eventually it became impossible to avoid the booths, and one by one, they became entrapped. Although the air was limited, neither Morton nor Dillon seemed perturbed. They were counting on the BoothTooth technology to release them. Grandpa, however, was growing just a little tired of almost suffocating to death.

Sure enough, the booths dissolved and the three of them found themselves on stretchers, hastily transferred to the triage train. Dr. Chomberg was back, flitting between the three of them. Grandpa had to get oxygen again. He lay there on his stretcher more frustrated than fatigued. His moustache twitched vigorously as if to resort to some form of communication while his mouth was occupied. After they had all passed through the decontamination units and all of the apparatus was cleared off, Grandpa was able to sit up and release his message at last.

"It is my inalienable right to be able to be breathe," he declared. "I would really appreciate it if you would stop denying me that right."

Morton didn't seem to hear Grandpa. He began pacing up and down the tiled coach floor, apparently absorbed in his own frustration.

"What's the matter?" Dillon asked him.

Morton just shook his head and continued to pace. Medical personnel who were moving between coaches had to step out of their way in order to pass him.

"We were saved by CAVE," Dillon said to him. "Everything is cool, isn't it?"

Morton glared at him, almost seething. "Just swell," he glowered. "Let's go somewhere where we can talk."

He directed Dillon and his Grandpa through all the coaches towards the back of the train, into a supplies coach loaded with numerous boxes and packets. Dillon felt as if he had been summoned into Mr. Rigler's office after the raid, although this time he had no idea what he had done wrong. As far as he could tell he had done pretty well in the mortgage site. In fact he had probably saved Morton's life by jumping into the numbers river when Morton had thought it futile.

Morton pursed his lips so tightly that all the muscles around his mouth crimped together like a string-bag. He began absent-mindedly tapping the sides of a supply box that read "RAM Vaccines for memory loss".

"You know what I'm wondering," he said without much vitality to his voice. "I'm wondering if your PDA survived the blasted liquid soup we were floating in. That's what I'm wondering."

He continued to tap his fingers. Dillon felt for his PDA. At least it was still there in his pocket. He withdrew it slowly. Morton stopped tapping, not even breathing for a moment or two. Grandpa also allowed himself a little agony of suspense, although this little contraption in Dillon's pocket held as much fascination for him as an Income Tax guidebook.

"Turn it on," Morton whispered, his voice taught and tenuous.

The PDA felt slippery and sticky in Dillon's fingers. He pushed the power button and nothing happened. He pushed it again and again. Still nothing. He shook his head slowly and looked up at Morton with trepidation.

"Oh, well," Grandpa said. He may as well have been expressing disappointment over a change in the weather. Morton's face seemed to grow redder than was humanly possible.

"I'm sorry," Dillon said feebly. "Maybe we should wait until it dries out before we try it again."

Morton let out a roar that frightened even Grandpa. His face was sweating and his hands were pounding the box next to him.

"You idiots!" he scowled. "You don't realize what this means."

Grandpa did not take kindly to this choice of language, but he also did not have the chance to object before Dillon spoke up.

"Mr. McAfnee," Dillon tried to say, "it just means that our experiment with the PDA will be delayed."

"Aaargh!" Morton raged.

"Quite the temper," Grandpa noted.

Morton suddenly laughed through his fury. "Temper. Temper? Just you wait. You haven't seen anything yet. You think you understand anything? You are both so naïve, so gullible. You trusted me – what kind of numbskulls would place their trust in someone who leads them to an infected site?" He edged towards them as if on a tightrope. He held out his hand and stared maniacally at the PDA in Dillon's hand. "Give that to me!" he ordered, trembling all over.

Dillon instinctually clutched the PDA to his chest. He was so overcome by shock that he felt his legs go numb. He dropped to the floor. Grandpa, now himself full of rage, tried to help Dillon up while he gathered the words of attack inside him. "Don't you come anywhere near my grandson!" he fumed.

Morton continued his deranged laugh as he came closer. "Shut up, you bumbling old fool. To think I've had to tolerate you all this time so that I could get a hold of this machine."

"But you're a Cyberian," Dillon stammered. "You're not allowed to touch a PDA."

"Not allowed?" Morton scorned. "Not allowed?" He quickly reached over and tried to bolt the inter-leading coach door, but it wouldn't stick shut. He picked up a box and pushed it up against the door. Then, with only a few words, he revealed the depths of his deception.

"I would also not be allowed to destroy all of Cyberia. Wouldn't you think?"

There was a silence so intense it seemed to suck out all the air of the coach. Morton's words had the effect of wrenching all sensation from Dillon's body for what seemed like an interminable period of time.

"It's you," Grandpa managed, aghast. "Grandma Burdock was talking about you. The threat was right under her nose. Well, I'll be…."

"Now," Morton said, instantly calm. "Dillon, I want you to give this PDA to me right now, and I want you to tell me the last character of your password. Just the last character." He spoke now with a voice of caring authority, almost parental.

Dillon could not even bring his jaw to close, let alone respond to this man.

"Don't tell him anything," Grandpa breathed resolutely, slightly more annoyed than terrified.

Morton ignored him. He inched closer, somehow imagining that he would win Dillon's trust. "Dillon, listen to me. I don't want to harm you. All you have to do is pass this thing over to me and give me a single letter or number. It's not anymore complicated than that."

A frown lined Dillon's forehead, but his eyes and his mind were elsewhere. Anywhere but the present: when his father cancelled the one and only camping trip they were to take together because of a business meeting; When the smiling owner of the candy store he'd always visit was arrested for tricking children into doing something disgusting; When his school principal left because of something called embezzlement. One thing seemed to lead easily into another, and Morton's frightening face was part of a collage.

Morton was so close now that his breath burned against Dillon's face. "That's right," Morton cajoled him, "Just give me the PDA."

At that point Grandpa had seen enough. "Get away from him, you scoundrel!" He lunged forward and with both of his hands pushed Morton to the ground.

This served only to heighten Morton's rage. Saliva bubbles popped out of the corners of his mouth as he picked up his glasses and struggled to his feet. He uttered something incomprehensible and charged Dillon.

He grabbed onto the PDA and tried to pull it away, but something stirred inside Dillon, snapping him out of his trance. His hands locked onto the PDA, his muscles forming solid ridges like robotic joints beneath his skin. He and Morton struggled in a tug-of-war, each trying to remove the other's grip with the force of their bodies. They rolled on the floor and slammed into a stack of rectangular BoothTooth frames, which crashed about them and boxed them in at sharp angles. Grandpa, in the meanwhile, was chasing the both of them as they moved about, hoping to latch onto Morton. But he was unable to keep up. Just as he would approach them, they would roll off in a different direction.

At one point, Dillon broke free with the PDA in hand and jumped up and over a side of a BoothTooth frame, but Morton caught him by the foot and pulled him to the ground.

Still unable to grab onto Morton, Grandpa looked about the coach, searching instead for something amongst the supplies that might help him. He quickly scanned the labels of the boxes lining the walls of the coach, stopping briefly to read one out of every few.

Spam Allergy Tablets;
Pixel Polish for Higher Resolution;
General Anesthetic for Hard Resets.

Grandpa didn't understand any of this jargon, but there wasn't much time to lose. Although Dillon was a strong boy, he would probably not hold out much longer against Morton. Grandpa pulled open the next box he saw, which read "Web Anti-freeze" and which carried some stern warnings that Grandpa simply did not have the time to examine. He pulled out a large oblong canister and put his finger on the nozzle, ready to spray

153

Morton with whatever this anti-freeze material was. He strode over to where Dillon and Morton were engaged in battle and tried to hold the canister over Morton's neck and back. But Morton kept on moving, and sometimes it would be Dillon who would shift into the line of fire.

"Try to keep still, Dillon!" Grandpa shouted, although his words were a blur, competing with Morton's maniacal yelling and the loud rumble of the train's engine.

Grandpa kept trying to aim the canister at Morton but there was no way to be certain that Dillon would escape harm once he pressed the nozzle. In those few seconds he had visions of a horrific twist of fate, grandfather harming grandson. His fingers trembled around the canister nozzle.

Suddenly Morton broke free and Grandpa saw that he had wrestled the little computer from Dillon's grip. Immediately, Grandpa raised the canister to Morton's face. He pressed on the nozzle and held it down fast. But Morton had detected the movement out of his periphery and he'd ducked in advance of Grandpa's fire. Instead, the thick pillar of smoke that emerged from the canister shot at the box behind Morton. As if time stopped for a moment, all eyes silently turned to the box, which did nothing immediately, but then began to soften like a marshmallow s'more. Then it lifted off like a leaf swept by the wind and began to float around the room.

A chime sounded. "Warning! Anti-freeze has been released in this compartment. Caution must be exercised in altering solid states to liquid or vapor."

Morton was staring crazily up at the voice as if it were visible. This gave Dillon, who had uncurled himself from a ball on the floor, the chance to leap up and make a grab for the PDA again.

In attempting to do so, he knocked Morton to the floor and the tug-of-war resumed. Grandpa raised the canister again and this time moved in much closer, coming within inches of Morton's head. He settled his finger on the nozzle, swooping in even closer so that he could be sure, and....

Morton swirled around in a flash and grabbed the canister out of Grandpa's hand. He jumped to his feet, and with a grin that spread like a splinter across his face, he waved the canister between Dillon and his Grandpa.

"The game is over," he said, his breath heavy and his grin persistent. "Give me the PDA, you little brat."

Dillon glanced at his Grandpa, whose eyebrows communicated that this was not a time to surrender.

"Give it to me!" Morton yelled. He aimed the canister deliberately a few inches above Dillon's head and fired a smoke blast, which struck the wall of the train. "If you don't give it to me, what happens to this wall of the train will happen to your brain."

A patch of wall behind Dillon began to sag and fold in on itself like a blanket, before coming apart at the seams and floating through the air like sand particles in water. The gap in the wall immediately allowed a treacherous noise to rush in and fill the coach. In the moment that Dillon turned to observe this spectacle, Morton snatched the PDA from Dillon's grip. Defying reason, Dillon jumped up again in order to reclaim the PDA. Morton was caught between trying to aim the canister at Dillon and protecting the PDA from being wrestled from his other hand. In the process, the PDA dropped to the floor. Dillon tried to curl it towards him with his foot as he battled Morton now for the canister. But Dillon felt his strength wane. He simply could not hold on much longer. He let go and scampered behind a pile of boxes. He could hear Morton chasing after him.

Out of the corner of his eye, he saw someone disappear through the inter-leading door of the coach. Was that Morton? Grandpa? He stood up, and there was Morton grinning, aiming the canister right at his head. His heart in his throat, Dillon leapt towards the gaping hole in the train wall and, before Morton could process anything, dove headfirst through the hole.

Nine

One winter when Dillon was about five or six, it snowed so hard that the guys in their snowplows just gave up and went home, if they were able to. The snow fell so fast it looked to Dillon like chunks of cloud were falling down around the house. His mother would not let him go outside until it stopped, even then it was only for a few minutes because she was afraid he'd get hyper-something or other. But those few minutes had been sheer bliss. The whole world was white: the sky, the air, the ground, the houses, the roads, the trees –especially the trees. You couldn't even see any evidence of bark on those trees. He'd started to make a snowman, but decided to just roll around and slip and slide in the stuff instead. There hadn't been a snowfall quite like that one since. Other times it would snow but not halt things, only decorate things in white. But that time it seemed the whole world had stopped for a moment, taking a break from all that spinning.

This was the first memory Dillon visited as he awoke with a pounding headache on the pure-white ground. His eyes faced the sky which was also white, an endless, consistent white that covered the entire horizon. But he wasn't cold. His fingers dug into the cookie ground around him, testing it for the soft malleable texture of snow. But it was just as firm as any other Cyberian soil.

He sat up slowly, one hand cradling the back of his head. No matter which way he turned, he was staring into formless white. It was impossible to determine where the ground ended and the sky began. If it weren't for the fact that he could see his own body, he might have thought his eyes had failed him. Where was this? His mind immediately raced with the final moments inside the train – Morton, the PDA, Grandpa. Grandpa! His stomach sank. His Grandpa was still on the train with that scumbag, Morton. He closed his eyes to shut out the images and pray that his Grandpa was safe. He tried not to think what Morton could have done with him, but he couldn't help but envision the worst. After all, Morton had been holding that ant-freeze stuff, not to mention the fact that the PDA was probably now in his possession. Anything was possible once he gained access to it. Maybe this white realm he was in was happening to everybody. Maybe Morton had succeeded in destroying all of Cyberia according to plan, and this was the result – a wasteland like the aftermath of a nuclear explosion. He had seen a movie like that. This place reminded him of the eerie quiet and complete absence of life that remained after an explosion.

On the other hand, Morton had yet to find out the final character of the password for the PDA. But if it was only one character, how difficult would it be to go through all the buttons on the keyboard, trying all the different combinations until he'd find the right one?

If this really was the end of Cyberia, was Grandpa still Ok? How would they ever get back to the real world? He could not believe he had allowed things to get this far in this crazy place. Whether or not Cyberia was real, the danger he and his Grandpa had experienced so far certainly felt unmistakably real. The blame was squarely on him for bringing them both here and for staying as long as they did. He should have insisted that they return home long ago. Now Dillon could not bear to entertain the possibility that he might be stuck here forever. Even if this white landscape was harmless, he could not survive without food. He put a hand to his stomach. Food. The last time he and Grandpa had eaten was at Mc Ronalds, which was quite a while ago - he wasn't sure exactly how long.

Well, he sure wasn't going to solve any problems by just sitting there. He hoisted himself slowly to his feet. His ankle hurt him. He'd probably strained it on landing. But it occurred to him that for jumping from a speeding train, a headache and a sprained ankle were very minor injuries. In fact, it was pretty miraculous, unless, of course, this wasn't your regular countryside by the railroad tracks. Which it wasn't. Not too many railroad tracks were bordered by cookies to cushion one's fall. He began to limp forward. He'd heard that in a desert, stragglers who had no way to tell direction would unwittingly walk in a circle, eventually ending up back where they started from. That would probably happen to him too. But he was hungry and he had nothing to lose by trying, so he moved slowly forward. The image of his Grandpa kept popping into his brain, as well as that of Morton. He shook his head as if to rid his mind of Morton's profile. The man had become a monster, not worthy of sharing space in his head with Grandpa. The deception was too much for him to deal with right now. The protector and trusted guide had somehow become the mortal enemy in a matter of moments. There was no safe place. There was no safe person. Except for his Grandpa. Thank God for his Grandpa. Dillon dragged his feet along the white cookie ground, kicking up a cotton-white cookie cloud behind him. He licked his lips. He began to notice how thirsty he was. He thought of soda and how it fuzzed and sparkled, and tasted so good and then their science teacher, Mr. Donovan, and how he'd showed them what soda did to a tooth that he'd dropped inside it.

What would his mother say about all of this? He pictured her quietly admonishing him, not looking directly at him as she scrubbed the walls of the kitchen with so much soap it could flood the room. "Dillon, you're making me very nervous. I can't sleep at nights when you go off on these adventures and I have no idea where you are. Do you realize what it does to my nerves? I was going to give a speech at the Haiku Luncheon but I had to refuse because I just couldn't get my thoughts together. I need my sleep otherwise I just can't function at all. Not even my yoga class can relax me...."

And his father, between a fax and an email in his study on a Sunday morning: "Dillon, your curiosity gets you into trouble and then you wonder why you're lost in a barren white wilderness with nothing to eat or drink. Your mother and I try to teach you responsibility but you insist on risky adventures. Do you know how hard this is for us to deal with? We are busy enough just trying to keep up with our chores and obligations without having to figure out now how to get you out of this mess. Can't you make it easier for us?"

The blank horizon in front of him became like a movie screen, drawing from the myriad archives of people, events and imagery that had been stored somewhere in his brain, now splashing across the screen in a kaleidoscope of colors. His life played out vividly in front of him. So many things he'd forgotten now resurfaced. When he was eight years old, he'd awoken very early on Thanksgiving morning, long before the sun came up. He'd decided to surprise his parents by setting the table for the guests all by himself. He dragged the spare table in from the garage, trying very carefully not to make any noise. Then he located the tablecloths and the fine china, making sure to gingerly transport each dinner piece one at a time. By the time his parents had awoken, the entire table had been set for his family and fourteen guests, each napkin folded in a different design. Each plate was also evenly spaced and each piece of cutlery perfectly aligned. When his mother saw it she shrieked like she had won the lottery and his father was equally thrilled and especially proud. They'd promised him that they would take him to the theme park and that he could get unlimited rides for the whole day. That night and every night afterward he'd lie in bed counting down the days to that special day, which was first delayed, then revised to half a day, then a couple of hours, then delayed again, then promised for a different time "when things calmed down a bit" and then....it was Thanksgiving again and he was nine years old.

Tears streamed down Dillon's face as he pushed forward, motivated by thirst, by hunger and by the determination to find his Grandpa.

A tiny speck of color appeared ahead of him. He stopped in his tracks and squinted at the speck. Something else he'd heard about being lost in a desert was the concept of a mirage. Well, there was only one way to find out if it was real. As he approached the object, he prepared himself that it might pop any moment. But he was almost on top of it and it was still there, now large enough to look like some sort of counter or....ticket machine. Train tickets! Maybe he could get out of here! He limped up to the machine and read the screen, which was a luminous yellow, the color that had drawn him from a distance. Digital instructions rolled across the screen. "Error 404: Cannot find server. You have reached a page that cannot be found. To contact an administrator, press here."

"Oh, I get it!" Dillon said out loud, clapping his palm against his forehead. He'd seen these before on his computer when he'd typed in the wrong address into the address bar or he'd interrupted the search query. His computer would take him to a completely blank white screen with the same error message at the top. And here, he'd jumped from the Noogle train and in so doing had interrupted the search ride. Now he was in nowhere land. This was not the end of Cyberia. At least, not yet. He was just in between web sites. All he'd have to do is get back on a train and he'd be able to find his Grandpa. He just hoped fervently that Grandpa was still okay. Dillon breathed a sigh of relief and pressed the green pincushion below the screen.

"Thank you for traveling with Noogle," it read. "Please enter your destination."

Dillon thought about this and keyed in "Grandpa Harley Wilson." This train would probably have a couple of stops or so, but one of them was bound to take him where his Grandpa was.

"Thank you," the screen read. "Please deposit 400 Cybercents in the slot to the right."

Any glimmer of hope vanished in an instant. He had no money. Grandpa had the money. There was no way he could buy the ticket. He tried to get the machine to issue the ticket anyway but it wouldn't advance from its position unless money was deposited.

Dillon shrank to the floor and dropped his head in his hands. He fought back his tears, because crying would be like giving one more victory to that evil man,

Morton. Why had the guy not yet destroyed all of Cyberia anyway? It must have been because he still couldn't work out the last character of the password. Or maybe Grandpa had even figured out a way to overpower him and grabbed the PDA from him. Whatever it was, the fact that Cyberia had not yet been destroyed, was at least somewhat encouraging.

As he sat there, he reviewed his entire experience with Morton. The more he thought about it, the more he realized how carefully thought-out Morton's plan had been from the start. He had led them to Mc Ronalds and to the infected site just so that he could watch Dillon input his password. That was why he hadn't tried to grab the PDA away from him right away. It would have been useless without the password. The thing was, what about Commander Burdock? Was everybody, the entire staff of CAVE in on this scheme? Their entire function was supposed to be to protect the people of Cyberia, and now it was possible that they themselves were the instigators of that attack they were "worried" about – some "mysterious" attacker that was going to wipe out all of Cyberia, that they wracked their brains about because they didn't have any clues who it was. And Bingo, what do you know? They were their own enemy! This wasn't just confusing, it was nuts. He let out a bitter laugh because it triggered a memory of a dog in his neighborhood that would howl and squeal as it spun around in circles, trying to bite its own tail as if the tail was attacking him.

But it was just so hard to imagine that Commander Burdock would seek to destroy the world she lived in. She seemed to be so proud of her grandchildren. Why would she want to see them hurt? Imagining her becoming evil and violent was like imagining his kindergarten teacher, Mrs. Saffer, suddenly seized by a crazed desire to upturn the chairs in the classroom and wreak havoc amongst the students. Then again, he was learning pretty quickly that the bad people in the world weren't necessarily the thick-browed, teeth-gnashing villains that populated storybooks and television programs. Sometimes they were really nice to you. Sometimes they helped you. And then they revealed who they really were. That was the scariest part.

What would motivate people to destroy everything around them? He wondered. They knew fully well that they themselves would also get destroyed in the process. Unless Morton had planned some sort of escape route, he would go down along with everyone else. How could he escape Cyberia if he destroyed it while still standing right inside it? A couple of years after the terrorist attack in New York, Dillon had reached an age where the motive for the attack had begun to occupy his thoughts. His father had told him that some people get it in their heads that it's worthy to kill innocent people and die while doing that. He had sighed and shrugged his shoulders, saying, "Yup, that's the world we live in now." It had seemed that his father couldn't understand it but had accepted it as part of life. He even returned to his computer screen after that and didn't seem to worry about it much. But it had taken Dillon a lot longer to let go of the images in his head. For several weeks, he'd pass ordinary people in the street and wonder if in their minds they had these insane plans to exterminate everyone including themselves. He'd had dreams about it too. When he'd awake from those dreams, he'd be in an especially suspicious mood. Even his mother wouldn't escape suspicion, although he would never dare say anything about it.

He forced himself to his feet again and began to walk on. After only a few feet he stopped. He realized that if this was an Error page, it would have no borders. There would be no end to the white and it would not contain anything other than the means to exit the site, which he couldn't afford. It would be pointless to continue walking if every part of the site was the same and there was nowhere to go. If he died here, would he really be dead? His parents would never find his body. The only way to do that would be to come after him into Cyberspace, somehow track down his movements and find him on the Error page. And then, he reminded himself, there was the problem that time really stood still for him back home, because if he were to return to the real world, he would re-enter at the same moment that he left. So his parents wouldn't even notice that he was gone in the first place. He could be dead for several years or even a hundred years in Cyberia, and as far as his parents knew, he was still in his room the same night he left! His head hurt him even more trying to contemplate all of this. He thought again of that neighborhood dog trying to chase its tail. That's what his mind felt like now anyway. He'd started feeling woozy and weak, and was just aching for a drop to drink.

There was a faint tapping sound behind him. He turned around and saw something moving towards him. It moved irregularly, more like a hobble than a walk. The tapping sound grew louder and he could make out a figure of a man.

Barely holding himself up, Dillon tried to study the man's face, but he was still too far to get a proper look. Dillon felt a spark of hope flicker inside him. Another straggler, he thought, who was still around, and with whom he could join efforts in trying to get out of here. As the man got closer, Dillon was about to call out to him when his face became discernable. Dillon's jaw dropped. Morton! Dillon's muscles froze. Should he run? Could he run? Should he face him? Demand where he his Grandpa was? Try to overpower him considering he had nothing to lose anyway?....Ask him why he looked the way he did?

Morton came closer. His eyes looked distant and his face was haggard. But he was moving faster than he appeared to be. In fact his hobbling was probably closer to the speed of a jogger, which didn't make any sense because he didn't seem to be pushing himself all that hard. Dillon began to retreat, stumbling over his feet. He did an about face and tried to limp away. But Morton was advancing. The uneven footsteps grew loud enough to send small vibrations through the cookie earth. Dillon tried to increase his pace but he couldn't find the strength. Although a vast expanse of white lay ahead of him, he may just as well have been up against a wall. "Leave me alone!" he heard himself yell, and then implore, as Morton's face swooped up close to his. Suddenly he heard a chime sound above him, its pleasant tone almost mocking the seriousness of his predicament. "Dillon. T Appleseed, you have received a web-form. CAVE cannot identify the origin of the message as you are located on an Error Page which is devoid of email streets nor web-form channels which are required to process the message efficiently. This message has had trouble locating you and has traveled extensively in search of you. Do you wish to accept this web-form message?" The familiar green and red pincushion buttons appeared off to the right. Morton's face had frozen, his mouth draped open as if stuck in the middle of a luxurious yawn. With some trepidation, Dillon waved a hand back and forth in front of Morton's face. No response. Oh, well, now he felt like a fool. This wasn't really Morton. It was an email, or rather a web-form from Morton. A web-form that had to criss-cross unfamiliar territory looking for him. And now the pincushion was flashing, waiting for Dillon to accept or decline what ever Morton had to say. His first instinct was to reject it. He had heard enough from this latest low-life con artist to enter his life. But the longer he thought about it, the more he realized that any information would probably be useful information, especially if it came from the source of the trouble itself. Maybe there would be mention of Grandpa. Reluctantly, he pressed the green pincushion. It was degrading, like submitting to the enemy.

Morton came alive again and spoke without looking directly at him.

"You little rat," he said by way of introduction. "I have your fat old lump of a grandfather with me. Let's put it this way: He's still alive, but it won't be that way much longer unless you return the PDA. Either you give it to me or sweet old Grandpa dies. It's your choice. You don't want to kill your own Grandpa, now do you?" Morton laughed, an oddly mechanical eruption, his neck bobbing up and down as if on a puppet-string.

The words spun wildly in Dillon's head. The PDA? Didn't Morton have the PDA? He had a memory flash of the instrument falling to the ground. Surely Morton had picked it up. Dillon's fingers dove into his shirt pocket just in case, but he was quite certain he didn't have it. If he didn't have it and Morton didn't have it, then where was it? If Grandpa had taken it, Morton would have searched him by now and snatched it from him. This was amazing. This put a whole new spin on things. He spent a moment more marveling at all the new possibilities, before castigating himself for ignoring the thrust of the message: His Grandpa was in grave danger. Morton was holding him ransom. But how could he meet Morton's demands if he didn't have the PDA? Maybe he could play along, pretending he had the PDA – that would give him the upper hand. Before he had a chance to mull this over, the web-form version of Morton continued. "Get on the Noogle and meet me at my blog, MortMac.blog. You'd better hand over the PDA. When you arrive with the PDA, I will allow you and your Grandpa time to return home before I execute my plan. If you don't, well, say goodbye to this whiny flabby wimp you seem to love so much."

With that, the web-form began to depart, hobbling along at an incongruously fast speed. Dillon suddenly had an idea. If he could latch onto the web-form he might be able to hitch a free ride out of the Error Page. If the web-form could leave this site without having to buy a ticket for the Noogle train, so could he!

So instead of running from the web-form, he now pursued it with all his might. He forgot his pain and his fatigue and sprinted towards the web-form, but just as he had been unable to escape it earlier, he was unable now to catch up with it. He watched it slip away from him, eventually swallowed by the great deep white horizon.

He was alone again in this land of nothingness. Now his hunger and thirst came to the fore, overshadowing all else. He sat down on the white ground. Even if he wanted to, he couldn't devise a rescue plan for his Grandpa now. He was just too weak and his mind didn't seem to want to work properly. The minutes became hours. And then time became completely indiscernible. He noticed at one point that the ground was up against his face, that he lay sprawled on it, that his cheeks were folded over the white soil. But it didn't matter. A whole string of colorful images continued to pour into his head, lingering and swaying as if floating in a pool.

Some of them he remembered from home and school, and some of them from films and commercials. Some of them didn't even make any sense. But that was okay. They all seemed to blend seamlessly. The visions were soothing like a pleasant dream, some of them entangled in Grandpa's custard, strawberries, and lemon juice. In fact, he felt strangely good now. The hunger was fading and the thirst evaporating, and the ground felt cozy against his ear. The brightness of the white landscape dimmed somewhat and it just felt right to close his eyes and sleep. That was all he wanted to do. Sleep. He relaxed his body against the ground and welcomed the enveloping darkness. And he would have continued to enjoy it were it not for the poking and stabbing sensations in his side, and the remote voices that accompanied them.

Ten

"**A**rthur, what are you doing? Get your walking stick out of his ribs. You could hurt him!"

"Well of course I could hurt him, Shirley. I'm not doing it to tickle him, for goodness sake. I'm not taking any chances with these wretched robots in this country." Nevertheless, Arthur let up a little on the pressure as he poked around Dillon's ribs.

"Oh, for goodness sake, he's just a boy. Can't you see?" She tried to wrestle Arthur's cane from him. The problem was that any amount of abnormal physical exchange between them tended to throw them both easily off balance. Thus, when Arthur resisted Shirley's stealthy grab for his cane, that was all it took to make them both topple over. And topple they did, right on top of Dillon.

Even Arthur was somewhat apologetic. "Oh, excuse me," he mumbled, trying to rise to his feet. But Shirley had decided to use her husband's arm as a lever to help her up. So every time he tried to stand up, she would pull him down again in a flash.

"Shirley!" he yelled. "For goodness sake, wait until I get up and then I'll help you up."

"Some gentleman you are!" she snapped back, although not that audibly. Her mouth was sort of pasted to the white cookie ground. "Typical. You help yourself before you help me. My mother was right about you."

Arthur managed at least to make it to his knees. "Shirley," he said, out of breath, "How many times have I told you in the past fifty six years to stop bringing your mother into our discussions."

"I never bring Ma into our discussions," she insisted.

"Oh, really? You just did!"

"That's because we never have discussions, Arthur. We only have arguments."

"Oh, for goodness sake!" Arthur exclaimed.

Shirley managed to hoist herself up to a sitting position. "Oy, my back. My back."

"My knees," Arthur rejoined.

"Arthur," Shirley said, suddenly calm and collected. "He's just lying there. If he was dangerous wouldn't he have tried to attack us by now?"

Arthur stared at Dillon who had barely moved during this melee. "I don't know. And I don't want to know. We've been tricked before."

Shirley's painted eyebrows curled in pity. "Arthur, feel his pulse."

"Shirley, please...."

"For goodness sake, Arthur. Feel his pulse!"

Arthur sighed. He lowered his hand gingerly to Dillon's wrist, ready to recoil at the slightest movement.

"Oy, it's very weak," he said softly.

"Oh, no!" Shirley cried, clasping her hands over her mouth. "What are we going to do?"

"What are we going to do?" Arthur imitated her. "We can't do anything. We don't know how to revive these Cyberian creatures."

"But what if he's human?"

"Well, how are we going to find that out? We can't ask him."

"Try to give him some of your seltzer water. You know they don't eat or drink anything. If he takes it, we'll know he's human."

Arthur grudgingly obliged, although he was privately quite concerned for the boy himself. Sometimes the dynamic between him and his wife got in the way of how he really felt. He withdrew the seltzer water bottle from his pocket, opened it and positioned it just above Dillon's lips.

"Nu, go ahead and drop some of it inside him," Shirley urged.

"For goodness sake, Shirley. I have to do it slowly. I don't want to drown him."

"Alright, alright. But just do it already."

"Shirley!"

With a quivering hand, Arthur let a few drops of Seltzer water drop onto Dillon's lips. Immediately, Dillon stirred and opened his mouth. His tongue emerged briefly to lick the water off his lips. His eyes shot open, and then closed just as quickly. Arthur swallowed as if to empathize with him. He let some more water drip into Dillon's mouth and this time Dillon coughed and bolted upright. His eyes were so bloodshot they were like ripe cherries. He saw the two figures crouching over him and tried to leap to his feet, but did not succeed.

"Don't be scared, young man," Shirley said, although she herself was frightened out of her wits.

"We are human like you are," Arthur assured him.

Dillon stared at them intently for a long while, and nobody said a word. "Am I back home?" his voice croaked finally.

"Well, I don't know where home is," Arthur replied. "But if you mean, are you back in the real world? No. You are still in Cyberia."

"Grandpa," Dillon said, his mind searching and finding, searching and finding. Everything replayed until he remembered the endless white.

Arthur glanced at his wife.

"He is not your Grandpa, sweetheart," she said.

"Sweetheart?" Arthur repeated.

"Well, for goodness sake, look at the poor boy," she chided him.

"No, I mean," Dillon said, "I'm looking for my Grandpa."

"Is he somewhere here?" Shirley asked.

Dillon nodded. "Not on this Error page, but in Cyberia."

"Well, that's a pretty big place," Arthur commented.

Dillon's eyes traveled to the seltzer bottle. "Thank you for giving some of that to me. May I have some more?"

"Well, of course you may," Shirley said, taking the bottle from Arthur and handing it to him. "You poor thing. What about food? Arthur, do we still have some of that turkey sandwich I packed this morning?"

Dillon's eyes lit up at the mention of these words. He had never felt such a yearning for a turkey sandwich in all his life.

Arthur gave Dillon the remainder of their lunch. "Eat slowly," she urged Dillon. It was hard for him to oblige. Each bite was like an injection of warmth to his body. Arthur and Shirley remained seated on the ground around him, watching him patiently.

"This is so great," Dillon managed to say between chews. "Where are you guys from? How did you land up in Cyberia, and on this page?"

Before responding, Shirley brushed the skin of her cheeks with her palms as if to powder her face.

"We're from Boca."

"Boca?" Dillon asked, puzzled.

"Boca Raton in Florida," Arthur explained.

"Oh," Dillon said.

"Yes," Shirley continued. "Yes, we live there six months of the year, and live six months in Cyberia to escape the Floridian heat."

Dillon was amazed and baffled at the same time. "You have a home in Cyberia?"

"Yes," she traced the sides of her mouth with a fingernail. "On the Cyberian Riviera. It's very expensive."

Arthur rolled his eyes.

"And we're really happy here," she said, her eyes repelling her husband's unspoken sarcasm.

"But still, how did you land up on this Error Page?" Dillon wanted to know.

"Well," Arthur cleared his throat. "I think the search train we were using was faulty."

"No, it was not," Shirley shot back immediately. "Sometimes it just pays to ask for directions, rather than figure it out yourself."

"Oh, for goodness sake, Shirley. I asked the lady for the Virtual Opera just like the instructions said."

"No, Arthur. You asked for the Virtuoso Opera."

"No, I did not."

"Yes, you did."

"No, I did not."

"Oh, for goodness sake, Arthur."

Dillon smiled. "You guys like to say 'for goodness sake' all the time," he observed, downing the last bite of the sandwich. He let out a groan after he was done. His stomach now felt distended.

"I told you not to eat so fast," Shirley admonished him.

Dillon forced a smile. "It's just that I haven't eaten in a while."

"Well, did you bring any food with you from home? You know you can't buy food here."

Dillon sighed. "I – I didn't know that when I left. How much food did you guys bring in? Enough for six months?"

"Well, actually we go back every day," Shirley responded, cupping the curls at the back of her head. "We simply can't schlep enough food for six months."

"You should see what we bring every day," Arthur piped in. "It's enough for six months each time."

"Oh, for goodness sake, Arthur," she snapped. "I just buy the necessities."

"Like the ten packets of veal we bought this morning?"

"That's protein!" she protested.

Arthur shook his head.

"Wait a minute," Dillon said, trying to piece this all together. "You live here for six months of the year but you go back every day?"

"Yes," Shirley smiled. "I know it sounds a little confusing, but it's got to do with time dimensions and I don't truly understand it myself...."

"Let me explain," Arthur interjected. "When we say we spend six months of the year here and six months of the year in Florida, it's not six months at one time and six months at one time. The entire year we travel back and forth so that we can go and get the supplies we need to live here...."

"And to visit the children," she reminded him.

"Yes, yes, to visit the children. So when we say six months, we mean a total of six months spent here if you add it all up, and a total of six months there if you add it all up. Time stands still for us in Florida while we're away, which is nice because we don't miss out on anything that's happening there."

"He means the football, "Shirley sneered. "Arthur can't possibly tear himself away from it."

"Wow, you guys travel back and forth a lot," Dillon remarked, dodging all the innuendo flying between the couple.

"Well, we don't mind," Shirley responded, although it wasn't clear she was speaking for both of them. "We go back and forth so many times that we qualify for Transalot."

"Transalot?"

"Yes, it's a special service for their important travelers.

"Oh, for goodness sake, Shirley. *Frequent*, not *important*."

She ignored him. "They have special speed-lanes for us when we go through the BiteFlite station."

Dillon stared at both of them. Were he not stuck on an Error Page inside a bizarre self-contained cyberworld, he would have felt completely normal around these people. He was very easily able to imagine this conversation taking place on a bus or shared cab in a regular city setting.

"How did you find out about Cyberia in the first place?" he asked them. "Travel agents don't know about this, do they?"

Both Shirley and Arthur found this amusing, at long last one sentiment they were able to agree upon.

"No," Shirley said, containing her giggle. "Our son, Michael, told us about it. He showed us how to get inside the computer. In the strictest confidence, of course."

Arthur sighed. "Yes. Michael."

There was a strained silence. They both looked down at the white cookie ground. "He's married to a Cyberian," Shirley revealed eventually, her fingers stroking the pearls of her necklace. "It broke my heart."

"She's a nice girl," Arthur offered less than enthusiastically.

Dillon sensed that this was an area he should avoid entirely.

"You know, I really want to thank you for giving me this food," he said cheerily. "I was really, really hungry."

"Well, we have plenty where that came from," Shirley assured him. "Why don't you come back to the condo on the Riviera with us? I can give you a nice hot meal."

Dillon toyed with this idea, but only for a few seconds. He was resolute about what he had to do next.

"I need to find my Grandpa," he said. "What would be helpful is if you could...if I could ask you for some money for a search train out of here."

Without delay, Arthur dropped 100 Cyber dollars into Dillon's hand.

"Awesome!" Dillon exclaimed. "You guys are so cool!"

He reached forward and hugged Arthur, who fell backwards onto Shirley, who in turn crashed to the ground, and they were all once again flat as pancakes against the cookies.

Dillon helped the couple onto their feet and onto their search train after it downloaded, and waved to them as it pulled it off. Shirley left him with a worried look from the passenger window. She had given him their address on Avenue P.C. de la Vista on the Cyberian Riviera, with the invitation to drop in anytime he wanted something to eat. Now he was alone again, staring at the screen on the ticket counter. He finally had the chance to type in Grandpa's name, but he was having second thoughts. He had to be extremely careful about this. If he turned up to the place where Grandpa was being held, he'd be facing Morton without the PDA. When Morton would see that, he'd have no reason to keep Grandpa alive. He might very well kill him because he served no purpose. It was essential that Morton continue to believe that Dillon still had his PDA on him. But how was this possible? He couldn't enlist the help of CAVE because for all he knew they were in this devious plan together. He wondered if there was a way to go behind the scenes and find out just what was Morton's story, what motivated him to want to destroy everything, himself included. Perhaps he could snoop around Morton's house and find something that would provide some sort of clue, something that Dillon could use against him.

He clicked on the Cyberian White Pages and entered Morton's name. The screen provided only one entry.

"McAfnee, Morton and Sandra. 5134 Fortran Drive, Cyberia 09756."

Dillon took a breath and clicked on the purchase tickets button. "Your train will be here shortly," the screen said after Dillon dropped in the money.

It was an immense relief to be able to board the train and finally escape the Error Page. He had gotten so used to the vast empty white that the sudden rush of color and variety of shape was both refreshing and disorienting. Even the coarse furry skin of the web crawler sitting next to him was a welcome sight. This web crawler sat quietly, absorbed in The Cyberian Express, and didn't seem to notice Dillon. There was one other passenger at the front of the train. She was a middle-aged lady dressed in her nightclothes and her hair was in curlers as if she had just awoken or stepped out of the bathroom. Why would this woman be traveling like this to see Morton and his wife? Dillon tried not to let his curiosity win this one, but it was no use. He found himself making his way to her row.

"Hi," he said quietly.

The woman was startled and pulled her night robe closer. "Hi," she responded anxiously.

"I'm sorry to disturb you," he ventured, "but I was wondering how you knew the McAfnees."

The woman cleared her throat. "Oh," she laughed. "I didn't think anyone would notice me. I was just doing a harmless search on Sandra. We went to high school together but we've lost touch and I haven't seen her in years. I don't intend on visiting her or anything. I was just relaxing on the sofa at home and wondering what she was up to. So I jumped on this search train. I didn't intend on visiting her, not like this," she laughed again. "I was just curious."

"Oh, so it's Sandra you know," Dillon nodded. "Do you know Morton at all?"

"No. I mean, I knew she got married and all. I read it in the newspaper. I heard it was a fairy tale wedding." Her eyes lifted to the ceiling and sparkled with the train lights. "I know he has a high position in some corporation or organization or something. But that's all I know."

Dillon looked away. This was just another innocent trusting Cyberian who would fall victim to Morton's murderous plan if Dillon didn't do something about it. He wanted to divulge what he knew about Morton, but couldn't bring himself to do it. He had wanted to warn Arthur and Shirley too, but couldn't imagine how they would react. They would sooner conclude that he was a nutcase rather than take him seriously. That's what Grandpa said about the terrorist attack in New York. Anyone who would have warned the public about it beforehand – that planes would go into the two buildings – would've been put right in a straightjacket.

"So how do you know Morton and Sandra?" the lady inquired, noticing Dillon's pensive expression.

"Oh," Dillon swallowed. "Uh, I think I'm related through marriage," he said stupidly.

"Oh, really? How?"

"Second cousins, five times removed," he responded, his tongue seeming to run away from him.

She had a puzzled look on her face and Dillon didn't blame her. "Anyway, nice to meet you," he said, a wave of embarrassment washing over him. He returned to his seat and tried not to look towards the front of the train until it came to a stop.

When he stepped off the train, it felt like he was back home in suburbia. The houses and tree-lined avenues were virtually identical. Even the night sounds were familiar, complete with random bird-chirping and dog-howling. Of course, the spectacled executive spider's foray onto the sidewalk and into the dark of the night would have caused quite a sensation back home. So some things were bound to be different. The house at the end of the street, for example, seemed to be spinning at creative angles off its foundations. It made no noise and didn't seem to pose any threat or disturbance to its environs. Dillon stared at it for a while, blinking several times just to make sure he wasn't imagining things. A young boy on a skateboard skidded to a stop next to Dillon. "Cool screensaver," he said, admiring the scene together with Dillon.

"Screensaver?" Dillon sputtered.

"Yeah, the Murrays are on vacation. They always put their house on really cool screensavers whenever they go away. I wish my parents would choose those images. Our house just does a boring flip upside down every twenty minutes. My dad says he doesn't want to attract attention. That's what he always says."

The boy sighed and Dillon watched him jump back on his board and fly off recklessly in typical skater fashion.

He wished he could show this to his Grandpa, whose image in turn spurred him to get moving. The street sign above him read "Fortran Drive." The rambler across the street had the numbers 5133 pegged to the beam across the front porch. He turned around and saw that he was right in front of 5134. It was a large double-story house rising above the tall poplar trees guarding the front yard. The house was mostly dark, except for a dim light emanating from somewhere inside. He turned nervously to his left and right, trying to remind himself that this was the right thing to do. It reminded him of the similar fear he had the day he traveled down the hallway past Mrs. Klondike's window towards Mr. Rigler's office, when he'd put everything on the line for the sake of justice. The sounds of her haunting radio music came back to him, mingling with several voices of doubt about his current mission. Even the voice of his Grandpa expressing dismay at Dillon's choice of action. His mind yelled back at the voices. *This was the right thing to do!*

It was a good thing nobody could hear the shouting match inside his head. He approached the gate, his heart doing loops inside his chest. He reminded himself that Morton wouldn't be home. After all he was holding Grandpa hostage on his blog. But his family was probably home. Should he wait until the morning when everyone was out of the house? But how could he keep Grandpa waiting? What was Grandpa eating? He hoped Morton was feeding Grandpa something just to keep him alive. He had to press forward. With one hand on the gatepost, he sprung up and over the low gate and he was on the other side. Rather than allow time for remorse, he darted toward the side of the house, out of the streetlight. He crouched underneath the first window. Slowly he rose to full height and peered inside. It looked like a living room but it was hard to be certain since it was so dark. He traced his fingers lightly along the window frame and found that the window was left very slightly open. The problem was that there was a screen just in front of it, making it impossible to pass through. He moved down the wall to the next window but that was completely shut. The only solution was to remove the screen of the first window without causing any disturbance. He had done this several times before at home, much to his mother's consternation. He'd always protest that no harm was done since he'd be able to replace it easily. "Look, Mom, it's as if nothing happened!"

It seemed that his mischief at home was paying off dividends. He couldn't wait to tell his mother when he got back…. If he got back. He swallowed hard as his fingers gently loosened the screen without a sound. He lowered it carefully to the ground and let it rest against the wall. Now he was free to climb inside. He squeezed through the window and dropped down slowly onto the hardwood floors. He sat there against the wall for a while, waiting for his eyes to adjust to the darkness. He hardly allowed himself to breathe, his ears alert for the slightest sound. Just above the fireplace he made out a family portrait, a couple posing with two kids. But he couldn't discern their faces. He leaned forward to get a closer view, but it didn't help. Through the doorway across from him, the hall was faintly illuminated. On the other side of the hall there appeared to be a room full of bookshelves. If there was a room in the house that might uncover some information about Morton, that would be it, Dillon surmised. He rose slowly to his feet, the bones in his feet clicking loudly, even echoing. Why did his bones always click like that when he was trying to be quiet? As he stepped forward the floors creaked but not very loudly. After each step he stopped and listened for any sound. It took a couple of minutes to make it all the way across the living room. He took a slow silent breath when he reached the threshold of the room. He peered into the hall and took a step inside. Just as he did so he noticed a bright red light flash on in the upper corner of the hall. And then the most terrifying sound pierced his body. A blaring, wailing noise rocked the silence and sent him reeling backwards in shock. The alarm! How stupid could he be! The alarm. He scrambled to his feet and dove for the nearest hall closet as all the lights turned on and footsteps pattered down the stairs.

"Sandra, just stay upstairs! Stay upstairs with the kids," a man's voice hollered. Dillon stood motionless, huddled amongst the coats and jackets. There were shoes and other paraphernalia strewn across the bottom of the closet, making it difficult to get a secure footing. The alarm continued to blast, its searing pitch practically scratching his eardrums and flipping his stomach muscles like pancakes.

The footsteps stopped several feet away, He heard a sequence of touchtone beeps and the invading sound was halted mid-screech. Dillon hoped they would dismiss it as a false alarm. An agonizing silence followed. Would they notice the open window? There wasn't much of a wind outside. Perhaps they wouldn't.

"Morton?" Sandra called meekly from the second floor.

"Sandra, I told you, I have it under control!" he said with a clear quiver in his voice.

Morton's voice sounded strange. It was different to what he remembered, definitely deeper and slower, and well....just different. Maybe it was because he was hearing it through the closet doors. The seconds passed excruciatingly slowly as if Morton was picking each second apart and scrutinizing it before letting it tick on. Eventually Dillon heard footsteps start up again at a more relaxed pace, accompanied by the slight creaking of the staircase, gradually getting softer until the sounds stopped completely.

Dillon closed his eyes and let out the pent-up air he had been afraid to exhale. He was free to escape now..... or should he just try to get a peek inside that library? Both desires were equally tempting. His left foot had gone to sleep as it rested at a crooked angle amongst the pile of shoes. He slowly straightened it and readied himself to open the doors of the closet. Just as he leaned forward, the immortal verses of Humpty Dumpty sparked to life, in the form of a battery-operated stuffed animal that was being crushed by his foot. Dillon let out a yelp and glared at the little black current eyes of the toy that was betraying him. He leaped from the closet, but not quick enough to escape sighting by Morton who was already halfway down the stairs armed with a baseball bat.

Dillon turned only for a second to see that Morton was in a fit of rage and fully intent on beating him to a pulp. Only thing was....it wasn't Morton. Not the one he knew, anyway. How could this be? Dillon sped through the living room and bolted through the window. He was less concerned now with being caught than with the fact that this wasn't even the right Morton. Whoever the man was, he pursued him across the yard and over the fence into the street. But the guy's name was Morton McAfnee. How many Morton McAfnees could there be in Cyberia? There had only been one listed in the phone book.

Dillon sprinted down the street widening the gap between him and this other Morton whose privacy he'd just invaded. He was getting closer to the house on screensaver, which was situated on a dead end. He stopped running. Breathless, he whirled around to see several dozen CAVE officers on his tail. This was hopeless. If only he had his PDA now. He'd use it to try to close off this website and escape, although he had never successfully accomplished that before. He sat down on the cookie road and waited to be arrested, calmly surrendering to whatever consequences they had in mind for him. The most debilitating part was that he also found himself surrendering to the unquestionable reality of this cyberworld, which had presented itself initially as an innocuous joyride into a fantasyland, but in fact had staged a crafty, gradual assault on his confidence and sense of reality. It had defeated him, leaving him with the frighteningly real prospect that he might never see his Grandpa again.

Eleven

"Ok, these are the rules," the almost-toothless warden hissed, as he tossed Dillon into his cell. Oddly, the cell didn't seem to have any walls or bars to it like the other cells did.

"This is your bunk." He pointed to an elevated board made entirely of rotten cookies. "You are to keep it as clean as you got it."

Dillon squinted at the warden. The man was not only toothless, but expressionless.

"Also, no noise. You can talk quietly with your cellmate, but if I ever hear you raise your voices, I'll turn the volume down in the cell completely so you won't be able to hear yourselves talk." His face wobbled as he spoke, his cheeks puffing like water balloons.

Dillon nodded slowly, suppressing an urge to laugh.

"One last thing," he said, finally grinning. "You're human, so you get food. But don't expect fine cuisine," he warned ominously, his eyes as narrowing as if to squeeze out venom. We get our contacts in the real world to send us the worst possible stuff. Something you guys call *junk* food." He laughed sardonically.

Dillon desperately wanted to laugh too, but he managed to hold it in. He wasn't about to spoil the moment. If junk food was a form of punishment in this place, he was more than happy to face the music.

The warden then stepped away and pointed his baton at a small control panel located on the ceiling. Immediately, black bars appeared stretching from the floor to the ceiling, sealing off the area. After the warden sauntered off, Dillon touched a finger to the bars. They were hollow, yet able to deflect him, like repelling laser beams.

"You ain't getting outa here with those bars," a voice said behind him. "They're called Wingdings."

Dillon turned around to see a figure lying on his own rotten cookie bed in the corner. His face was hidden in the shadows.

"Wingdings?" Dillon asked, clearing his throat.

"Yup. That's what I said. You know, from those word-processing programs - those funny-looking characters people can stick on the page they're typing?"

He didn't wait for Dillon to answer. "Well, that's what these bars are made from. They can pop on and off at the click of a button. Cheap security but does the job."

Dillon ventured closer. "My name's Dillon," he said.

The face emerged from the shadows. It was a boy about his age or maybe slightly older. He wore a bandana and had tattoos of various PDA brand names running down his arms. The boy noticed that Dillon was trying to read them.

"PDA's," he said quite proudly. "They're banned. If only I could get my hands on one."

Dillon's sentiments were the same, but he wasn't ready to explain that quite yet.

The boy extended a hand. "Name's Vincent," he said, almost managing a smile.

Dillon shook his hand. "So….what are you uh…." he began without thinking.

"What am I in for?" Vincent proposed. "You cut straight to the chase, huh?"

Dillon blushed. "Sorry, I didn't mean…."

"No problem. You think I care?" he swung his legs off the bed and sat on the edge. "Substance abuse."

Dillon nodded, but then frowned in confusion. "But you guys don't put anything in your mouths. Do you inject it?"

Vincent grimaced. "Inject it? That would probably kill you."

Dillon remained puzzled. "So how do you…."

"There's only one way to take Batterijuana."

"B-Baterrijuana?"

"Yeah, you never heard of it?"

Dillon shook his head.

Vincent clapped his palm against his cheek. "Wow, man. You are so pure."

Dillon hadn't thought of himself like that.

"Batterijuana is a little disk made of chemicals," Vincent explained. "You plug it into your recharge socket, and man, you get such a supercharge that you think you can do anything."

Dillon considered this. "And obviously it's illegal."

"Dude, you are such a brain. What do you think I'm doing here?"

Dillon smiled. "But, why would it be illegal? I mean, it sounds like it helps you do things you find difficult."

"Yeah, well you're preachin' to the choir." Vincent's face flushed red. "Ok, so it can make you do stupid things. I broke a bank window. But hey, I didn't hurt no-one. If they don't keep their cash in vaults, how can they expect someone who accidentally breaks their window not to take the cash?"

Dillon didn't quite know how to respond. "Ok," he said finally, shrugging his shoulders.

"Yeah," Vincent went on. "And you know what, I heard that some parts of Cyberia are fighting to make Batterijuana legal. It helps you feel better, man. I say, more power to them, dude. More power to them."

Dillon pondered this for a moment. "Who sets the laws in Cyberia?" he asked.

"I don't know, dude. It just seems I was born into it, you know what I'm sayin'? I don't question it."

You just break it, Dillon thought. He sat down on his board-bed. It was rock-hard. He wondered if there was some organization that made the laws, an organization that wasn't corrupt that he could approach about Morton's plan.

"Hey!" Vincent said with a frown. "You do a lot of askin'. You don't do a lot of tellin'. What are you doin' in here?"

Dillon didn't know where to begin. There wasn't really a quick summary he could dish out, so he settled on his last accomplishment.

"Breaking and entering," he replied.

Vincent was duly impressed. He stared at Dillon for a while, and then pressed him for details.

"What'd you score?"

"Nothing," Dillon answered. "I wasn't really looking to steal anything."

Vincent's face cracked like a jigsaw puzzle. "What?"

Now Dillon had gone and done it. He'd have to start all the way from the beginning in order for his last statement to make sense. Why not? He thought. There wasn't much else to do in jail anyway.

The warden came to deliver Dillon's food just as he was talking about the struggle with Morton on the train. Vincent had been riveted from the start, and became agitated when Dillon was sidelined by the warm crusty doughnuts placed in front of him. The warden gave a satisfied smile as if to delight in the apparent torture he was inflicting.

"Dude, don't stop," Vincent begged. "I wanna hear more."

But Dillon was temporarily oblivious to anything but fluffy fresh fried dough drenched in oil. Only when he swallowed the last chunk did he speak.

"Wow, that was good," he breathed, wiping his mouth with a sticky hand.

"It looks sick to me," Vincent commented. "You put all that stuff in your mouth. Gross, man."

Dillon chuckled. "And you stick a plug into your body," he retorted. "Now, that is gross."

"Hey, that's just natural, man," Vincent argued.

"Anyway, so back to the story," Dillon said.

"Yeah!" Vincent exclaimed, striking his palms together.

At the end of it, Vincent's jaw hung low, his lips drooping and his eyes inflated like balloons. "C-o-o-l," he said finally.

"Cool? What's cool?" Dillon asked.

"This Morton guy is going to destroy Cyberia. I mean that's big time, man."

"Yeah, it's big time," Dillon said dryly. "So big that we'll all be dead."

"Dude, this is so cool. So cool."

Dillon shook his head. "I don't get it. Why would that be cool?"

"Dude, dude, this is big. Morton is from CAVE and it's CAVE who's keeping us here in jail. Think about it."

Dillon still didn't get it.

"If Morton is really a bad guy and CAVE is really bad, then why do we have to listen to their stupid rules? Huh?"

Vincent became excited. He stood up, his mind racing with questions and possibilities. "Are we being bad if we break the rules? Bad people are ruling us in the first place. Bad people are putting us in the slammer. Why should we let ourselves be ruled by criminals?" His own soliloquy rapidly inflamed his passions.

"I – I don't know if CAVE is really bad," Dillon said. "I'm not sure, I mean it could be. But maybe it's just Morton who's really bad."

Vincent's enthusiasm, however, was not about to be dampened. He paced the length and breadth of the cell, deep in thought.

"You know what, dude?" he whispered, stopping close to Dillon's ear. "We don't belong here. We don't deserve to be here."

"Wait a minute," Dillon protested, sitting back. "What are you saying? You want to escape?"

"Shhh!" he urged. "Some kind of prisoner you are. You don't go sayin' the e-word just like that. You've never had jail time before, have you?"

Dillon was almost ashamed to admit that he had none.

"But you're right," Vincent resumed his whisper. "We should get out of here, man. My dad tells me to stay out of trouble. And this is trouble, man. We need to get out of it."

Dillon squinted at him. Vincent's logic didn't sit so well with him. "I don't know," he said, yawning. He hadn't slept in a while, not on a full stomach anyway, and for now the rock-hard rotten cookie-bed looked appealing. "I want the chance to tell CAVE about Morton," he said, settling back against the board. "I want to see Commander Burdock again. If she's also bad, then I guess you're right. We have nothing to lose by escap...."

"Shhh!" Vincent admonished him mid-syllable.

"Sorry," Dillon yawned. "Anyway, I want to see what she says."

"You trust people too much, dude," Vincent remarked, returning to his bed. Dillon stared blankly up at Vincent for a while. Nothing Vincent had said thus far had penetrated like this last off-the-cuff remark. He folded his arms behind his head and drifted off to sleep to the words lodging in his mind and becoming enmeshed like skin caught in a zipper.

When the warden came the next morning to deliver Dillon's chocolate cream puff, Dillon asked him if he could speak to Commander Burdock. The warden nearly banged his head on the bars laughing, pouches of his skin wriggling like rooster necks. "Next you're going to ask me if you can have a suite on the Cyberian Riviera."

Dillon thought of Arthur and Shirley. Although he was itching to, it would be no use to tell the warden that he did, in fact, have an open invitation to join them on the Cyberian Riviera.

He thought quickly while the warden was still there. The warden was about to disappear when Dillon called out, "Wicker Chairs."

The warden turned around.

"Wicker chairs. Commander Burdock has wicker chairs in her office."

The warden stared at him.

"And pictures of her two grandchildren, uh ....Tyler and Kaden. They go to Weltzheimer Elementary."

The warden returned to the bars with a sober expression, his eyes narrowing to a fine laser-sharp focus, the kind Columbo delivered unexpectedly along with his verdict. Dillon returned the intensity with a triumphant smile. "Yes, I've been in her office before. And I'd like to speak with her," he declared proudly.

The warden continued to glare at him for a while and then left quietly, leaving Dillon to deal with Vincent's annoyed expression, which was his preface to a string of protests and arguments.

The warden returned a few minutes later with a stiff look, his nose upturned as if pulled upwards by a string, and his eyes looking everywhere but Dillon.

"The Commander wants to see you," he sniffed, deactivating the Wingding bars.

Vincent pointed to his chest and raised his eyebrows in a sort of plea.

"No, not you," the warden snapped, leading Dillon out of the cell. "Only this little critter."

Vincent switched quickly to a tone of indignation. "What? You don't think the Commander would wanna see me? I've learned a lot from the streets, man. Stuff that she doesn't know because she's never been out in the cold. Stuff that I could teach her."

"Like what? How to sell stolen watches on the World Time website?" the warden scoffed, and then followed that with raucous laughter. He reactivated the bars and walked Dillon toward the exit. Vincent growled through the bars, banging against them until the two of them were out of sight.

Soon Dillon was crossing the bridge leading to Commander Burdock's office. "Pretty cool view, isn't it?" he remarked to the warden as he looked down to the valley below. He got a mere grunt in response.

Commander Burdock rose from her chair when she saw Dillon. This time she had no smile, but she didn't appear angry either. It was more a look of mild concern, the way Mrs. Saffer would tense up when she noticed one of her students had a nosebleed or had spilled the paint all over the floor.

"Dillon!" she rushed towards him, but stopped abruptly a few feet short of him.

"Hi, Commander," Dillon said cheerfully.

The Commander nodded very slightly to the warden who took his cue and withdrew into the background.

"Dillon, I….I just heard about this," she began, wringing her hands. "Usually I hear about relevant happenings from every corner of Cyberia within seconds of their occurrence. But this one eluded me, probably because my team only tracks those that are relevant to our mission. A single act of breaking and entering is usually not worthy of my team's antennae."

Dillon had nothing to say. He was studying her expression, which appeared to be genuine. If this was an act, she was not providing any clues. But then Morton had never intimated that he was harboring even the slightest agenda. Certainly not one that was as devious and sinister as it turned out to be.

"Which makes me wonder," she continued. "Why did you do such a thing? It doesn't seem at all consistent with your personality. You seem like a balanced, well-behaved young man. And Morton told me that you just got up and ran from him."

Dillon's eyes lit up. "You spoke to Morton?"

"Yes, just a couple of minutes ago. I contacted him when I found out that you had done this. He told me that he had been showing you and your grandfather a mortgage site when both of you just fled. It's all very puzzling."

Dillon tried to speak but his mind was working faster than his tongue could move.

"Grandpa," he said finally. "Where's my Grandpa?"

"I don't know," the Commander shrugged. "Those three words are hard to say as the chief officer of a national intelligence operation. But I truly don't know. I was about to ask you the same question."

Dillon took a deep breath before spilling everything that he was holding in check. He didn't know whether or not he could trust her, but the desire to find his Grandpa superceded the need to be cautious. He tried not to be too vindictive about Morton, just to tell the details like a news reporter laying out the facts as they happened.

Commander Burdock hardly blinked as she listened. At the end of it, she ran her fingers through her hair and then brought them to her lips as if to stall what was about to pass through them.

"That's preposterous," she declared, turning to pace the room. "Morton McAfnee has been with CAVE for fourteen years. He is one of my most trusted advisors, and he didn't earn that title easily. From his start in the email room as a fresh college graduate, he displayed integrity and tenacity in his desire to make Cyberia a safer, and ultimately, better place. We have shared numerous hours in intensive strategic planning, in crucial brainstorming and in saving CAVE from an infinite number of predators who would just as soon see us fold." She turned to face him. "You are an interesting young man. You are intelligent and creative, and I am afraid the latter is causing me consternation."

Dillon dropped his stare. He caught the gist of what she was saying, which was essentially that he was making this all up. How could he convince her? He shut his eyes and forced control amongst the chaos in his mind.

Of course. He shifted his feet and began again. "Morton is holding my Grandpa hostage and I...."

"You claimed that already," she shot back.

"I know, but I think there's a way to prove that he's on his blog. He sent me a web-form that...."

"Morton is not on his blog. When I spoke with him just a few minutes ago, he called from his office as usual."

"But you can, or the CAVEMEN can track down that web-form and you can see for yourself that...."

"This is getting out of hand," she said, raising her voice slightly, a glimpse of the underlying toughness that had made her Commander.

Dillon was undeterred. He had to unload the evidence as fast as he could so that all of it would pile up and possibly pierce her resistance. He made a show of digging his hand into his shirt and showing his empty palm. "And what about my PDA? I don't have it anymore. Morton took it. Doesn't it concern you that I don't have it?"

Commander Burdock's eyes seemed to spin with anger, although her expression was calm. "Of course, it concerns me," she said, straightening her posture. "I've told you before how dangerous a PDA is in the wrong hands. I don't know where your PDA is, and frankly, I'm more inclined to believe that this problem is a result of adolescent negligence or mischief than a betrayal by my trusted advisor of many years."

She turned her back and began to return to her desk as if the conversation was over. It amazed Dillon that the Commander of this entire operation had been duped by Morton's fake show of loyalty. As if to address his thoughts, Commander Burdock spoke casually as she made herself comfortable in her chair. "I am not one who falls easily into traps, young man." She flipped through a file on her desk. "I also don't think you're out to deceive me. I think your creative mind has created a blur between reality and the evocative stirrings of wild fear. And that, I'm afraid, has succeeded in deceiving your own mind."

Dillon frowned at her. She still did not look up. "Think about it, Dillon. Do you really understand where you are? Do you understand Cyberia? I'm sure some of it feels like a dream to you, doesn't it?"

Dillon swallowed, his frown deepening.

"In dreams, many things happen," she continued. "Some of them are strange, some of them downright ludicrous. And the funny thing is, while you're dreaming it all seems to make sense, frighteningly so. You could swear it's so real. Cyberia may just contain a similar element of deception. I mean, your grandfather is not with you right now as he was before, so to you there is real urgency and fear and despair. But, as I asked you before, do you understand where you are? Here, things don't run the way they do back in the world you come from. What you're sure of there, you cannot necessarily be sure of here. And if your mind easily fills with spectacular ideas and imagery, who knows how much that has contributed to your perceived reality?"

Her voice was thickly sweet. Dillon shook his head as if to bat away the words. "I – I don't....that's not true." He trembled as he spoke.

She turned a page and perused it. "Oh? How can you be so sure? In the world you come from, the floor is not made of cookies, there are no web crawlers, people do not plug themselves in at night, they don't just download themselves....if someone like your grandfather goes missing, a police report is filed." She laughed politely, the way Mrs. Saffer would react to a student's misuse of an adjective. "Sometimes I think I know too much about that world for my own good."

She closed the file and glanced up at him with a sympathetic smile. "This must be so hard for you," she said. "What you're feeling is completely normal for someone who is learning to adjust to the rhythms of Cyberia. You have been exposed to many different and startling images in a short space of time. It tends to overwhelm your sense of normalcy, which in turn causes you to inject life into fantasy and to minimize actuality. You are so sure of certain things, but that can very deceptive. The fact that you made outrageous assumptions about Morton is very understan...."

As she spoke, it felt as if Dillon's brain was being squeezed, her words like a wrench, winding tighter and tighter. He opened his mouth and screamed with every fiber of his being, although it wasn't something even he himself expected.

"Shhh," the Commander said calmly. "Oh, poor boy. You're hoping to wake up from the dream, aren't you?" Her eyebrows arched like two half-moon ginger treats. "Dillon, you can't get out of Cyberia as easily as that."

He stopped screaming abruptly and switched to speaking, the words pouring furiously from his mouth.

"If I'm imagining things, then I've also imagined breaking and entering. I shouldn't be in jail." His eyes searched hers. But she returned to the file on her desk.

"That's very good, Dillon. But we have to make a distinction between what you claim and what we see. In other words, granted that the individual might very well be blending fantasy with reality, but the group who observes cannot be collectively mistaken. If we return to the dream analogy, you as an individual can dream about something, but it is highly unlikely that an entire group dream the same thing. Do you follow?"

Dillon refused to answer. She did not wait for his answer either.

"So what I'm saying is that an entire group of CAVE officers chased you down for breaking and entering.

They cannot all be imagining it. You, on the other hand, are alone in claiming such as you have about Morton's fidelity."

Dillon shut his eyes. If he had been confused and scared beforehand, now he felt like everything was spinning and he was going to crash. It was true that he didn't really understand Cyberia. The Commander's voice was so confident and assuring. Although it infuriated him, it was hard to completely dismiss what she was saying. Was it just another fact of Cyberian life that one's memory and imagination got played with? Was everything that he had recalled accurate? Could he have imagined things? But how was it possible for him to have imagined the whole episode on the train with Morton?

The Commander seemed to anticipate his quiet contemplation, glancing up at him every so often from her papers. After a while, she said something that brought Dillon keenly into focus.

"As for the PDA, it has to be somewhere. It's just a matter of finding it."

It's just a matter of finding it. The words penetrated like bullets. It dawned on him how Morton and Commander Burdock would make the perfect team. The PDA was what it was all about. The corruption was so skilled and the scheme so brilliantly devised that absolutely no-one would suspect anything. In fact, any suspicion would be turned onto the victims of the scheme. It was an incredibly powerful mind game they were playing. Rather than sink into despondency and defeat, Dillon immediately began to fill with an inspired sense of purpose here in Cyberia. He would be the one to save the nation from its horribly corrupt leadership. But just as he felt strongly about his mission, he was crushed by another realization: After this conversation,

Commander Burdock would probably alert Morton that Dillon didn't have the PDA. That would make his Grandpa useless to Morton as a hostage. And that would probably be the end of his Grandpa.

"Just don't harm my Grandpa," Dillon found himself saying before having the chance to evaluate his words.

Commander Burdock rose slowly to her feet. "I beg your pardon?"

"My Grandpa is all I have. Please don't take him away."

The Commander edged slowly forward as if treading a precipice. "I like your grandfather. I think he's charming. Why on earth would I try to hurt him?"

Dillon's teeth chattered, although he was more impassioned than frightened.

"I don't.... know," he stammered. "I just want my Grandpa back."

The Commander peered into his eyes, her own eyes like laser beams that could slice cleanly through anything. "You suspect me, don't you?"

Dillon's body went cold. At this moment Commander Burdock was the furthest thing from Mrs. Saffer Dillon could imagine. It was now obvious that not all grandmothers were always sugar and spice. He could not answer her. All he could do was return her stare. In any case, it didn't seem she was waiting for an answer. She turned and nodded her head very slightly to her right, at which point the warden appeared out of the shadows and began to escort him back to his cell.

"That's it?" Dillon shouted, struggling against the warden's iron grip. "I trusted you," he called back over his shoulder. He caught a glimpse of her stroking her chin in deep thought or, perhaps, satisfaction. It was hard to tell.

The warden said nothing throughout their trip back to the cell. He had probably been listening to the whole thing. This was another question he had: if the Commander was a part of this whole classified plan, why had she not been concerned about confidentiality?

Dillon entered the cell to find Vincent picking at Dillon's leftover cream puff, dabbing his fingers into it as if to test its resilience. As soon as he saw Dillon, Vincent withdrew his hand faster than a hummingbird's flutter. The warden left and the bars went up. "So you found my cream puff interesting?" Dillon inquired.

"I don't know what you talkin' about, man."

"Come on, Vincent. I saw you touching my food."

"I wasn't touchin' it."

"Yes, you were, Vincent. I saw with my own eyes. Look, you even have some of it on your fingers."

"Dude, I didn't touch your cream-puff. My hand musta brushed against it when I was walkin' to the other side of the cell."

"Oh, give me a break."

"I sure will if you don't quit. A break that's gonna hurt real bad."

Dillon rolled his eyes and lay back on his bed board. He let out a long sigh. "Vincent," he said.

"What?"

"What about a different kind of break?" His voice was reduced to a whisper.

Vincent was still on the offense. "That's what I'm talkin' about, dude. I'm gonna come over and..."

"Vincent, Vincent," Dillon stopped him. "Think about it. A....different....sort....of....break." He injected a little mischief into his voice to help Vincent catch on.

Suddenly Vincent understood. His mood morphed from seething resentment to joyful enthusiasm in less than a second, just as Dillon anticipated it would.

"Wow, you serious, dude?" Vincent sank to his knees alongside his bed, as if to dodge any radar that might already have picked up signals. "And I am so proud of you, dude. You managed to say it without using the e-word."

"You mean escape," Dillon asked playfully.

"Shhh!" Vincent admonished him, only to break into giggles moments later.

"There's only one problem with this plan," Dillon said soberly.

"What's that?"

"I don't have one," Dillon replied. Vincent rolled around on the floor unable to control his laughter.

They were interrupted by a loud rap on the bars. The warden's few teeth were exposed and his tongue swiped back and forth across his lower lip like a windshield wiper. "You know what I think about noise," he growled. "Consider this your warning. One more time and I'll turn the volume down in here for good."

"Yes, sir," the two of them chimed in at once.

After the warden left, Vincent stood up and began pacing, deep in thought. At one point he raised his hands in the air and turned to Dillon. "I know!" he enthused in a raspy whisper, before diminishing his voice until it was barely audible. "When the warden brings you your food, you ask him to come closer because you think there's a bug in it. And when he does, *wham!* You slam the food into his head, knocking him unconscious. And we escape through the open bars."

Vincent's eyes whizzed in circles as he envisioned the whole thing. They came to rest like pinballs in their slots as he waited for Dillon's reaction.

"That's….kinda….interesting." Dillon tried hard to be polite but the upturned lines at the corners of his mouth were giving him away.

"What?" Vincent demanded. "You think it's funny? You come up with something better than that."

There was truth to that. Dillon was blanking on any compelling strategy himself, so it wasn't his place to dismiss any of Vincent's ideas. The two of them spent a couple of hours in clandestine discussion before both of them drifted off to sleep in the midst of detailing some strange escape plan involving a web crawler and a giant bottle of insect repellant.

Dillon woke up to use the facilities. He had to call the warden who grumpily deactivated the bars and lead him to the bathroom, which in Cyberia, he'd learned was called a WD, or Waste Depot, where Cyberians would discharge their toxins. When he got back to his cell, he lay back down but couldn't sleep. His eyes were drawn to the only light seeping into the cell from the doorway at the end of the hall. It made a small arc on the ceiling like a faint spotlight. He thought of the cookie floor that lit up around his feet on the Congo.com website when he and Grandpa had toured it. He remembered how the voice welcomed him personally because it had read the cookies, and Grandpa's funny remark afterwards about reading cookies. He suppressed a chuckle, and then some tears which seemed to want to follow on its heels. He mouthed his Grandpa's name and closed his eyes, the arc of light lingering in his mind as he began to drift off to sleep…. Wait a minute! His eyes shot open and he stared again at the arc. That's it! All the elements of a plan began to congregate in his mind so rapidly that he was afraid he wouldn't remember the order. He sat up and through the murkiness studied the points where the

Wingding bars met the ground. He sat there allowing all the details to build in his mind. Then he turned to Vincent who was snoring into his rotten cookiebed.

"Vincent," he whispered.

There was a slight pause in the snoring but it resumed at full capacity.

"Vincent!" he urged a little louder.

There was a slightly longer pause, but nothing significant.

Dillon went over and shook his shoulder gently.

"What?" Vincent cried out, bolting upright. His eyes were red like fire.

"Shhh!" Dillon cautioned, and proceeded to tell him about the escape plan he had hatched.

"That's way cool, dude," Vincent said at the end of it. "Are you sure you can do that?"

"No, of course I'm not sure. I mean, we are escaping from jail, here. It's a new experience."

Vincent cleared his throat.

"For me," Dillon clarified. "It's a new experience for me."

"Let's do it," Vincent declared. "My dad used to say that it's all about timing. I live by that rule, dude. I wouldn't be where I am today without it."

Dillon wanted to laugh but he was afraid Vincent was being dead serious. He decided to press on with the plan. "Ok, Vincent, we'll need something sharp," he whispered.

Vincent nodded and surveyed the area around his bed. "I know." He scrambled under his bed and withdrew his nightly recharge chord. "There's this one part with a sharp edge that comes off. I mean, it's not like a knife edge, but it's pretty sharp." He pulled off a small metal cylinder with a flat tip and handed it to Dillon.

"Great," Dillon said, and moved over to the bars. He brought with him a bottle of soda that the warden had provided. He kneeled and began to cut into the cookie floor with the metal piece. The cookies were harder than he imagined them to be, but with some effort he was able to slice a circle about half an inch deep in the floor around one of the bars. Vincent kept watch for any sign of the warden as Dillon worked. Drops of sweat clouded Dillon's vision as he tried to scoop up the cookie soil contained within the circle. The soil crumbled in his fingers.

"Don't let it break, dude," Vincent urged.

"I can't stop it," Dillon countered, clumsily trying to balance the crumbs between his palms. "Let's try it while I still have most of it left." He held the scooped up soil at a right angle to the bar, a few inches away from it and the same distance off the ground. They both waited. Suddenly the foot of the bar plucked itself out of the ground and swiveled upwards to meet the soil in Dillon's hands, without making a single sound.

Dillon's jaw dropped, his eyes bulging. "It worked!" he exclaimed, a little too loud.

"Shhh!" Vincent cautioned, although he was just as ecstatic. "You are a genius, dude. Ge-ni-us!" He rubbed his hands together. "Did you see that? The bar got confused and just took itself over to where the soil was. Man!"

"Now pour a little bit of soda onto the crumbs in my hand so I can paste them to the bars," Dillon instructed Vincent.

Vincent picked up the bottle and examined it. "What is this gunk?"

"Just pour it, Vincent. Quick!"

Vincent let the bottle drop a single glug into Dillon's palm. "How did you come up with this, man?" he asked, shaking his head.

"Well, that's the advantage of working with cookies," Dillon said, trying to paste the remainder of the soil to the bottom of the bar. "I figured if there were cookies especially for me on Congo.com, there'd be cookies especially for the bars. Each bar would go where its cookie goes. Simple."

"Dude, I've lived in Cyberia all my life and I tell you, I have no idea what you're talkin' about. But, hey, if it works, it works."

They repeated the procedure with the six bars next to the first one, until there were seven bars sloping from the ceiling to a point several inches inside the cell, where they just hung in mid-air. Vincent did the last two, partly because the work had exhausted Dillon, and partly because he wanted to prove his proficiency as an escape artist.

Now that there was a sizeable gap, they both looked at each other beaming, and Vincent made a gentlemanly gesture for Dillon to go first. He crawled easily under the bars and stood on the other end waiting for Vincent, who seemed to be suddenly seized by fear. "Dude, if they catch us…."

"Vincent, remember what your father said about staying out of trouble," Dillon hit back quickly with the irrational rationale that Vincent himself had employed earlier.

Vincent bit his lip. "Ok, man. If this fails, it's your fault." He slipped under the bars and stood nervously alongside Dillon.

"Let's go," Dillon said. "Remember, now. It's early morning. No noise."

They tiptoed to the doorway where the warden sat asleep on a stool, his body propped up against the wall. They inched past him, watching every heave of his chest until they were out of the doorway. Vincent couldn't help emitting a tiny squeak of triumph.

Dillon immediately smothered it with his palm, giving him a stern look that quickly soured his euphoria.

Returning the stern look, Vincent shrugged off Dillon's hand and lead them down the hall to an open area where several CAVE employees briskly moved about.

"Where are we?" Vincent whispered.

"I have no idea," Dillon replied in a normal voice. "But we have to act naturally or else people will become suspicious. Don't whisper anymore and stand up straight."

"Ok, so where the heck are we going?" Vincent spoke up, adding bounce to his step.

Dillon cringed. "Our goal is to find the train station so we can get out of here."

"Sounds good to me, fellow CAVE employee. Wait, fellow CAVEMAN."

Dillon rolled his eyes.

When he and Grandpa had visited CAVE with Morton they had been downloaded from place to place. Dillon had no idea how to do that. In any case, he didn't want to risk losing some body parts in the process. They found a door to a staircase and entered. Vincent peered down through the gap in the railings. "Whoah, dude! Check that out. This is like the stairs to the Empire State Building you have in your world."

Dillon joined him at the railing. It was true. The stairs spiraled downwards further than the eye could see. There didn't seem to be a bottom. "I remember when we pulled into the station the first time, I looked up and couldn't see the roof. So this makes sense. If we want to get back to the station, we'll have to go down."

Vincent clucked. "Dude, ever heard of an elevator?"

"Sure I have," Dillon retorted, and immediately proceeded to descend the stairs as if Vincent hadn't said a thing.

"Wise guy," Vincent muttered and followed after him.

It took almost an hour to reach the bottom. They were both so out of breath that they couldn't talk. They sat down on the bottom step to rest before braving the door in front of them. It had a small worn sign that read "Lobby".

"Ok, we'd better make a move before the warden wakes up if he hasn't already," Dillon puffed. They opened the door and stepped into the lobby. Even at this early hour the reception area was full of people. "This is good," Dillon said, and began to stride confidently across the center, Vincent trailing him. He could see and hear the trains through the revolving doors at the other end. "I smell freedom," he said through gritted teeth. The doors were only a few seconds away.

"I smell someone who hasn't taken a shower lately," Vincent retorted.

"Just a second, gentlemen," a voice called from behind them. The words may just as well have been arrows.

Twelve

They both turned around to see a woman standing there with a clipboard in hand, smiling.

"Yes?" Dillon croaked, trying to appear calm.

"Both of you neglected to sign out," she said. Dillon recognized her from the front desk. Jan. Yes, her name was Jan. He hoped fervently that she would not recognize him.

"Uh….sorry," Dillon said dully.

"He's lazy," Vincent added, shaking his head in apparent disdain. Dillon served him a stare that drilled right through him. Fortunately Jan found it amusing. "Just sign here, guys." Dillon took the pen, quickly selected a name on the list at random and signed under the "logout" column. Whether Justin Grosvenor knew it or not, he was signing out early. Dillon handed off the pen to Vincent who was about to sign off as Sally Richmond when Dillon bumped his elbow to Wilbur Van Wild beneath that. "Oh," Vincent grinned sheepishly.

"Watch what you're doing, Wilbur," Dillon nudged him with a friendly smile.

Jan waited politely, following the dialogue with only marginal interest.

She took back the clipboard and began to walk back to her desk, glancing briefly at the two signatures she had just obtained. Dillon and Vincent wasted no time in heading through the revolving doors towards the trains. After passing through the doors, Dillon glanced back over his shoulder to see Jan stop in her tracks as she stared at the clipboard.

"Let's uhh....increase our pace," Dillon murmured in Vincent's direction. They dashed through the crowd towards a ticket booth, where several people waited in line.

"Let's go to the next one," Dillon urged, almost sprinting now. He couldn't bring himself to look back. Suddenly a man appeared before him, and Dillon crashed into him head-on.

"Morton!" Dillon screamed. A couple of passengers turned their heads before moving on. "I have your Grandpa. This is your final warning...." It was a blasted web-form. These things were so excruciatingly realistic. In between the pangs of fear, Dillon was dizzy with relief and excitement from the news that his Grandpa was still alive. It had the effect of blanking out the remainder of the web-mail message. The next booth was thankfully much less crowded. There were only two people in line. As he and Vincent took their place, Dillon found himself looking back over his shoulder through the revolving doors. He caught a glimpse of Jan speaking to a couple of CAVE officers. Then his view was blocked by passengers.

"Hurry up," he pleaded quietly.

It was their turn. Dillon still had some of the money Arthur and Shirley had given him. He hoped it was enough for two more tickets. "MortMac.blog" he told the cashier, who looked displeased to be working at this early hour.

"That'll be 800 Cybercents," she told them. Dillon fished frantically inside his pockets.

"In a rush?" the lady asked in a tone that implied she had all day.

Before Dillon could respond, the floor underneath his and Vincent's feet flashed a blazing red and an alarm the sound of a city bomb raid alert began to sound. Cookies had provided their method of escape back in the cell, and now these cookies had recognized them and were going to send them right back into jail. The red was so blinding and overwhelming it was as if the ground was going to open up and swallow them alive.

"Run for it!" Dillon yelled and they both dashed towards the nearest platform where a train was downloading. Dillon could hear the CAVE officers' footsteps gaining on them.

"Jump on the train!" he shouted to Vincent who was coughing as he struggled to keep up. A number of passengers were boarding the train and Dillon tore his way through them, creating a path for Vincent who almost trampled a couple of passengers as he launched himself onboard. Some very disgruntled passengers brushed themselves off and glared at the two of them. A few took to offering them a piece of their minds, but all Dillon could see were the doors of the train inching closed, just managing to shut out the hands of the officers. The train pulled off gently and Dillon looked around. The coach was jammed with passengers, providing a good opportunity to merge with the crowd. The departure announcements and instructions were muffled and unintelligible. Wherever the train was headed, it looked to be a popular destination. Almost all the passengers were dressed sharply and carried briefcases. The combined scent of cologne and hair gel threatened to replace the oxygen in the air.

"What's the first stop?" he asked the man next to him, who was holding onto the overhead handles.

"Stock exchange," he replied, absorbed in a list of figures he was studying.

Dillon turned to see that Vincent was grinning from ear to ear.

"What?" Dillon asked.

"Dude, we did it. We escaped."

"Shhh!" Dillon chided him. "Now it's your turn not to use the e-word. It's definitely not over. They're going to be waiting for us on the other side, for sure."

The train soon slowed down and the passengers straightened their ties and collars, snapped briefcases and adjusted glasses.

"Just go with the flow," Dillon whispered, stepping into the isle where everyone was gathering to disembark. Vincent straggled after him. "Dude, maybe we should stay on the train."

"No way. The officers will board it and we'll be trapped. Let's go. Just blend in." They moved towards the exit. "Talk to me about stocks," Dillon nudged him.

"Stocks of what?" Vincent asked with a panicked stare.

Dillon bumped him a little harder. "They say technology stocks are going up," he proclaimed in a brash voice.

"Yeah," Vincent nodded, limply. "That's a good way to go. Up."

"Forget it," Dillon hissed. "Just don't say anything and keep inside the crowd."

"Dude, you're confusing me."

The platform was swarming with passengers. Over the bobbing heads, Dillon glimpsed several CAVE officers standing off to the side, scrutinizing the crowd. He had the urge to duck but restrained himself, trying to appear as normal as possible. Vincent, on the other hand, was having a tougher time. When he saw the officers, he began to twitch. "They're gonna get us," he said, squirming as he walked.

"Vincent, stop! Calm down."

"I can't," he squeaked.

"We're almost past them. Just a few min...."

But it was too late. Vincent broke into a run, pushing aside the passengers in front of him. Dillon didn't have much of a choice now. He would be easily spotted at the center of the commotion, where startled passengers were trying to catch themselves from falling. He broke free of the crowd and began to chase after Vincent. The officers were on their trail within seconds. Vincent sprinted under a giant archway, which formed the entrance to a vast, crowded room. Dillon caught up with him. Security guards stationed at the archway tried to stop them but were unable to get a hold of them. The two of them just kept running, heading straight for a center arena that was cordoned off with barriers. Multiple skull and cross bone signs appeared in front of them, the kind that signaled minor safety issues like an impending cliff edge or quicksand region. They both glanced at each other and without any deliberation, bounded over the barriers into the darkened arena. There was a gasp from the crowd, followed by a stunned silence.

"What is this?" Vincent sputtered, staring at the ground and then at the crowd, feeling as if he were a circus animal.

"I don't know," Dillon huffed back. "But it's obviously dangerous. And I guess we're going to find out why."

Even the officers had stopped at the barrier, frustratedly shouting commands at each other. Through the murkiness Dillon discerned thousand of black ropes on pulleys filling the arena. It reminded him of the elevator cables in those black and white movies, whining eerily as they pulled up a rattling black cage.

Suddenly he heard a whistle sound above him and he looked up in time to see an object falling from the dark sky and screeching to a halt only a few inches above his head. The object was a gleaming three-dimensional form of the words, "Cyberian Textile Group."

Then there was a whir to the left of Vincent as another object lifted upwards rapidly on its pulley. It was also an illuminated word form that read "CyberCare Industries".

"Oh, I get it!" Dillon exclaimed.

"You always do, dude," Vincent said dryly.

"We're at the stock exchange, right?"

"If you say so."

"These must be the stocks going up and down in price. In Cyberia, they don't just go up and down in numbers on a board. They go up and down in reality."

"Great," Vincent remarked, unimpressed. "I think we're dead, dude. Something's gonna fall on us."

"Not if we catch a ride," Dillon said, scouting the area for gleaming objects.

"What? Dude, there's no way. I'm scared of heights."

The officers were yelling indiscernible threats at them from the side.

Dillon turned to face him for a moment. "Which are you more scared of? Heights or being squashed?"

Vincent grumbled. "You see anything?"

"Not yet," Dillon said. "Let's go further in."

"Dude, stop!" Vincent yelled suddenly.

Dillon froze. Vincent pointed downwards. Dillon had stopped an inch a way from the edge of an endless black pit.

"Whoah," was all Dillon could say. "Hey," Vincent said, "what's that coming up the pit?"

"It must be a stock," Dillon said. "This is our chance."

As the stock reached ground level, both of them threw themselves on top of it. It did not slow at all in spite of the weight of both boys clinging to its three-dimensional letters. They ascended rapidly, enough to make Dillon nauseous. Vincent's eyes were shut tight, and he had no plans to open them any time soon. "What stock are we on?" he squealed.

"I…. I think it's gold," Dillon replied.

Somehow that made Vincent feel better.

"Gold must be doing well," Dillon remarked dryly. Their ascent began to slow, and then the stock halted with a slight jerk, which made Vincent whimper. Dillon could see the crowd below, pointing excitedly up at the two of them. The CAVE officers seemed to be arguing with several people in an observation booth perched on a platform. Dillon wondered what they were up to. He glanced at Vincent whose eyes remained glued shut. After a few moments the people in the booth emerged through its glass doors and called the crowd to attention. This took several minutes. Then they all shouted something in unison, one word that sounded, like "….ell" or "sell"? Sell. Yes, it was sell. The gold perch started to slip downwards. It gained momentum as the chanting increased below.

"They're causing us to come down," Dillon groaned.

"I'm not complaining," Vincent said.

"I guess that's it. It's over," Dillon lamented, resting his head on top of the giant "g". They accelerated towards the lobby level. Dillon noticed that they didn't seem to be slowing down. He caught a glimpse of another fracas between the officers and the stock monitors as they tried to reverse the shouts of "sell" to "buy". But it was too late. They sunk below the lobby level into pitch darkness and continued to fall. Eventually the pulley slowed and they came to a stop, still suspended above an unknown bottom. The stock swung from side to side like a pendulum. Dillon surveyed the area around them.

"Vincent, look!"

"No way, dude."

"Vincent, it's Ok. We've stopped moving. You can look now.

Vincent allowed one eyelid to roll open slowly like a garage door. He saw a lit platform only a couple of feet to his right. His eyes shot open. "Ground!" he cried.

"Well, not quite," Dillon said. "We have to leap across this uh….abyss to get there."

Vincent cringed. "Oh, man. Why can't it ever be easy?"

"Vincent, do you see that sign there?"

"No."

"That's because your eyes are shut again, Vincent. Just open them and read that sign."

Vincent braved sight once again. "The 1987 Stock Exchange Crash Museum," he read.

"Exactly," Dillon said. "If we can jump across to that ledge, we can get inside that museum."

"You know what, dude? This time I'm not even going to think about it."

"But Vincent…."

"I'm just going to do it," he elaborated. And with a booming jungle cry, he launched himself off the gold stock and onto the ledge.

"Hey, Vincent! That's awesome," Dillon cheered. He stepped back and then took a flying leap towards the ledge, but to his horror, his foot slipped on the edge and he fell underneath it, grabbing the edge with his hands and dangling from the precipice.

"Dude! Dude, Grab my hand!" Vincent urged

Dillon screamed as he held onto the ledge with only one hand so that he could grab Vincent's with the other. With all the energy he could muster, Vincent managed to pull Dillon up and over the edge. They both lay there utterly spent.

"Thank you," Dillon breathed, patting Vincent on the shoulder.

"No problem, dude."

They located a door leading into the museum, but it was really a fire exit. Obviously they were not accessing the museum through the standard channels.

"It's locked," Dillon reported, his shoulders sagging.

"Well, let me see…." Vincent said in a strange voice. His eyebrows curled as if to endear himself to anyone who might appear. He withdrew something card shaped from his pants pocket and did something with the lock. Dillon heard a click and the door opened. "Let's just say, I've done this kind of thing before," he said sheepishly.

Dillon had no comment. He was just grateful to be inside a well-lit room and on solid ground. He looked back through the broad window of the museum just in time to watch the gold stock rise back up again.

They ambled along the isles, feigning interest in the displays, which were horribly mangled and crushed stock names in glass boxes, preserved for public awareness.

A recorded voice played in the background. "....fell to the level you are standing on, completely destroying many stocks and funds."

They exited the museum through the front door into a narrow hallway with a ticket counter. Dillon was overjoyed. "Vincent, look!" He tried to contain himself. "We can get on a train now and rescue my Grandpa."

"Well...." Vincent demurred.

"What?"

"I think I've had enough for one day. Don't get me wrong, dude. It's been fun, but I just wanna go home. Know what I'm sayin'?"

"You're kidding, right?"

Vincent avoided his stare. "No, you gotta understand, dude. I'm not built for this."

"But if you go home, they'll find you and arrest you again."

"I gotta take my chances. What can I say? You know what I'm sayin'?"

Dillon sighed and stared down at his feet. "Yes. Yes, I know what you're saying."

"Dude, don't be angry."

"I'm not angry. I'm just...." His hand flopped to his side. "Look, Vincent. You saved my life. I can't be angry at you."

They stared at each other for a few awkward moments.

"Stay out of trouble," Dillon said finally.

Vincent smiled. "Dude, you're soundin' like my dad."

Dillon bought tickets for each of them and they boarded different trains.

Dillon's train to Morton's blog was empty. The blog could not have been all that popular. Some of the kids in his class had blogs and they talked about it all the time, more than Dillon particularly cared about. Carla who sat behind him would go on about the alleged popularity of her blog any chance she got. Once, just to quiet his suspicions, he visited it to discover that the visitor comments contained the same misspelled words that were located in the blog copy. He decided not to confront her about it, rather to grin and bear it every time she gushed about the latest self-generated praise she'd received.

He braced himself as the train began to near its stop. He hadn't really strategized about confronting Morton as he had done upon leaving the Error Page. At this point he was just driven to find his Grandpa and rescue him somehow, anyhow. In any case, Commander Burdock had probably revealed to Morton by now that Dillon no longer had the PDA, or wait a minute!....He sat up straight. The web-form he'd gotten from Morton was a warning to bring the PDA! Either it was an old web-form floating around from long ago or.... could it be that Commander Burdock had neglected to tell Morton? That didn't make any sense, unless.... The doors opened. There was no more time to think. He found himself in a fairly large room that was sparse except for a hologram of Morton with a nauseating smile in the center of the room, and a little silver plaque at his feet containing an "About me" paragraph.

Dillon came closer, not to read the plaque, but to read the green pincushion button across Morton's chest.

"Click here to read my blog."

Dillon couldn't resist giving the pincushion a little punch rather than a regular tap, since it was so neatly located on Morton's chest. As he did so, the walls around the room folded open like the sides of a box and the room began to fill with inserts, a maze of sheetrock that immediately blocked his view with a thousand different corners and angles. Hanging from each wall was a picture frame containing the words of one of Morton's blog entries. Dillon had no interest in reading the entry in front of him, but he had his eye on the comments box underneath it, which was a small screen with a microphone projecting from it. He cleared his throat and spoke into the microphone. "What an idiot you are," he enunciated carefully, and to his delight, the words as he spoke them typed themselves across the screen.

"Enjoying yourself?" a voice asked coolly from behind him, causing Dillon to jump in fright.

Thirteen

Dillon slowly turned around to face Morton, who stood stiffly with a peculiar, glazed expression. Was this another web-form?

"Where's the PDA?" Morton asked, gnashing his teeth.

There was no mistaking that look. This was the real thing. Dillon swallowed, stepping back a little.

"Where's my Grandpa?" he asked back.

"You don't learn, you little rat. If I ask you a question, you answer it. Where's the PDA?"

Dillon dug a hand inside his pocket and pretended to hesitate before withdrawing the PDA.

"It's right here," he said, his strategy forming rapidly on the spot.

"And I've figured out how to delete you," he added out of nowhere.

Morton turned pale. He tried to speak but his lips couldn't form the words. Dillon couldn't believe he'd struck a nerve using something he'd sucked out of his thumb only a second ago.

"Now, tell me where my Grandpa is," he asserted, capitalizing on the wave of panic washing over Morton's complexion. Morton shifted his weight and glared at Dillon's hand still buried in his pocket.

"You figured out that I was spyware," he said, swallowing.

"Uh-huh," Dillon said right away, trying not to nod his head too obviously. Spyware. Wow! A zillion wows! He knew what spyware was. Mr. Halfinger had explained it a couple of times in class. He remembered how freaky it had felt to find out that people could surreptitiously place programs on your computer that could basically take over your computer functions. Spyware was a cool term too. It brought expectations of dark mystery and intrigue. Never did Dillon anticipate, though, that one day he'd be staring down a human form of spyware. The man standing in front of him was really nothing more than a bug! He recalled that eerie sensation he'd felt when Morton had fluffed his hair. So there weren't two Cyberians by the name of Morton McAfnee after all. There was the real one, whose house he'd broken into in suburban Cyberia, and there was this....bug, spyware that disguised itself as a Cyberian Anti-Viral Enforcer. All of these thoughts raced through his head at light speed. He had to remember to breathe. This was so nuts it was almost....cool. "Sure," he added nonchalantly. "I figured you out. And it's pretty easy to delete spyware." He even signed off his sentence with a smile.

Morton's eyes narrowed and then locked onto Dillon's, scrutinizing his expression. "Why aren't you taking out the PDA?" he questioned him after a few moments.

Dillon took a long breath to buy some time. "Because....I know that if I take it out, you'll try to take it away from me again," he responded.

Morton's eyes continued to penetrate him. "I don't believe you," he declared finally. "I'm starting to think you don't have the PDA."

"That's up to you to decide," Dillon shot back. "You could be right. But then again, what if you're wrong?" Dillon held on tenaciously to the smile he was wearing. The bluff was wearing thin but he wasn't about to give it up.

Morton folded his arms. "Your grandfather is right above you."

Dillon's eyes bolted to the ceiling. There, in a little glass box, was his Grandpa. He was seated in a lounge chair, reading something. It appeared that he couldn't see anything below him. Dillon was overcome by a blend of joy and pain at the sight of him. "Why can't he see me?" Dillon demanded, his eyes filling with tears.

"It's a one-way mirror. He's up in the Links section. It's a sound-proof room where I've been keeping him, feeding him his stupid custard and strawberries that I had to import for him or he threatened a hunger strike."

"Grandpa!" Dillon shouted over and over again, leaping off the ground as high as he could. In his excitement he'd forgotten, for the moment, his charade about the PDA. Nor did he notice Morton creeping up on him. Dillon turned aside too late. Morton pushed him fiercely to the ground and pinned his arms down with his knees. Then he fished inside Dillon's pocket and withdrew his hand in disgust as if he had inserted it in sewage.

"You little liar!" he raged. "You don't have the PDA. You lying devil! You and your Grandpa will suffer from this. I gave you both a fair chance to return safely to the real world and you just blew it. Forever."

Morton flipped Dillon onto his stomach and locked his wrists together in a vice, shoving them up the length of his back so that Dillon cried out in pain. Morton lifted him off the ground by pulling up on his interlocked wrists and the hair at the back of his head. The pain was so great that Dillon's vision blurred. Morton started to lead him away but stopped to press a green pincushion with his free hand. The glass box above them began to descend like an elevator. Grandpa was startled and he put aside his book. When the box reached ground level, the front glass wall slid open and Grandpa stood up.

"Dillon, my boy!" he shouted ecstatically, his cheeks flushing red and his moustache quivering uncontrollably. But he quickly withdrew when he saw Morton and noticed Dillon's dazed expression.

"Are you letting us go now?" Grandpa asked cautiously.

Morton laughed sardonically. "Yes, I'm letting you go now. You could say that."

Grandpa's eyebrows clamped down over his eyes like eagle claws. "I don't know what you're up to now, but you promised me you'd let us go home when Dillon brings you the instrument."

"That's exactly right, you ancient fool. I would've let you go home had Dillon given me the PDA."

Grandpa turned to Dillon. "Please, my boy, just give it to him and let's go home."

"I don't have it, Grandpa. I don't know where it went," Dillon said meekly, unable to straighten up in Morton's grip.

"Please, don't hold him like that," Grandpa begged.

"Like what? Morton asked. "Like this?" In one swift movement he kicked Grandpa in the stomach, causing him to double over, then grabbed him by the skin of his neck and started pushing both of them along the corridor of the maze.

Dillon heard his Grandpa moaning in pain. This was unbearable.

"Where are you taking us?" Dillon asked.

"Well," Morton said smugly, "Let's just say that conscientious people are always mindful of disposing of the things they don't need any more. I guess I am one conscientious bug." He exploded in laughter, which was interrupted by an electronic jingle, the kind that sounded when customers entered a retail store.

"Darn it!" he cussed. "I never get visitors, and now of all times...."

For a brief moment while Morton considered his next move, Dillon felt the grip on him loosen. With every bit of strength he had, he rammed himself backwards into Morton, who let go of Grandpa and tumbled to the ground.

"Grandpa! Quick, let's go!" They both bounded down the hall of the maze, Grandpa hopping erratically after Dillon.

"How do we get out?" Grandpa puffed.

"I don't know. I don't see any exit signs," Dillon answered, grabbing Grandpa by the arm and pulling him along. They heard Morton charging after them. Dillon spotted an opening in the wall leading to another path. He led them through the opening. Immediately there was another opening to their right. Dillon figured the more turns they made, the harder it would be to find them, so he pulled his Grandpa down that path and then through yet another opening and another until he lost count of the number of turns they had made. Eventually they just stopped and sat down which was a good thing because Grandpa couldn't really continue at that pace. They tried not to make a sound. Dillon began to wrack his brains for a new strategy. Something that involved a pincushion somewhere perhaps. Suddenly the walls around them began to vibrate, then fold open flat as the walls had done on the home page of the blog. Dillon and Grandpa jumped to their feet and began to run again, but there were no walls now.

"Bingo!" Morton exclaimed a couple of yards away. "I am so glad the blog came with a merge function."

They both continued to run, but Grandpa was not able to move very fast. Morton seized Grandpa by the arm and began pulling him along in the opposite direction toward the outer boundaries of the blog. Dillon returned to fight off Morton's grip, but Morton shoved him off and led Grandpa through a doorway near the exit.

"Let him go!" Dillon yelled after him.

"Absolutely," Morton replied and Dillon could hear Grandpa's cry as he fell through the air. "I let him go," he said with a satisfied smile.

Dillon filled with rage and launched himself at Morton, who simply moved aside, hoisted Dillon in the air and threw him into the pit where his Grandpa was. The wind was knocked out of him as he landed amongst some bobbing debris. When his breath returned, he immediately called for his Grandpa.

"I'm right here, Dillon. I think I broke some bones," Grandpa croaked. He was floating all the way along the side of the pit. Dillon swam through the thick murky fluids towards his Grandpa. Above him, he could hear an electronic voice say, "If you'd like to delete the contents of Trash, click here."

No, no. Dillon tested the walls of the trash pit. They were surprisingly coarse and jagged, which allowed him to get a good grip. He climbed up a couple of steps, and then returned to grab his Grandpa's hand. "Come on, Grandpa. I'll lift you up."

"Alright. But I think my arm is broken."

Grandpa winced in pain as Dillon attempted to pull him up the wall.

"I....I can't do this, Dillon."

"Grandpa! Don't give up now. It's not far to the top."

His muscles quivering at their peak, Dillon tugged his Grandpa slowly up the jagged stones. He could hear another electronic chime above him. His hand reached the top. He tried to hoist his body over the edge while still holding on to Grandpa.

"Are you sure you want to permanently delete the contents of trash?"

Dillon's grip on the edge was weakening. Grandpa's weight was just too much for him.

"Dillon," Grandpa begged, "just let me go."

"No!" Dillon cried, his muscles going numb. Tears poured over the rigid muscles of his face.

"Dillon!" Grandpa yelled. "Listen to me. I am your grandfather, and I order you to listen to me. I have lived my life. It's been a good life. You have your whole life ahead of you. Now let me go before it's too late."

Morton's hand reached for the green pincushion.

"Dillon!"

"No, Grandpa!"

"Let me go!"

Dillon screamed hysterically as he released Grandpa's hand and struggled to clamber over the edge. His muscles were numb and failing him. He shut his eyes.

"System Error. Spyware has been removed. Press here to return to previous command."

Dillon flopped his arms over the edge of the pit, his body hugging the wall. A torturous silence prevailed. He opened his eyes. Morton was gone. What trick was this now? He looked down to the trash surface below. Grandpa was still tossing about in an assortment of deleted files and emails.

"Grandpa, are you ok?"

"I've felt a little cleaner than this. But other than that and perhaps a couple of broken bones, I'm fine, my boy."

Dillon used all his strength to climb over the edge of the trash bin. His breathing was so heavy it felt as if his lungs were grinding against each other.

"Wait there, Grandpa," he called down.

"Thank you. I wasn't really planning on going anywhere."

Spyware has been removed. Was it possible that Morton was removed? Dillon wasn't going to take a chance. He slowly scanned the area all about him, his eyes penetrating every inch of space, his ears fine-tuned to the slightest sound.

"Dillon."

He spun around, his breath caught in his throat. It wasn't the voice of Morton. In fact, it wasn't even the voice of a man.

The woman emerged from the shadows and smiled. She was holding the PDA.

Dillon's jaw dropped. "I – It's you. You're that girl who...."

"Susan," she laughed. "Susan Dandelion. The girl who was out to save Cyberia."

"Yeah," Dillon breathed. "Susan, with the petition from Mem...."

"MemFriends."

"And you...." Dillon stammered. "You just saved our lives."

She shrugged her shoulders and flashed the PDA. "These things are handy. It's much easier to remove spyware with this external device than from within Cyberia."

She peered over the edge of the trash bin. "Hello, sir," she said matter-of-factly.

"Susan!" Grandpa exclaimed.

"Are you all right?" she asked.

"Well, I suppose I'd feel a lot better if I could just get out of...."

"I want you to know something, sir," she interrupted him, directing her words down the pit in a voice filled with emotion.

"You can call me Harley."

She smiled broadly. "Harley." Her voice echoed off the Trash walls. She bit her lip and seemed unable to continue for a moment. "I want you to know that...." her voice faltered, "what you said to me that day I first met you, was.... I mean it may sound a little crazy to you, but...it was just the nicest thing anyone has ever told me. No-one, and I mean no-one, had ever said anything like that to me in my whole life." She brushed away tears. "The thing is, you may not remember the words – they seem like simple words, I know – but I can tell you that I know them by heart by now. It's easy because there's not a day that goes by that I don't hear 'you're a good soul' playing in my mind."

Everyone was silent. Grandpa was transfixed, bobbing between deleted emails. His mind was racing with the shock and the euphoria of having achieved one of his life-long goals here in the bowels of cyberhumanity.

Dillon was the first to clear his throat. "H- how'd you do this? I mean, how did you get hold of my PDA? How'd you figure out the password?"

"Well," Susan began calmly. "I followed you and your grandfather around quite a bit."

Dillon's eyes scurried about like tiny squirrels. "That was you."

Susan blushed, shrugging her shoulders. "Well, yes, that would be me. The thing was that your grandfather intrigued me. Also, I pretty much suspected something interesting was going on when we met the second time. So I decided to follow you guys around. You know, I'm a political activist and lobbyist so I do quite a bit of snooping around for information." She smiled briefly. "I figured I'd research your story. Boy, I did not expect to find out what I did. I mean, Morton's act was such an unbelievable scoop."

Dillon stared at her. "So you knew about Morton?"

"Dillon, I was on the train with you," she said emphatically, almost berating him.

"Oh, right....I guess. But I mean why did you kinda.....keep it to yourself?"

"Oh, I didn't," she replied in a cheery melody.

"You didn't?"

"Of course not. Commander Burdock and I have been working very closely together on this."

"What!" Dillon stammered.

"You heard me. The tough part was cracking your password. We had to use a special electronic code-cracking device imported from government sources in your world. When we finally got hold of it, it blitzed through all the different permutations and gave us the answer we needed."

A frustrated voice from the depths reminded both of them that they had neglected him.

"Oh, uh....Grandpa, I'm sorry. We'll pull you out of there in a minute. Did you hear that Susan was working together with Commander Burdock all this time?" Dillon asked him excitedly.

"Of course, it was in the strictest confidence," Susan continued. "It has always been a dream of mine to work closely with the Commander on issues that would improve the lives of all Cyberians everywhere." She shook the hair from her face, cherishing the sweet sound of the words she was uttering. "Now that I have my foot in the door, she's even open now to discussing MemFriends. We're working on memory-saving strategies, and I just can't be happier. And basically, it's all thanks to your grandfather."

They both peered down adoringly at the man who floated beneath them.

"Perhaps you'd like to thank me on dry grou...." Grandpa tried to say, but was drowned out by Dillon's bewilderment.

"I don't get it," he said to Susan. "I thought Commander Burdock was collaborating with Morton."

Susan resisted a giggle. "Yes, yes I know. She told me how difficult it was for her to put on that act in front of you. She is definitely not mean by nature. But you have to understand, in Cyberia, the walls have ears."

Dillon turned to the wall of the Trash room and studied it.

"It's an expression," Susan said dryly.

"Hey, in Cyberia, you never know," Dillon responded.

"Anyway, Commander Burdock had to be exceedingly careful not to let on that she was onto Morton. She was afraid that if any word got out that she suspected him, Morton would become desperate and not only harm your grandfather but many other Cyberians as well as a kind of last stand. As long as he thought his plan remained a secret, he would simply wait for it to come to fruition without causing harm in the meanwhile."

The thought crossed Dillon's mind that there was no way to know whether Susan herself could be trusted. But then again, she did get rid of Morton. He swallowed, wiping his forehead from all the dirt and sweat.

"So," he sighed. "When Commander Burdock tried to make as if I was dreaming it all up, it was just a.... a trick, or what?"

"Now, Dillon," Susan asserted. "The warden was standing there in the background. There are audio-waves that other Cyberians can tune into. It was imperative that she turn the suspicion onto you, so that everyone would have no doubt about absolving Morton. But the truth is that Commander Burdock has had her suspicions about Morton for many years. She told me so herself, in the strictest confidence, as I have mentioned. Some of his actions had led her to wonder if he was corrupt. Apparently the way he would react nervously to the subject of spyware in particular, would give her real cause for concern. So she was worried all along that the big disaster that was looming, the one they had called you in about, might come from within the ranks. But she didn't have the evidence. She was delighted when I came along and told her what I had witnessed between you and Morton. She finally had the information she was looking for. But she had to handle it delicately, as I've explained, or the whole thing would explode prematurely. So she entrusted me with the mission of trailing you, and ultimately protecting you from him. She had to face the very difficult decision of temporarily overriding the ban against Cyberians possessing PDA's so that I could get a hold of it. In view of the importance of my mission of protecting you and all of Cyberia, she approved it." She raised her chin proudly.

Dillon studied her expression. He couldn't tell whether or not this whole thing was genuine. "But you weren't with me all the time."

"I know! For the most part I had you safely in sight, even in that horrible mortgage website with that Trojan Horse chasing you guys. I was the one who contacted CAVE and got them to activate the isolation booths. I managed to get on board the train afterwards, but then you decided to go ahead and jump out of it, and heck, I was not about to do that." She laughed, examining her long, painted nails. "So you were in some no-man's land and it was impossible to locate you. Believe me, I tried. And then, after you decided to get yourself arrested, we had to come up with a plan to get you released. Commander Burdock spent hours trying to figure out how to bypass some Cyberian statutes in order to allow your release. Fortunately for us, you pre-empted us and decided to escape. Way to go! What a nifty idea you had with those bars!" She threw her head back in laughter.

Dillon was quiet. He peered down at his grandfather whose eyebrow was raised far up his forehead. "She's fine," he declared nonchalantly, having read Dillon's doubt in his expression.

"Oh, I get it," Susan said awkwardly. "You're not sure if I'm telling you the truth. I can understand that," she nodded, although her smile vanished.

Dillon's first thought was to reassure her, but at this point, he was not about to apologize for his lack of trust in anything that moved. Experience had taught him well.

"Why don't we go directly to the Commander," she suggested. "I think your doubts will be dispelled that way."

"One way or another," Dillon retorted. He turned to look over the edge of the pit. "Come on, let's go, Grandpa."

"Oh, I'll give you a good spanking," Grandpa said with a twinkle in his eye, lying back helplessly in the murky waters.

Dillon was uneasy at the first sighting of CAVE officers strolling the Reception area. He glanced at Susan who smiled at him assuredly.

Grandpa was nursing his injured arm, wincing at the pain.

"She's not like Samantha, is she?" he whispered into Dillon's ear with a broad smile that defied the pain.

"Samantha?" Dillon said, frowning. "You mean from school?"

"Yes, Samantha from your school, and from the prom of every other school, in fact."

Dillon blushed. "Yes, she is not like Samantha. Definitely not."

"She probably doesn't think you're weird either," Grandpa added.

Dillon looked at Grandpa briefly. "Probably not, Grandpa. Now let's leave it alone."

Grandpa's smile stayed a while, nevertheless. And Dillon couldn't quite leave it alone either.

Susan ushered him and Grandpa into full view of the people who had been chasing him earlier. Dillon was prepared to make a run for it but nobody seemed to even notice he was there.

"Come on," she urged, as she led them in the direction of none other than the receptionist, Jan. Dillon looked down at his feet as they approached the desk.

"Oh, hello, Justin Grosvenor," Jan teased him with a broad smile.

Dillon continued to look at his feet.

"The Commander is ready to see you all," Jan said, and began the downloading process.

Commander Burdock was reading the same folders Dillon had last seen her with. Dillon stood stiffly alongside Grandpa and Susan at the entrance to her office. His heart was doing gymnastics, his arms almost completely numb. She looked up from her work. Dillon braced himself for her deceptively sweet voice. He resolved to be firm and resist it. Immediately the lines around the Commander's mouth dissolved into a wide smile. She jumped up from her desk, raced across the room and gave Dillon such a tight hug, it caught him off guard and somehow squeezed away the doubt, bringing him instead to tears.

"Oh, Dillon," Commander Burdock said. "I am so glad you're all right. I worried about you so much."

Dillon squeezed his eyes shut, trying to hold back the tears. He tried very hard to resist, but the warmth of her embrace spoke so many words. He knew it wasn't wise, but he simply let go of all the suspicion, of all the mistrust, of all the fear.

"It's ok," she said through her own tears. "It's all over. It's all over." Neither Grandpa nor Susan could restrain themselves either. Even the security guard had to fight the moisture in his eyes.

Dillon had always wondered what it must be like to be hounded by the media. He'd seen many of the Hollywood celebrities have to ward off journalists by raising the palms of their hands at the screen. He'd never imagined that he'd ever attract such attention. Although this was not exactly Hollywood, the media was not any less persistent. A multitude of microphones hovered near his face waiting for his response to their garbled questions as he made his way to the platform of the CAVE press room. Apparently he had single-handedly saved Cyberia and millions of people definitely wanted to know more.

"Actually, it's all my Grandpa," he croaked into the microphones, his words reverberating throughout the enormous room. "My Grandpa doesn't know much about computers or Cyberspace, but he understands people. If it wasn't for him, Susan here would not have pursued us."

Susan smiled broadly and gave a sweeping wave to the crowd.

Commander Burdock had to field the questions that were being fired at every pause.

"Did you at any point think you would not make it alive out of Cyberia?" one woman asked matter-of-factly and then gave a little sniff of triumph that she had been selected.

Dillon glanced at his Grandpa before answering. "I think....I could say that there were many times I was sure that I would....die in Cyberia." He swallowed hard. "And I didn't really know what that meant. Just that I would be responsible for it, and worse than that, that I would be responsible if something happened to my Grandpa." As he took a breath, a man in front managed to sneak in another question. "What have you learned from your experience in Cyberia?"

Dillon looked squarely at the man who was tapping his foot. "I think it's got to do with trust." He could not, or perhaps, would not, elaborate. There was just so much to talk about, he wouldn't know what to say and what not to say.

Grandpa Harley dipped a spoon into his imported custard and lemon juice. Commander Burdock observed him with a bemused expression, as they sat comfortably in her wicker chairs.

"Harley, I cannot believe you consume such a thing," she said, her hands playing with the curls at the back of her hair.

"Well, if you would be able to eat, you would understand," Grandpa replied. "There are very few pleasures in the world that compare."

"Grandpa, I am able to eat, and I still don't understand," Dillon teased him.

"Ah, but there are a lot of things that require maturity, young man, and you will in time develop a penchant for custard." He then proceeded to regale Commander Burdock with the history of custard and how it was originally used as a binder for fillings in medieval flans and tarts.

Dillon stood up. "Uh….I think I'll just go to say a couple of goodbyes," he announced.

Grandpa turned to face him and broke out in a broad grin. "Oh, how I wonder whom you wish to bid farewell."

Dillon blushed. "Grandpa, it could be anybody."

"Of course, it could," Grandpa nodded. "Give Susan my regards, will you?"

Both he and Commander Burdock laughed, and resumed their culinary discourse.

Dillon exited the train at the MemFriends website. The entrance was very narrow. He almost had to walk sideways in order to get in. As he crossed the threshold, the floor creaked like old wood, and a number of chimes began to ring. He found himself in a dark, cramped lobby that reminded him of those poky souvenir stores in quaint historic districts. The walls were smothered with Gothic posters, somber shaggy-haired musicians and large banners that read "Memory should not be forgotten" and "Legalize Batterijuana."

He squinted through the dark, musty air to discern another room ahead, where he could see figures hunched together. But as he stepped towards it, he bumped into something furry.

"Ah!" he shouted.

"Ah!" the web crawler echoed.

"Oh," Dillon said, relieved. "You're a crawler."

The crawler was well-dressed, his suit crisp and immaculate, perfectly molded to his brown torso. "I'm sorry," he said. "I'm a little nervous. I have to admit I find this place a little creepy."

A spider, commenting on how creepy something was. Now that was another one for the books.

"I guess we all have different....uh, tastes," Dillon offered.

Suddenly two people burst into the lobby from the other room. One of them was Susan.

"I don't see why I have to be the one who applies for the perm....Dillon!" Her face broke into a smile and she immediately dished out the clipboard she was carrying to the girl beside her.

"Hi, Susan."

"You came to see MemFriends!" her face beamed. "I am so honored. Dillon this is Becky. Becky, Dillon."

Becky smiled sheepishly. "I....I know who you are," she said, her butterflies quite obviously running amuck inside her. There was that celebrity gawk again.

"Ahem," the crawler said, now even more uncomfortable. "I...I think I've gathered all the information I need for the day, and will be moving on.

Good day." He did a semi-bow and disappeared out the door.

"So, what you think?" Susan asked, throwing her hands to the corners of her domain, clearly expecting only accolades.

"Uh....I'm still taking it in," Dillon said. "There's a lot to look at."

"I know, so much to see all in such a small space," Susan said, eyeing his expression.

"Was that deliberate? I mean, you campaign for saving memory space, so you intentionally kept the site small?"

Both Susan and Becky laughed. "I wish I could say that was our motivation," Susan regretted. "The truth is that we just didn't have the funds for a larger site. But!" She raised her finger like a starter-gun in the air. "Thanks to you, I have a great relationship now with Commander Burdock and things are going to change."

"Great," Dillon said, biting his lip and staring down at his shoes.

"What's the matter?"

"Oh, nothing. I just came to say goodbye, that's all. I wanted to say that uh....thank you again for all that you did for me and my Grandpa, and I hope that uh..." he swallowed hard. "That maybe uh.... that maybe...."

"Yes, it would be great to see you again, Dillon," she smiled.

"Great," Dillon said again.

"Maybe we can meet at Cyberbucks next time."

"Cyberbucks?"

"Yes, you never heard of the chain? It's a coffee-charge store."

"A coffee-charge store," he echoed again stupidly.

"That's right. We plug ourselves into coffee cells and get a wonderful caffeine boost."

"Oh. But....but aren't you against chain stores expanding and taking up space?"

She grinned, and replied in a hushed tone. "They make great coffee."

All three of them laughed. Dillon thanked her again and backed out of the store, almost knocking over a stack of protest signs.

"Say goodbye for me to your Grandpa," she called after him. He boarded the downloaded train, found a seat and lost himself in thought for the journey.

Commander Burdock had to order a special guided escort for Dillon and Grandpa so that they would reach the BiteFlite station without being harassed by reporters. At the station, Grandpa caught a glimpse of the front page of The Cyberian Express. There he and Dillon were in 5 x 7 color, right at the top, smiling nervously into the crowd.

"Dillon," he nudged his grandson with the arm that wasn't in a cast. Dillon was looking over the instructions for Image Particle Transfer. "Let's take this newspaper back with us. We'll have evidence that we weren't making this all up."

Dillon pointed to his Grandpa's thickly bound cast. "There's the evidence right there, Grandpa."

Nevertheless, Grandpa bought the newspaper. The clerk at the newsstand looked absolutely thrilled to serve them.

"We're celebrities," Grandpa smiled proudly.

"Not where we're going now," Dillon reminded him. "Everything will still be the same as we left it. At least, I hope so."

Under armed guard, they took their positions in front of the departure screen and promptly left Cyberia without a sound.

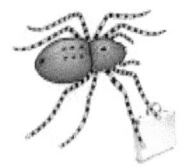

Fourteen

"**D**illon, did you pack your lunch?"

The urgency in Eileen Appleseed's voice was not excessive for a typical weekday morning. Behind her, the juicer whirred and the coffee maker crackled. Next to him, Nicole was wriggling in her seat. Everything was moving at a pace that was just a touch too fast for someone who was suffering from severe Cyber-lag.

"Uh….no, Mom," he croaked, hardly able to raise an eyelid in his mother's direction.

"What's the matter with you this morning?" she quizzed him as she struggled to seal a Tupperware tub. "You're so groggy. Are you feeling ok?"

Dillon peeled back his eyelids and faced her. "I guess I had a rough night."

"Was your sleep disturbed?"

Now that would be the understatement of the year. He was not able to hide a smile.

"What are you grinning at?" she asked him as she scraped some leftovers into the trash. The thing was, she was facing the opposite direction, so how on earth did she know he was smiling? His mother always knew everything. It would probably be a matter of time before she found out about his and Grandpa's adventures in Cyberspace, even though he would try his darndest to keep it secret. He could only imagine her reaction, and how he would have to revive her afterwards.

"Oh....I'm just thinking about how much I love orange juice," he said stupidly, although there was truth to that, considering how difficult it was to obtain anything to drink or eat in Cyberia.

His mother squinted at him briefly before returning to her chores.

"I love orange juice too," Nicole said, "but I don't smile about it like that."

Dillon gave her a light rap on her knuckles.

"Ow! Mom, Dillon hit me!"

"Dillon, she's your baby sister," Eileen chided him as she zipped a lunch bag.

"Yeah, baby is right," Dillon retorted under his breath.

"I heard that!" Nicole cried.

"The two of you stop that right now. I don't want my day to start off like this. Now, where is your grandfather? I told him to set his alarm. He's got a doctor's appointment this morning."

Dillon blanched. "What doctor?"

"His physiotherapist, Dr. Weltzheimer. Why?"

Dillon almost choked on his orange juice. It spouted from his nose like Jacuzzi jets. Nicole began to laugh hysterically. Dillon's mother looked at him like he had just arrived from another planet. Funny that.

"Uh, mom?" Dillon squeezed his voice through the orange sediment that had fallen down his windpipe.

"What? Dillon, what has gotten into you?" She dropped the dishtowel she was carrying on the counter and scrutinized him.

"Umm....well, I had a rough night, but Grandpa had an even rougher night."

Her eyes narrowed. "What do you mean?"

"Well, Grandpa fell out of his bed and broke his arm in several places. We had to go the doctor in the middle of the ni...."

His mother was already downstairs before he could finish. He wished he had been more polished. He wished he had given more thought to the explanation he'd give his mother other than the lame one he'd just invented. But they had been so tired and so relieved to get back inside his room after their trip back, that all they could think about was crawling into their warm, familiar beds right away. There hadn't really had any time nor any desire to plan things. The next words from his mother, after her piercing shriek, were inevitable. "Dillon T. Appleseed, get down here at once!"

Dillon reluctantly descended the stairs and entered his Grandpa's bedroom. Dillon couldn't believe that his Grandpa was smiling bravely from ear to ear in spite of his daughter's hysteria. She let out a series of yelps as she discovered the extent of his bandages.

"I'm fine," he tried to tell her.

"You're fine? You're fine?" she repeated with such a sharp edge in her voice it could slice through metal. "One minute you go to sleep as the father I know, and the next minute you wake up embalmed like a mummy. Dad," she breathed, "tell me what's going on." She turned to her son. "Dillon?"

"I can explain," Dillon said.

"Yes, he can explain," Grandpa agreed nervously.

Dillon took a breath. "Mom, uh…. what would you say if I told you that Grandpa and I went inside my computer and discovered a whole world there, and Grandpa broke his arm when he fell down the Virtual Trash Can?"

Grandpa glared at Dillon with golf ball eyes.

"Dillon, my patience is running short. Either you tell me the truth or you're grounded for a month."

"I'm sorry, just kidding," he said. "The truth is that Grandpa and I got into an argument last night."

"What?" She demanded.

"Yeah, and it got a little out of hand. I'm sorry, Mom." He stared down at his feet.

"You hit your own grandfather?"

"Well, while we were fighting. It was a mistake. I did the bandaging myself."

Grandpa interjected. "I forgave him."

Eileen drew her hands to her hips. "Well, I don't forgive him." She approached her son and bore down on him. "Shame on you. You are grounded for a month anyway."

"Dad," she said, turning around. "I'm canceling the appointment with the physiotherapist and taking you to the hospital for X-rays instead. This is unbelievable."

She ascended the stairs. "And Dillon, get ready for school. You'll be late."

Dillon's stare didn't leave his feet.

"Well, very clever, young man. You did it."

Dillon shrugged his shoulders, still not looking up.

"What's the matter?"

"It doesn't feel right, Grandpa. I lied so bad."

"On the contrary, you lied pretty well," Grandpa retorted with a chuckle.

Dillon sat down at the edge of Grandpa's bed. "Grandpa, I think I should tell her the truth."

"You tried to tell her, my boy. It's just somewhat difficult to convince someone that you've been sucked inside a computer where you saved an entire nation from destruction, all in a night's work."

"I know," Dillon said. "It must sound crazy. I wouldn't believe it either if I were her."

Just then the footsteps that they thought had disappeared, returned. Eileen Appleseed had only pretended to ascend the stairs completely, but in reality had remained at the threshold of the room, listening in, just in case there was something that was being concealed from her. She paused mid-descent where her son and father were visible to her and studied them for a long while, a deep frown all she could muster as a reaction to what she had just heard.

The doorbell rang, thankfully bringing an end to the interminable silence. Without losing her frown, Eileen returned upstairs to answer the door.

"Oh, boy," Grandpa said.

"Maybe I won't be grounded after all," Dillon said, smiling.

The maid, Dora, appeared now mid-way down the staircase. It was she who had rung the doorbell. As soon as she saw Dillon and Grandpa, she let out a whoop.

"Hi, Dora," Grandpa said. "Didn't mean to scare you."

"No speaka English," she said in a flurry and then sprinted back up the stairs.

"What happened there?" Grandpa asked.

"She's just weird," Dillon responded.

They were all about to leave through the front door, Dillon and Nicole to school and Grandpa and Eileen to the hospital when someone came up the path.

"I don't believe it," Grandpa stammered.

"I called her just a couple of minutes ago to tell her what happened to you," his daughter informed him.

Great Aunt Babette, or GAB, hobbled down the path as fast as she could, her breath billowing whole clouds in the cool morning air. She was holding on to her mauve hat which threatened to fly off in the wind.

"She's probably come to curse me that I don't heal," Grandpa muttered.

"Dad!" Eileen wanted to give her father a little tap on the arm, but the bandages left her no room.

"I had to come as soon as I got off the phone with Eileen," GAB heaved, stopping just in front of her brother.

"How can I help you to…." Grandpa began, but GAB cut him off.

"Harley, I want you to promise me something."

Grandpa raised an eyebrow. "Let me hear the 'something' first and then we'll see if I'll consider it."

"Please, please," she begged him in a tone that he hadn't heard in decades. "Harley, don't ever, ever go there again."

Grandpa and Dillon's mouths fell open in unison. Eileen's followed suit a moment after that and the three of them just stood there gawking in silence. Grandpa stared at his sister. She actually had tears in her eyes.

Then, as quickly as she had hobbled towards them, she hobbled back down the path and turned the corner.

"Why do I feel like the world has conspired against me?" Eileen wanted to know. But there was just no time to find out. There was school, the hospital, carpool and grocery shopping that took precedence over this nutty interlude from the twilight zone.

It felt like ages since Dillon had been in school, even though he had attended the day before. And perhaps it *was* ages, just that time had stood still for him. Whatever. He wasn't about to wrap his head around it so early in the morning. Mr. Groll was a welcome sight even though he was at his dreariest, reciting so many historical dates today that Dillon wondered if he was reading them off a screen somewhere at the back. It was difficult enough to concentrate at the best of times, but now it was particularly difficult to stop the image of GAB standing there, seemingly speaking with knowledge about their adventure the night before.

Carla, the blog starlet, had an eager report for him on her latest entry. Apparently a visitor had disagreed with a point she'd made, but after some intense back and forth on the subject, quickly realized the truth of her reasoning.

"He just admitted that there wasn't anything he could find wrong with what I was saying about the existence of extra-terrestrial creatures. He even apologized," she gloated, flicking her pencil merrily back and forth between her fingers.

So did you accept your own apology? Dillon was itching to ask her, but chose not to. Blogs were not a subject close to his heart at the best of times. After visiting Morton's, he would be glad if he never had to hear about them again.

As the day wore on, Dillon began to wonder what his father would say to this all, whether he would pause between one critical legal case and another to consider the scenario of his son's disappearance inside a computer. Considering the history of their relationship, there was not much to hope for. Nevertheless, there was one thing about his father that Dillon came to realize after narrowly escaping from Cyberia. After having endured wave after wave of deception there, Dillon was grateful that his father simply was who he was. He didn't pretend to be a fantastic father. What you saw was what you got. And the truth was, when it came down to it, his father was doing all that crazy time at work because he believed he was helping his family. It was not a tremendous amount of consolation, but it did count for something. His mother, too, loved him in her own weird way.

Dillon was anxious about seeing Mr. Halfinger in Computer Science. How would he respond to all that Dillon reported? He hoped his teacher would be proud of all Dillon's accomplishments. He debated about the right time to tell him all that happened, and concluded that although he was bursting to tell him right away as he saw him, it would probably be best to wait until after class when all the other students weren't around. In any case, this bought him time –he'd have the whole class-time to think about what he'd say.

When the students entered the classroom, Mr. Halfinger was studying his notes. His wiry hair popped into the air like antennae, and his thick glasses hovered over his notes like observation robots on a seabed. When he looked up, it was sudden, with intense purpose. The students became quiet as all eyes watched him scan the classroom. Clearly, he was looking for someone. His eyes rested on Dillon and stayed there. He looked very surprised to see him. Mortified, in fact.